Lucky Lady

Russell Stickney
with Guy Bates

Story and text copyrights, Russell Stickney, St. Louis, MO, 2004. All rights reserved.

Book layout and cover design, Red Ink Publishing Services, Phoenix, AZ, 2004. All rights reserved.

www.redink.biz
guy@redink.biz

ISBN 0-9679472-2-7

Acknowledgements

Fran Baker provided the energy and enthusiasm for pursuing a dormant story. She literally breathed life into Lucky Lady. She introduced the author to Guy Bates, who helped smooth over rough spots, provide cohesion, and move the story along. His service in the U.S. Navy was a valuable complement to the project. Sally Rosenthal was an invaluable proofreader, with her sharp eyes and very shrewd suggestions.

Preface

This is a true story about an old sea-going oil tanker during World War II. Historical dates are correct and geographical locations in the South Pacific are accurate.

The story unfolds in the form of the ship's log. Incidents of the ship and crew are based on actual events. Over the two years of the story, the tanker experienced several unusual occurences that could truly classify her as a Lucky Lady!

The names of the ship and crew have been changed, although the personalities remain true to the characters.

Contents

Chapter		Page
1	The Ship	1
2	The War	6
3	The Captain	10
4	Underway	28
5	The Change	67
6	Action	93
7	Chewing Guam	109
8	R&R	133
9	The Tow	168
10	Spiked Beauty	213
11	Home	236

Chapter One
The Ship

28 December 1941
New Caledonia, South Pacific Ocean

The SS Ellen Hagerman eased out of the harbor in Noumea, New Caledonia, under the cover of night. The 485-foot, steel-grey tanker was a familiar vessel in the shipping lanes between Samoa and Australia. She was steam powered and sailed with a crew of 14 merchant marines. Carrying 50,000 barrels of crude oil, Ellen slipped quietly among the small tropical islands of New Caledonia until she had to turn southwest and navigate 600 miles of open sea to Brisbane.

Just three weeks after Pearl Harbor, the Japanese controlled most of the island groups and atolls in the South Pacific. However, New Zealand and Australia were too big, too well defended, and too far from supply lines to occupy so soon into the war. Allied shipping—military and civilian—became the principal target of the Japanese imperial navy.

29 December 1941
New Caledonia

Christened in 1901 in the Chesapeake Bay by Standard Oil Company, the Ellen Hagerman was older than most of the ships operating in the South Pacific. When she carried a full load—70,000 barrels of crude oil—the tanker weighed almost 17,000 tons. Top speed was less than 10 knots. Even without full tanks, she would travel dangerously slow during daylight in a war zone. The trip from

Noumea to Brisbane would take almost a week.

Still, Ellen was solidly built. And her captain cruised south of the usual commercial shipping lanes to avoid Japanese submarines hunting Allied ships. He also doubled the watch and secured all of the watertight hatches. If the tanker were hit by a torpedo, the watertight compartments would keep the ship floating a little longer. His cargo was valuable but the lives aboard were more valuable.

Just before noon, the wind picked up as thick grey clouds drew together. One of the lookouts spotted the white caps of a torpedo breaking through the turgid, uneasy sea. He called the bridge on his sound-powered headset.

"Mast to bridge. Over."

The helmsman answered. "Bridge. Go ahead."

"Torpedo! 600 yards off the starboard bow. It's headed for the stern. Over."

The helmsman relayed the message to the captain. Lifting binoculars to his eyes, the captain turned to his right and searched the water for the torpedo. "Damn!" he said. "Left full rudder. Sound general quarters."

Eyes wide, the helmsman spun the helm and punched the large red button on the control panel to his left as he spoke into the microphone of the ship's announcing system. "Now hear this. Now hear this. All hands, general quarters. All hands, general quarters. This is not a drill. I repeat. This is not a drill."

Speakers up and down the ship blasted the loud, intermittent bong-bong-bong of general quarters. The crew scrambled to get to their stations. The lookout rushed down from the crow's nest on the mast but before he could get to the deck, the torpedo slammed into the hull and exploded in the engine room. Everyone in the black gang was killed instantly. Fortunately for the ship, the torpedo hit starboard aft. Had it hit amidship near the storage tanks she would

2

have been ripped apart by a series of gigantic, fiery explosions.

However, damage to the tanker was severe. The turbines were blown apart and the men who manned them were dead. Water quickly rushed into the stern and spread into some of the adjacent compartments. Fearing another torpedo, the captain ordered the crew to abandon ship. As the aft half of the ship steadily slipped below the waterline, two deck hands swiftly lowered a single lifeboat into the water. They, the captain, and remaining crew clambered into the small boat and pushed off.

Thinking they had dealt a fatal blow to the tanker, and saving the limited number of torpedoes for more targets, the Japanese sub surfaced. Three sailors climbed out of the hatch and pulled the tarpaulin off of the 3-inch, 50-millimeter cannon on the bow. The Japanese captain ordered them to fire on the lifeboat. The first shot was a little wide and long. The second shell exploded in the middle of the lifeboat.

2 January 1942
Coral Sea

The crippled and unmanned ship did not sink. The secured watertight compartments kept the Ellen Hagerman afloat. Wind and current carried her, leaking oil, a few hundred miles west and north until she was spotted by a mail plane flying from Rockhampton, Australia, to the New Hebrides, an island chain 250 miles north and slightly east of New Caledonia. The pilot radioed the small air station at Rockhampton, and the station telegraphed the shipyard at Townsville to report the ship's coordinates. They dispatched two ocean-going tugs to bring her in.

16 January 1942
Townsville, Queensland, Australia

Townsville was not much more than a rural fishing community before the war. But all of the small villages along the northeast coast of Australia gained strategic importance not long into the war. A long coral reef provided natural protection from submarines and the villages were relatively close to the island-hopping campaign that the Allies must surely wage to reach Japan.

The shipyard notified the Standard Oil office in Canberra that the Ellen Hagerman was in Townsville. They reported the ship's engine destroyed, the giant propeller torn from the rudder, and a gaping hole in the starboard aft hull and cargo holds. Without sending anyone to look at the ship, Standard Oil wrote off the tanker as a loss and reported it to the United States Navy—standard operating procedure during time of war.

18 January 1942
Washington, DC

Commander Andrew Johns was a member of the Naval Planning Board for the South Pacific. He was 51 years old with sharp blue eyes and shortly cropped white hair. Johns graduated third in his class at Annapolis and had a mind for logistics. Reading Standard Oil's report, he realized that the war in the South Pacific would need hundreds of ships: warships, supply ships, hospital ships. Those ships would need fuel and tankers carried fuel.

Johns contacted Leeder Shipbuilding Company in Sydney and asked them to send someone to assess the damage to the torpedoed tanker. A major overhaul might be cheaper—and quicker—to refit a Patoka-class tanker in

Australia than building new one from scratch and sailing her to the South Pacific from the west coast of the United States.

28 January 1942
Washington, DC

CDR Johns reviewed the salvage report from Leeder. Except for the starboard aft hull, the engine, shaft and prop, the ship was structurally sound. Johns authorized Leeder to refit the Ellen Hagerman.

He agreed to replace the turbine with a diesel from an old, large tanker decommissioned just before the war. Because the diesel came from a much larger ship, Leeder would have to jury-rig many fittings to connect it to Ellen's propulsion system. Top speed would be about 10 knots. That, too, was fine with Johns. He needed a floating refueling station, not a speedboat.

He told Leeder to add berths, heads, and showers for more than 100 officers and men. And, because the tanker would be in a war zone, Johns contracted for a few guns. Four 20-millimeter anti-aircraft guns—2 port and 2 starboard—and a 3-inch, 50-millimeter cannon—at the bow—were added. All included gun tubs for protection and secure storage for ammunition.

30 January 1942
Townsville, Australia
Leeder towed the ship down the Australian coast to Sydney and began work.

Chapter Two
The War

December 1941
Central Pacific Ocean and South China Sea

Japanese forces attacked Pearl Harbor, Hong Kong and the Kowloon Peninsula, Singapore and Malaya, Siam, and the Philippine Islands. The Marshall Islands, Gilbert Islands, and northern Solomon Islands were occupied not long after.

A Japanese submarine torpedoed the SS Ellen Hagerman.

February 1942
South China Sea

Japan took Singapore and invaded Burma from Siam. Borneo, Tarakan, Celebes, Timor, Bali, Ceram, and Sumatra fell. American naval forces, under the command of Admiral Chester A. Nimitz, began raiding the Solomon and Gilbert Islands.

The Ellen Hagerman received a dry-dock berth at Leeder Shipbuilding in Sydney.

March 1942
South China Sea

Japanese forces invaded New Guinea. An American task force, built around the carrier USS Hornet, sailed within 600 miles of Japan. Colonel James A. Doolittle commanded 16 Army medium-range bombers and successfully attacked Tokyo, Yokohama, Nagoya, and other targets in southern Honshu, Japan.

American troops landed in Fiji. The United States set up a chain of naval bases and air stations spanning the Pacific and consolidated supply lines from Australia to the Central and South Pacific islands. New Caledonia was made a main support and supply base and a secondary base was established in the New Hebrides.

Leeder began removing damaged sections of Ellen's aft hull, stern, and engine room.

May 1942
Coral Sea

Japanese forces attacked Florida Island, a small island just north of Guadalcanal, and advanced on Tulagi, the main town. Two American carrier groups arrived and attacked the Japanese navy. Although the Battle of the Coral Sea was statistically a standoff, it was a strategic and moral victory for the Allies because it was the first time a major Japanese force was pushed back.

Leeder requisitioned the diesel of a large tanker decommissioned before the war and ordered a shaft, propeller, four 20-mm anti-aircraft guns, and a 3-inch-50 cannon for the Ellen Hagerman.

June 1942
Central Pacific

The Japanese attacked Midway Island. In two days, the Japanese suffered defeat in one of the most decisive naval battles of the 20th century. They never recovered from their losses. American forces paid a high price in lives and equipment but the Central and Southeast Pacific were secure for the Allies for the rest of the war. The Naval

Planning Board for the South Pacific established offices in Noumea, New Caledonia.

Japanese forces occupied Attu and Kiska in the Aleutian Islands off Alaska.

Most of the damaged aft hull, stern, and engine room of the Ellen Hagerman were removed. Inspectors double checked adjoining hull sections, bulkheads, and storage bays for stress and underlying structural damage. Renovation began on crews' and officers' quarters.

February 1943
South Pacific

Allied forces took Guadalcanal in the Solomon Islands.

Ellen's engine room was nearly finished.

March 1943
South Pacific

US Liberator and Flying Fortress bombers sank more than 20 Japanese transports with 15,000 troops bound for New Guinea.

Leeder began work on the tanker's shaft and propulsion system.

August 1943
South Pacific

US intelligence intercepted and broke Japanese codes. Admiral Yamamoto, the architect of the attack on Pearl Harbor, died after his plane was shot down by American P-38s.

US troops retook Kiska in the Aleutians.

Work on Ellen's hull was under full swing. Topside, the guns were being installed.

November 1943
South Pacific

Allied forces captured the most northern of the Solomon Islands and advanced on the Gilbert Islands.

Ellen's engine was connected to the propeller shaft. Berthing compartments were ready, guns fully operational, hull and cargo bays nearly complete.

February 1944
South Pacific

Allies took Kwajalein Island and Eniwetok in the Marshall Islands.

Rechristened the USS Osage IX731 by the US Navy, Ellen Hagerman left dry dock. A skeleton crew sailed her to Tulagi, Florida Island, in the Solomons to wait for her new captain and crew.

Chapter 3
The Captain

10 March 1944
0900 Hours
Noumea, New Caledonia

CDR Johns pushed his chair back from the large teak desk and stood. Johns wore tropical whites—short-sleeved white shirt and shorts cut to the knee, white shoes and socks that rose over the calf—the uniform of the day for officers in the South Pacific. He picked up his white and blue coffee mug and walked to the large, bay window.

"Damn!" he said aloud, "Where am I going to find a crew for that tanker?" The Ellen Hagerman, now the USS Osage IX731, had been in Tulagi Bay for a little more than a week. Johns had been sifting through files of available enlisted men and officers to man the Osage. The Naval Planning Board for the South Pacific had a staff of more than 40 men and women to help plan, assign, and move material and personnel. But Johns took a personal interest in this ship. He stood at the window for a moment and took a long gulp from the mug.

There were lots of new recruits coming out of boot camps in naval training centers and plenty of graduates from officers candidate school back in the States. But the Ellen Hagerman needed veterans, men with experience and sea legs—especially the commanding officer. Coast Guard, he thought. They have experience. The Navy has used them in the past to man ships during war. Johns turned, walked back to the desk, set down his coffee, and picked up one of the officers' files at the top of a neatly arranged stack. He opened it and read.

Honas Michaels. Lieutenant Commander. 48 years old. Grew up in Lokken, small fishing village on north sea coast of Jutland, Denmark. Graduate, Copenhagen Maritime Academy. Captain of The Vulcan, Danish schooner now in Portsmouth, VA, harbor. Joined the US Coast Guard a couple of months after his ship arrived stateside in October 1940. Outstanding seamanship. Basic English-speaking skills. Requesting active duty, preferably Europe.

"I'll bet there's no love lost between you and the Germans." Johns spoke directly to the file. "They danced through your country on their way to Sweden. Not much of a fight. That's why you want duty in Europe. And you probably know the North Sea like the back of your hand."

Johns looked up from the folder but his eyes did not focus on anything in particular. "A three-masted schooner is no match for a U-boat, Honas. I think I have something for you in the South Pacific."

14 March 1944
1330 Hours
Portsmouth, Virginia

LCDR Honas Michaels shuffled into the yeomen's office with his cap under his arm. He had the dark, ruddy, weather-beaten face of an old salt, a man who spent a lifetime at sea. His wide mouth was slow to smile and quick to command. Most men were more comfortable walking on land than on a ship. Michaels was more comfortable walking on the weather deck of a ship rolling and listing in the open sea. He stopped at the duty officer's desk.

"I am Honas Michaels," he said. The words almost ran together in his Danish accent.

"I have orders for you, sir," replied the yeoman second class. He fingered through a row of large manila envelopes standing in a rack at the edge of his desk.

"Orders." It was more command than question.

"Aye, sir. Here you are." The yeoman handed Michaels one of the envelopes. "I've included copies of all your records, and a brief history and description of your command."

"Vell, back to Europe—finally."

"Sorry, sir. Your orders aren't for Europe."

Michaels' eyes grew narrow, his brow furrowed and lips pursed. His thick, calloused hands anxiously broke the seal on the flap. He pulled out the top sheet and searched for his duty station and billet. A few seconds later he looked at the yeoman.

"Vhere in hell is Tulagi?"

28 April 1944
1000 Hours
Solomon Islands

All four engines of the gunmetal-grey, Navy seaplane purred as it descended through low-lying, thick white and gray clouds. Michaels shifted nervously in his seat as the plane rattled in a pocket of turbulence. He looked out the small oval window at the cluster of islands below and gripped the arm of the seat. "Great Hamlet's ghost," he whispered, "get me to the vater alive, in vone piece."

The seaplane set down in the harbor and tied up to one of the long wooden pier. Michaels waited for the other passengers to file past him before he stood and pulled his tan and brown suitcase from under the seat. He walked aft to the cargo hold. The cargo handlers had just boarded the plane to unload luggage and freight. Michaels spotted his duffle bag next to a young seaman lifting a large brown box.

He waited for the seaman to give the box to another sailor on the pier and then asked him to pass the duffle bag. He also asked for directions to the Navy personnel receiving station and the port authority.

The island was a sight to Michaels. It was the first time he had seen palm trees. They stretched high and narrow into a sky that seemed a much softer, paler blue than the sky over Denmark and the North Sea. It was certainly warmer and more humid here than it was in Copenhagen. Only twenty yards from the plane, he already felt beads of sweat roll slowly down the middle of his back.

When Michaels checked in at personnel, he asked if any of his crew had arrived. The yeoman replied that he needed specific names to check arrivals. Michaels didn't have names so he shrugged it off. On the way to his temporary berth assignment, Michaels found the mess hall and the officers' club.

The officers' barracks was a long and narrow, one-story building with evenly spaced tall opened windows. It was divided into three dormitories. The duty petty officer led Michaels to his assigned dorm. Military cots, ten on each side of a wide center aisle, lined the north and south walls of the large rectangular room. Each cot had a small pillow, fitted white sheet, white top sheet tucked smartly between a thin mattress and the wire-spring base, and a green cotton blanket folded across the foot of the bed. Half a dozen ceiling fans ran a straight line over the center aisle from the door to the head. The blades of five fans rotated slowly counterclockwise. The blades of the third fan from the door were not moving. Michaels picked an unassigned bunk and stowed his gear in the empty locker behind the bed. After a quick shower, he hung up a fresh shirt and pair of pants, and took a short nap.

1430 Hours

"Vhat you mean, you do not know vhere it is?" demanded LCDR Michaels. "It is big ship!" Michaels held his arms wide, palms opened, fingers extended.

"We believe it's here in the harbor, sir," replied the port authority supervisor. He wore wire-rimmed glasses, and was short and thin and stood behind a waist-high counter that ran from wall to wall and divided the room. Four fans whirred briskly on the ceiling above. The supervisor was thankful the counter was between him and the agitated officer. The officer had a barrel chest and thick forearms. "We just don't know where—exactly."

"How you lose a damn ship almost 500 feet long and 50 feet high?"

"The crew never checked in with us. They just dropped anchor, put the paperwork on the counter during lunch, and left without a word. And, with all of the ships coming and going north, we haven't had time to look for it."

Michaels' nostrils flared and he breathed heavily. He pounded his fist on the counter. "I vant my ship, mister! I have orders!"

The supervisor grabbed a legal-sized green ledger on the counter. He fumbled to open it at the bookmark. "Let's see," he said running his forefinger down the page. "I can give you a skiff and a cox'n. You could look for it, sir."

"Vhen?"

His finger stopped two thirds down the page and he looked up over the rim of his glasses. "Umm…first thing, day after tomorrow. 0800."

"That is Sunday!"

"Yes, sir. The duty watch can take you."

"Not today?"

"It's too late, sir. The boats are all out. Sorry."

"Tomorrow?"

"Nothing available. A lot of brass are on the base. They've got everything. Day after tomorrow is the best I can do. You can use the boat all morning. The cox'n will take you anywhere you want to go."

"Great Hamlet's ghost!"

Michaels turned and strode to the door. The supervisor closed the book, took a deep breath, and watched the officer leave. Just before Michaels reached the door, he stopped, turned, and pointed at the supervisor.

"0800. Sunday," he said loudly.

"Aye, sir. 0800."

Michaels looked at him for a moment. The muscles in his face relaxed. "Thank you," he said softly.

30 April 1944
0815 Hours
Tulagi Bay, Florida Island

LCDR Michaels sat in the middle of the skiff bouncing over small waves kicked up by the morning wind that blew across the bay from the west. The coxswain held the rudder with both hands. Michaels estimated close to 50 ships in the southwest end of the harbor: destroyers, destroyer escorts, a cruiser, some tankers for refueling, cargo ships, two hospital ships, and a carrier laden with a full air wing secured on the flight deck and in the hangar bay. Tulagi was a vital stop on the way to the northern Solomon Islands and the Gilbert Islands.

Michaels first wanted to check the south rim of the bay because it was close to the commercial shipping lanes. The skeleton crew sailed the tanker north from Australia. If they had been eager to ditch it, perhaps they left her close to the south entrance of the harbor. He hoped the supervisor at the port authority wasn't lying. He didn't want to navigate a tiny powerboat around so many huge warships to look for a tanker he had never seen.

About half a mile from the mouth of the bay, the water became choppier. As they passed the cruiser, Michaels had a good view of the port side of a tanker sitting high in the water just off the headland. From that distance the tanker didn't look so bad. With empty cargo holds, the deck was approximately 50 feet above the waterline. Two superstructures on the deck—one forward, one aft. A slender 90-foot mast in front of each. Large smoke stack in the center of the aft superstructure. Rounded stern. A fine ship. He thought it odd, however, that there were no hull marks to identify it as the USS Osage IX731.

The small boat approached the tanker's stern. Michaels saw the top of a giant new propeller and asked the coxswain to circle the ship counterclockwise—slowly. The coxswain throttled down to a crawl. Portions of the stern were obviously new. The giant, shiny steel plates were a stark contrast to adjacent plates covered with reddish-brown surface rust streaked with dark-grey oil stains that dried long ago.

As the skiff crept along the ship's starboard side, Michaels looked up and noticed a new gun turret atop the corner of the rear superstructure, paint peeling. At the midsection, he saw a rusted metal ladder that rose from the waterline to the deck. The forward superstructure was a little farther down. The bridge, command central, was enclosed with large glass windows.

Coming out the side of the bridge, on the front of the superstructure, a short flat wing stretched horizontally over the side of the ship. At the edge of the wing sat another new gun glistening in the tropical sun. And, finally, the starboard anchor chain. Between the deck and the portal where the chain entered the forecastle, Michaels saw the ship's name faded and scratched, SS Ellen Hagerman. "Here you are," he said under his breath.

The skiff rounded the bow. A gun, much bigger than the other two, sat back from the front of the ship. They passed the port anchor chain and another smaller gun on the edge of the port wing. Just before the port ladder, Michaels told the coxswain to stop.

"I vant to look around," he said. "Come back at 1600."

"Sorry, sir. It takes almost an hour to get here. I have muster at 1630."

"Vell, come back at 1500."

"Aye, sir. 1500."

Michaels stepped onto the ladder and the coxswain pulled away from the ship.

At the top of the ladder, Michaels swung his legs over the side and stood on deck. He pushed the brim of his cap higher on his forehead and looked across the ship, then aft, then forward. He walked to the rear bulkhead of the forward superstructure. Two sets of metal stairs, one on each side of a closed hatch in the middle of the bulkhead, led up to the first deck and the captain's quarters. From there, a second set of stairs continued to the bridge.

The new captain of the USS Osage IX731, the Ellen Hagerman's new name, stepped up the starboard stairs. At the first deck, he opened a hatch and stepped inside. The room ran the width of the superstructure. To his right, a heavy wooden table, the size of a dinette, was bolted to the floor. A heavily padded chair sat next to it. Another was on its side under the table. Michaels walked over and pulled the chair out from under the table and turned it upright. A large wooden bookcase was bolted to the bulkhead behind him glass doors covered the front of the bookcase and a small key was inside the lock of the door on the right. On either side of the cabinet was a porthole, closed and secured. He stepped up to each porthole and opened them. The room desperately needed fresh sea air. The salty breeze slowly cut through the stale smell of musty bedding and mildew.

He walked to the other side of the room where the bed rested against the bulkhead. To his right, also against the bulkhead, was a mahogany rolltop desk and chair. No doubt, he thought, a relic from the Standard Oil days. To his left, just past the foot of the bed, he saw a large closet and the entrance to his private head and shower. "Ya, this vill do," he said.

Michaels stepped out, closed the hatch, and continued up the starboard stairway to the bridge. He opened the hatch and stepped inside. The bridge ran long and narrow athwartship, port to starboard, directly above the captain's quarters. Immediately in front of him, was the captain's chair. It looked like a small swivel recliner mounted on a barstool. The radio shack was just behind it. In the center of the bridge stood the helm, a large round steering wheel.

The ship's compass sat between the helm and the front bulkhead. On the other side of the helm was the engine room communication panel. The chart room was to the rear. To his right, the entire front was a wall of glass panes from his waist to the ceiling. Below his waist, the wall was solid bulkhead.

Michaels walked up to the glass windows and looked at the island's natural harbor. A tangle of glittering pinpoint shadows embraced the sun on the water. Florida Island, dust brown with long pockets of lush tropical green, cradled the ships slowly rising and falling in the tides that filled Tulagi Bay. And just beyond the bay, the dark blue-green Coral Sea faded into a pale-blue sky strewn with high, wispy cirrus clouds. The CO took a deep breath and exhaled slowly. With the day's heat and humidity, it felt like he was breathing through a damp washcloth.

He turned to port, stepped to the corner of the bridge and out onto the wing. Michaels walked up to the 20-millimeter anti-aircraft gun that he hoped they would never have to use. The gun tub was round and shallow. The barrel was five feet long and slender, the housing no more than a thick stem to lift it off the deck. The barrel pointed up—about 45 degrees between the opening of a thin, u-shaped plate in front of the gun. A small canvas sheath covered the tip of the barrel. The other end came right up to a metal seat bolted to the stem. The seat reminded him of his uncle's old tractor on the farm south of Copenhagen. The captain nodded and returned to the bridge.

From the bridge, he walked down the metal stairs to the deck. He turned around to face the superstructure. Michaels opened the large oval hatch in the center of the bulkhead and ducked into a passageway that ran fore and aft through the center of the superstructure. A few feet in, it connected to another, wider passageway running athwartship. Michaels stopped. He looked up and down the passageway before he turned to starboard.

He passed a head and showers for officers. The passageway ended at two officers' staterooms, one on each side of the passageway. The rooms were mirror images of each other: standard Navy bunk wedged into the near corner between the bulkhead and a floor-to-ceiling locker; small, wooden desk and bookcase bolted to the floor against the far bulkhead; secured porthole over the bookcase; a small fan bolted in the upper corner across from the bed.

The captain reentered the passageway and turned to port. At the opposite end of the passageway, he found more 2 more staterooms and heads. Michaels walked back to the center passageway and turned to forward. On his right was a spacious rectangular room, the officers' ward-room. He looked in. A large, wooden table was bolted to the floor in the center of the room. It was covered by a green, felt-like cloth.

A dozen heavy wooden chairs were scattered loose-ly around the room. In the center of the far bulkhead was another hatch, closed and secured, that led to the weather deck. On both sides of the hatch, two portholes were closed. Behind him, on the other side of the passageway, he noticed the stewards' room where the officers' food was prepared. It was half as deep and nearly as long as the state-room.

He continued forward to another passageway run-ning athwartship. Four more staterooms, he thought. A few feet more and the captain arrived at a closed hatch in the middle of the bulkhead. He opened it, ducked out, stood on deck, and waited for his eyes to adjust to the sun glaring on the metal deck.

He walked to the bow and looked at the 3-inch-50. The gun sat in the center of a large gun tub on a raised deck. Michaels stepped onto a short ladder and climbed to stand behind the gun. The housing was chest high and four feet wide. The long, slender barrel came out of a wide slit front and center at the top of the housing. It was parallel to the deck. A short canvas sheath covered the end of the bar-rel. At the rear, a round hatch was shut and locked. Michaels sat in the seat attached to the rear of the housing and gripped the firing wheel. He shut one eye and looked through the sight. "Boom," he said. "I bet you're a loud vone." The CO patted the butt of the large gun, lifted him-self out of the seat, and climbed down the ladder to the deck.

To the side of the ladder, he opened a secured hatch

and descended a spiral staircase. At the first deck below, he found a short passageway that ran athwartship. Across from the spiral staircase, the captain discovered a hatch secured in the middle of the forward bulkhead. It was the entrance to the forecastle. The forecastle held the chain winches and the huge vertical lockers that stored the port and starboard anchor chains. There will be time enough to look at these, he thought.

Traffic aboard ship usually followed a set of guidelines—especially during general quarters—to avoid congestion and allow quick movement from one place to another. Normally, men walked fore and up ladders on the starboard side of the ship; aft and down ladders on the port side. Michaels was alone. He walked aft down the starboard side of the ship.

The first hatch on his right was open and secured to the latch on the bulkhead in the passageway. Michaels stepped into the room. In the dim light, he saw 20 metal-framed triple bunk beds. The bottom bunk in the frame was on the floor; the middle, waist high; the top, eye level. Each bunk was a single thin mattress and pillow resting on a shallow metal locker the length and width of the mattress. He also saw 8 wooden card tables bolted to the floor in the center of the room and a host of chairs strewn about.

The next compartment forward was the crews' head and showers. No need to stop, he thought. After the head, another passageway ran athwartship. It was much darker here because the natural light, from the opened hatch forward, faded quickly around the corner. In the center of the aft bulkhead, another secured hatch led to the decks in the center of the ship between the forecastle and the fantail.

The 'tween decks—as they were called by sailors—held pumps, tanks, hoses, and other storage. They also provided safe passage fore and aft during rough seas and heavy weather.

With the engines cold, the ship had no electricity, no lights. The ship's commanding officer knew he would have to wait to inspect the 'tween decks until the black gang came aboard and fired up the diesel. He walked forward in the port passageway and climbed the spiral staircase to the weather deck. Again, he waited for his eyes to adjust before he walked aft.

Inside the other superstructure, Michaels briefly inspected four more officers' staterooms, the crew's mess hall and kitchen, refrigerated walk-in storage for perishables, a room for dry storage, and the supply office. On the port and starboard sides of the aft superstructure, metal stairways led to the decks below. He descended the port stairwell. As much as the sparse natural light allowed, he looked at another crew's quarters and searched for—and found—the aft entrance to the 'tween decks.

The captain also found a hatch that led to the engine room and steerage but delayed going in until he had good artificial light deep in the recesses of the ship. Even if he had thought to bring a flashlight, it wouldn't provide enough light to check the engine, shaft, rudder, and fittings. Time enough, he rationalized.

The CO returned to his stateroom and secured the hatch to the exterior bulkhead. He brushed the dust off of one of the padded chairs and sat. He wanted his officers and crew aboard ship now. There was a lot to do: get the diesel up and running, double check the shaft, propeller, guns, communications; bring supplies aboard; clean the ship and paint her; carry out drills; schedule shakedown cruises to get the crew and officers familiar with the ship and how she handled; iron out any kinks or problems they found.

"Great Hamlet's ghost, ve have a lot to do here," he

said aloud as he patted the arm of the chair. "But ve are going to fix you up, Ellen. You deserve better than this."

The ship's captain looked at his watch. It was nearly 1400 hours. The coxswain would arrive in an hour. Michaels made a mental list of things he wanted to bring the next day and went down to the deck to wait for the skiff.

At 1500 the powerboat pulled alongside the tanker. Michaels descended the ladder and stepped into the boat. When the officer was seated, the coxswain shoved off and returned to the dock. Ellen's captain had a couple of errands to run before dinner at the officers' club.

Michaels walked to the port authority office and asked to see the supervisor. The little man stepped slowly to the counter.

"Thank you for the boat," the captain said. "Can the cox'n take me to ship in morning and pick me up in afternoon?"

"Tomorrow?"

"Every day this veek," replied Michaels.

"It's a bit unusual, sir, every day." The supervisor hesitated and Michaels' brow became tight and furrowed. "But I'll arrange it."

Michaels thanked him and left.

At the personnel receiving station, he approached a different yeoman than the one he spoke to the day before. This yeoman was stout with thick black hair that curled up at the tips. The captain asked the yeoman to notify him when officers or senior petty officers checked in with orders for the USS Osage IX731. He gave the yeoman his temporary barracks billet.

"Vone last thing," Michaels said.

"Yes, sir?" asked the yeoman.

"I vould like some pencils and pads of paper. Vere is the supply office?"

"Don't bother, sir," the yeoman said. "You'd probably retire before you finish filling out the paperwork." He grinned, reached into his desk drawer, and pulled out two pads of legal-sized paper and six black-ink pens. "Will this be okay?"

The Dane smiled. "Ya, this vill do. Thank you."

1800 Hours

Michaels sat on a barstool, back to the bar, elbows on the rail. His empty dinner plate rested on the bar directly behind him, silverware propped up on the rim, napkin in a wad. His left hand clutched a glass mug of beer. He took a drink and snarled. Weak, he thought. American brew had no flavor. It paled in comparison to the rich, darker, full-bodied European beers—especially his favorite: Elephant Beer from Denmark. American beer reminded him of the watered-down brew that adults in Lokken gave their children when they first took interest in what their parents were drinking.

The officers' club was built like a high school gymnasium with its tile floor, no interior walls, and high ceiling. Tables were placed in rows to fill the center of the spacious room. Two perpendicular wide aisles split the tables into four quadrants.

It was a little too noisy for Michaels. Giant floor fans circulated the air filled with sweat, cigarette smoke, and the smell of beer and whiskey. At the far end of the room, a six-piece combo played the latest and favorite swing tunes of Goodman, the Dorseys, Miller, James, Ellington, and others. Perhaps 250 officers, in dress whites or work khakis, sat at tables and ate or drank; strolled around the room; or stood and chatted about war exploits, families back home, and the latest rumors.

Officers' clubs and enlisted men's clubs were rumor mills and every sailor, soldier, and fly boy seemed to have an inside story or the latest hearsay about orders for ships, infantry, and aircraft. And everyone had something to say about the progress of the war in Europe and the South Pacific.

Michaels spun around to face the bar. "Vhiskey please, bartender. No ice," he said.

"Put that drink on my tab, bartender. And bring me one as well," said someone to his left.

Michaels turned and looked at the officer standing next to him. Roughly his own age with sharp blue eyes and shortly cropped white hair, the officer was a commander in tropical whites. Michaels disdained tropical whites. He thought the shorts and high socks were prissy—much like the men who wore them. Michaels always wore work khakis.

"Vhy you buy me drink?" asked Michaels. His eyes narrowed.

"It's the least I could do for bringing you here from Virginia. I'm Commander Andrew Johns." Johns smiled and extended his hand to Michaels.

Michaels stood and shook his hand. "I am Honas Michaels."

"I figured as much—with that accent." Johns smiled.

"How you know I am here?" asked Michaels.

"This is a small island with only one officers' club. We were bound to run into each other sooner or later."

"Ya, sure."

The bartender set two whiskeys, neat, on the bar. Johns thanked and paid him. Both men reached for a high-ball glass. Johns extended his to Michaels. "To victory," he said.

Michaels clanked the side of Johns' glass with his.

25

"Victory," he repeated. Each took a short swallow and set his glass on the bar.

"Did you find your ship?" asked Johns.

"Ya. South end of bay. She needs vork."

"Well, your crew arrives this week. At least, half your crew."

"Half?"

"I was only able to fill about half the billets," replied Johns. "But they're all Coast Guard, like you."

"How vill I fill the other billets?"

"Coast Guard is bringing in a ship that's pretty damaged. I think I can swing most of the crew to your ship."

"Vell, that is good. Ven do they get here?"

"Toward the end of the week. You should have a full ship's company this weekend—although some still need to find their sea legs."

Michaels picked up his glass and took another swallow. "Ven do I get orders?" he asked.

"In two or three weeks you'll sail north and support fleet ops. First, get the Osage sea worthy. Take 'er out for a couple of shakedown cruises and get to know 'er. How do you like 'er so far?"

"Topside is okay, I think. I not yet see below decks. No electricity until the black gang comes aboard."

"They should be here tomorrow. Your supply officer should also report tomorrow."

"Good. I have plenty for him."

"Had to give you a diesel engine. And to make it fit the old rig, they used a lot of couplers. The diesel has a lot more power that those old turbines but she'll be damned slow." Johns picked up his glass and sipped. He watched Michaels to see how he would react to the news.

Michaels eyes slowly grew wide. He sighed. "Great Hamlet's ghost, she vas slow before. And you say she vill be slower."

"You won't be on the front line and you have more guns than other tankers. The Japs are pulling back. True, they're tough as nails, but they are losing ground."

"She vas torpedoed vonce—not very lucky. Vonce unlucky, alvays unlucky."

"Unlucky? No, no, Honas. Think about it. Ellen gets torpedoed but doesn't sink. A mail plane just happens to spot her in the middle of the ocean. Instead of getting scrapped at her age, she gets refitted. Although I only found half a crew, two days ago I received word that the Coast Guard is bringing in a ship we might have to scrap. There are enough men on that ship to fill your billets. If you ask me, she's a lucky lady. Though, it might not hurt to pray her luck continues."

"Ve vill see." Michaels picked up his glass again. This time he raised it. Johns followed in kind. "Victory," said Michaels.

"To victory," replied Johns.

Chapter 4
Underway

8 May 1944
0830 Hours
Tulagi Bay, Florida Island

As late as Sunday evening, men checked into the personnel receiving station on the island. They were given temporary berths and orders to board the Osage at 0600 the following morning.

On Monday morning, the tanker was still anchored near the mouth of the bay. She sat high in the water and slowly turned with the tide. Although still early in the day, little ripples of heat started to rise from the deck. This was the first morning the Osage had a full ship's company. Officers and enlisted men were checking into their divisions and getting familiar with work spaces, living quarters, and passageways fore and aft.

On the bridge, Quartermaster First Class Hal Emerson, the helmsman, keyed the microphone for the ship's announcing system. Tall and slender with a cleft in his chin and jet-black hair that looked indigo blue in dim light, Emerson's long aquiline nose added a breathy, almost weightless, quality to his voice. "Now hear this. Now hear this. All hands muster on deck. All hands muster on deck."

"Ya, that vill do, Emerson," said Michaels. He turned to Ltjg. Rick Jackson, the first lieutenant. In the ship's chain of command, the captain was the undisputed authority. If anything happened to him, the executive officer assumed command of the ship. If something happened to him, the first lieutenant took over.

Jackson was in his middle twenties, well groomed,

and had the reputation of a smooth-talking smart ass who avoided eye contact. He was also an abernathy: He had one green eye and one blue eye—a characteristic that was very popular with women, single and married.

"Mr. Jackson, you have the bridge," said Michaels. He handed Jackson a pair of binoculars.

"Aye, sir. I have the bridge," replied Jackson. He took the binoculars with his left hand and saluted with his right.

Michaels returned the salute and left the bridge. He stood at the top of the ladder and watched his crew assemble for muster.

Officers and enlisted men quickly arrived on deck to listen to their new captain for the first time as a crew. They joined other men in their division. Basically, Ellen had two divisions: Engineering and Deck. Deck hands included boatswains mates, gunners, quartermasters, cooks and stewards, and the supply officer. They numbered close to 60. There were a little more than 40 in Engineering including machinist mates, electricians, and radiomen. Both groups mustered between the superstructures. A ten-foot aisle separated them.

Each division had 6-8 lines, 8 men in a line, facing to port. A few aimlessly shuffled their feet or fidgeted with something in their hands. Almost everyone looked around at other crew members and officers. Silently, they measured each other for their worth: likely coworkers, would-be friends, and potential rescuers in a fight at sea with the Japanese.

Division officers called the ranks to parade rest: feet shoulder-width apart, back straight, chin up, right hand in the palm of the left hand resting in the small of the back. Michaels left the bridge and slowly, deliberately, stepped down the ladder to the deck and walked to stand midway between the two large superstructures. Hands on his hips, he faced the crew. Deck was to his left; Engineering, to his right. He was not smiling.

The executive officer, Lieutenant Donald Morton, walked up to Michaels and saluted. Morton was 30 years old with big hands and a face that always looked like he was blushing. Under his cap was a crop of thick, unruly dark-brown hair. He spun around on his heels to face the men assembled on deck.

"Company, atten-hut!" Morton barked.

Officers and enlisted men snapped to attention: shoulders back, arms straight down the side, hands next to their thighs and fingers closed, chin up, eyes straight ahead.

"Your captain wants a few words with you," he continued. "Pah-rade rest!" Officers and men took the position. Morton stepped back three paces as Michaels dropped his arms to his side and took a couple of steps forward.

"Vell," began Michaels, "this is the USS Osage IX731 and you are its crew. I am the captain, Lieutenant Commander Honas Michaels." Michaels' voice was sound and sure. His thoughts were not. He did not like public speaking. He preferred not to speak much at all. "I do not know vhat brought you to this god-damned rust bucket but I know vhat you vill do to get her shipshape. In two or three veeks, ve sail north. Ve vill be ready. Orders now are simple. Today, check into your division and find a berth. Division officers vill assign billet and GQ station. Then, look around the ship. Know her vell. Traffic moves forward and up ladders on starboard; aft and down ladders on port. No exception! Tonight, check out of barracks on the island. Tomorrow morning, all gear vill be aboard. This is your new home."

Michaels stopped and cleared his throat. He shifted his weight to his left leg and continued.

30

"First priority is make this ship good for living. Lieutenant Clark is supply officer. He has cleaning supplies. Tomorrow, everyone cleans this floating rust bucket. Also tomorrow, Lieutenant Morton vill post duty sections and chain of command in mess hall and vardroom. Ve vill have 2 duty sections—day on, day off." Michaels paused for a moment.

"After ship is clean, ve take shakedown cruise to Espiritu Santo. Ve vill learn how to handle this old sea whore and learn to vork together. Very important."

Michaels paused again. He shifted his weight to his other leg.

"Vone last thing. This is oil tanker. Fire from cigarettes is dangerous. Today is last day to smoke freely. Tomorrow, smoking lamp is out except in designated area—one fore, one aft. No exception. They vill be marked." Michaels cleared his throat. "I vant to see officers in vardroom in ten minutes. Company dismissed!"

The crew relaxed and broke ranks. The men slowly left the deck like ants probing the back porch for food on a summer afternoon. Michaels walked to the ladder on the forward superstructure, climbed it, and entered his stateroom.

Three machinist mates, walking aft, struck a conversation.

"Whadcha think of the old man?" asked the youngest. Machinist Mate Second Class Bill Kraft was only 26 years old. He was a thin, 145-pound walking book of engine knowledge with blonde hair and deep blue eyes. Having recently graduated from technical school, he lacked the experience—and confidence—of his two comrades.

Chief Machinist Mate Bernard Edwards answered. "He shaw ain't fum Georgia." Originally from Atlanta, his short grey hair was almost white and made him look older

31

than his 37 years. Chief Edwards knew engines—turbines, diesels, and gas powered—like the alley behind his house when he was growing up.

Before he joined the Coast Guard, Earl Frederickson, Machinist Mate First Class, spent most of his adult life in the merchant marine on oilers and tankers in the Great Lakes. His face and body were hard and very symmetrical with no really outstanding features. In a crowd, no one ever noticed him. And, occasionally, he used it to his advantage. "He sounds German," he offered. "Wonder what he's doin' in the South Pacific?"

"I heard he's fum Denmark," answered Edwards.

"Where'd ya hear that, chief?' asked Kraft.

"Walls talk, boy. 'Specially at sea. Listen but don't pay 'em no never-mind."

"Whadcha mean, chief?"

"You'll find out soon enough, mister." replied Frederickson. "Get below. We haven't got all day for sweet talk and bullshit."

Frederickson pointed to the ladder that led from the aft superstructure to the engine room. Kraft descended. Frederickson stepped aside for Chief Edwards and followed him down.

After muster, Lt. Roger Clark walked alone to the wardroom. He wore horn-rimmed glasses on a narrow face with high cheekbones. Clark was an unwilling serviceman. He didn't want to go to war and his attitude showed it.

Clark seldom spoke unless spoken to and usually answered only what was asked. When he came aboard a week ago and met the captain, Michaels asked him to take a quick inventory and submit requisitions to supply the ship. Inventory was easy. There was almost nothing aboard. Filling out requisitions forced Clark to seek out division commanders and talk to them at length. For that, he disliked Michaels a lot and immediately.

At 6-foot-4, Ensign Pete Russell was the tallest officer aboard the Osage. He was also the youngest, barely 24 years old, and had no sea experience. Tall and lanky, he was probably the only man aboard ship who enjoyed writing. He kept a journal. For that reason, Michaels made him the ship's communication officer.

As he approached the entrance to the forward superstructure, he met Ensign Fritz Lycovec. Lycovec was a few months older than Russell. He was a tough ex-cop with broad shoulders, a large square jaw, and a long vertical scar on his right cheek. Lycovec came aboard that morning.

Russell extended his right hand and smiled. "Hi. I'm Pete Russell, communications officer."

Lycovec shook his hand but did not smile. "Lycovec. Gunnery officer."

Russell ducked inside, took off his cap, and tucked it under his arm. Lycovec followed in kind. They walked down the passageway to the wardroom.

"When did you come aboard?" asked Russell.

"This morning."

"I got here last Thursday. The ship seems okay but I thought tankers were bigger."

"This is a tanker, not a carrier."

Russell stepped into the wardroom, Lycovec right behind. Clark already sat at the table.

"Mornin', Clark," said Russell. Clark raised his right hand, palm forward, shoulder high, and returned it to his lap. His face remained expressionless.

Russell looked at Lycovec. "Have you two met?"

Lycovec shook his head. "Not yet."

"Lieutenant Roger Clark, this is Ensign Lycovec. Sorry, Lycovec, didn't get your first name."

"Fritz. But Lycovec will do just fine."

Clark nodded once. So did Lycovec. Lycovec wondered about Clark. A man who didn't talk or shake hands when introduced usually had something to hide.

Both men took a seat opposite Clark.

Lt. Henry Becker, the engineering officer, stepped into the wardroom. He was 5-foot-7 and weighed more than 200 pounds. Becker was self-conscious about his weight but never, in his 31 years, considered going on a diet. A good mechanic, he was as efficient as men his size could be. Becker was looking at the man behind him.

"I don't want to give him up," he said. "With that jury-rigged propulsion system, I'll need every man I can find. And that includes Frederickson."

Lt. Phil Harkel, the fueling officer, followed Becker into the wardroom. "But he's got lots of experience as a fueler. And that's what this ship does. It refuels other ships," Harkel said empathically. He wasn't afraid to argue or take charge and he seldom backed down. With his sandy-brown hair, Harkel still looked like the boy next door, although he was pushing 30.

A third man entered the wardroom. Older than the other two, he had thin lips, crooked teeth and oily, uncombed hair. Mel Cook was a warrant officer and nearly 40 years old. Warrant officers were in command limbo somewhere between commissioned and noncommissioned officers. Noncoms became officers through the warrant officer program. It was the eternal hope of chain-of-command wannabes who wanted to rise above their station as enlisted men. Cook passed the written exam when he was a chief electrician.

"But we need him," whined Cook.

"That's not what you need, Mr. Cook," laughed Harkel.

Michaels entered his stateroom and walked to the

table. He picked up his coffee cup, a pad of loose leaf paper with notes scribbled in Danish on the top sheet, and a pencil. He turned and left the stateroom.

When muster ended, Morton walked up to Chief Boatswain's Mate John Stacek. The division officer for Deck was the first lieutenant. Because Jackson had the watch on the bridge, Chief Stacek called the men to parade rest at muster. He grew up on a farm in the Midwest.

To Stacek, a ship was a lot like a farm. If you took charge and made sure everything was done right the first time, there were few problems. He was 5 feet 9 inches tall, big boned with strong hands and shoulders. He knew his job. And he knew how every job in the division should be done.

"Chief."

"Yes, sir?" Stacek saluted and Morton returned the salute.

"Send a man to the bridge. Tell Mr. Jackson that the captain wants him in the wardroom."

"Yes, sir."

"Thank you, chief." Morton turned and slowly walked away.

Stacek looked around. One sailor, just ten feet away, knelt on one knee to tie his shoe lace. "You there, sailor."

The seaman looked up.

"Yes, you." He pointed at the sailor. "Double time it to the bridge. Tell Mr. Jackson the captain wants him in the wardroom."

"But, chief . . ."

"No buts, mister. Move it."

"Aye, sir."

The seaman stood and ran up the metal staircase to the bridge. He relayed the captain's orders to the first lieutenant.

35

Jackson turned to the quartermaster. "Can you handle the helm, Emerson?"

"I believe so, sir." He raised his eyebrows and looked directly at the first lieutenant. "We are at anchor."

Jackson looked away and set the binoculars on the console of the communication panel. He walked toward the hatch. "Just making sure. I'll be in the wardroom if there's a need."

"Aye, sir. The wardroom." Emerson's eyes followed Jackson to see if he would look back. He didn't.

Jackson was the last to arrive. Michaels sat at the head of the table. Jackson took the vacant seat next to Clark and smoothed down his carefully parted hair with the palm of his hand.

"Now, ve are all here" began Michaels, "Have you met each other?"

All of the officers nodded.

"Good. Ve can get to business. Mr. Morton, the duty roster vill be ready tomorrow?"

"Yes, sir," replied Morton. "This afternoon, I will receive the names of everyone who reported aboard this morning. The duty roster will be posted as you ordered. And, captain, shouldn't we give two copies each to Deck and Engineering so they can post the roster in their offices?"

"Ya, sure. Do it."

Morton nodded.

"Mr. Jackson, go ashore this afternoon with Mr. Lycovec and Mr. Russell. Ve need all the chipping hammers you can find. And ve need enough red lead and blue-grey paint to cover this piss pot."

Jackson, Lycovec, and Russell responded together. "Aye, sir."

"Mr. Clark," continued Michaels, "do ve have room

36

in cold storage enough for 50 cases of beer?"

"Not 50, sir. Maybe 30. I might be able to squeeze in 35—tops."

"Mr. Jackson, add beer to list."

Jackson released his carefully rehearsed smile and looked at the captain. "An excellent idea, sir."

"Ve have food for the crew, Mr. Clark?" asked Michaels.

"We've been bringing food aboard since Thursday, sir. Today, tomorrow, and Wednesday, meals will be a little thin. After that, we'll be fine."

"Acceptable."

Michaels turned from Clark and addressed all of the officers. "After ve are shipshape, this tanker vill become most efficient ship in South Pacific. Mr. Morton, set schedules for gunnery practice, refueling drills, and general quarters. I vant schedule day after tomorrow."

"Yes, sir."

"Every officer on vatch, keeps written log. Include veather, drills, course changes, everything that happens. Mr. Russell, you vill combine rough logs and create one smooth log. Use good English, ya?"

"Yes, sir, good English."

"Mr. Lycovec, look at guns. Check ammunition. Make damn sure they vork good. Tell Mr. Clark anything you need."

"Aye, sir." Lycovec looked across the table at Clark. He was fumbling with a pencil and did not look up.

"Mr. Becker, does black gang understand jury-rig fittings?"

"I think so, sir." Becker's green eyes glanced nervously around the table. "There are an awful lot of them. Not just for the screw and propulsion. Everywhere the turbines are hooked up: electric, heating, the works. Mr. Cook

37

is writing down everything. We hope to have extra couplers onboard before we sail north. But it might take awhile to get them if we have to order off the island for anything."

"I vill come down at 1300 hours to see this jury rig. Ve cannot afford problems. Ve must have spare parts. Order vhat you need soon!"

"Aye aye, sir."

"Mr. Harkel, have you checked hoses and stations for refueling?"

"Yes, sir. Equipment is fine."

"No problems?"

"Well, one sir."

"Explain."

"Engineering has a good fueler with experience. His name is Frederickson. I need him. I'm short-handed."

Cook whined, "But, sir, he's assigned to Engineering. We need men more than Mr. Harkel needs them. We have a jury-rigged engine room. His hoses are fine."

"Great Hamlet's ghost! Ve are vone ship. All vork together. Frederickson is a fueler, ya? He reports to Mr. Harkel. But, Mr. Harkel, you vork with Mr. Becker. Mr. Becker, you vork with Mr. Harkel. Help each other. Understand?"

Both men said, "Yes, sir." Becker nodded and sighed.

"Mr. Harkel, talk to yeoman to change billet. I vill sign papers."

"Aye, sir." Harkel smiled softly.

"Okay, at 0800 hours ve meet here every morning until shipshape. Questions?"

Russell raised a hand. "I have one, sir. How do you want me to arrange the smooth log?"

"You have a personal journal. You decide. But keep rough log on bridge. Keep smooth log on the table in my stateroom."

"Aye, sir."

"More questions?" No one raised a hand. "Dismissed."

1330 Hours

Michaels stood in the engine room with Becker, Cook, and Edwards. A pungent aroma of diesel fuel, engine oil, and human sweat filled the room. Michaels tolerated the smell because it was the life's blood of his ship. The engine room was three decks high. Each offered access to different areas of the gigantic machine. The decks were plates of steel grating laid end to end and bolted to a welded frame. Standing on the middle deck, he could see the deck below and through the deck above.

For the past 15 minutes, Edwards explained all of the gauges, indicators, and dials on the console that faced the diesel. They were, he said, connected to a series of pressure valves and electrical circuits which helped monitor the diesel. The console was waist high with a large, four-panel sheet of plexiglas framed from the top of the console to the deck above. The machinist mates stood or sat at the console, monitored the gauges, took readings, and watched the diesel from behind the plexiglas panels.

The huge pistons created so much noise that Edwards shouted for Michaels to hear him. Michaels had never seen a diesel so large, so loud. Until he sailed into Portsmouth, VA, a few years ago, Michaels had been to sea only on 19th-century sailing vessels with jibs and booms and sailcloth.

Sailboats, no matter how large, were relatively quiet. Other than storms, the only noises were sails flapping in the wind, the ship rolling and pitching in the sea, wooden

39

planks creaking, and birds crying overhead when they were close to land. Those noises were calming and reassuring in ways that he could not—and did not want to—describe with words.

Michaels had questions about the machine, the step-up and step-down couplers, the black gang who took care of this unnatural metal monster. But he decided to wait until he didn't have to shout to ask them.

Jackson, Lycovec, and Russell descended the port ladder to the skiff waiting below. At first, no one spoke. Jackson broke the silence.

"When we get to base, I'll do the talking. I'm the senior officer."

"That's fine with me," said Lycovec. "Although, I am sorry that I left my tissues in the head."

"Why do you need tissues?" asked Jackson.

"Well, if you handle people anything like you handled the captain this morning, you'll need the tissues to wipe all that brown off your nose."

Lycovec smiled. Russell laughed out loud.

"Lycovec, how clever. I didn't realize you were such a comedian," said Jackson.

Lycovec did not take the bait.

"Sometimes a little flattery goes a long way," continued Jackson. "It's not how you get what you want; it's that you get what you want. Those who give it up want to, and believe they're doing the right thing. It's an art, really."

"Art or not, Jackson, we're at war in the middle of the god-damned Pacific Ocean. Just who are you gonna smooth-talk? Are you gonna flatter the Japanese to death?"

"We shall see, Lycovec. We shall see."

In the crew's living space near the forecastle of the Osage, Boatswain's Mate Second Class Billy Philips stowed his gear under a top bunk in the back of the room. He had
40

a quick smile and a high brow that made his small green eyes look beady, almost shifty, especially when he told jokes, his favorite pastime. He was a slender long-distance runner in high school—more from necessity than desire—but grew into a 180-pound body.

"Man, the captain's no Quasimodo," he said to a yeoman second class lying down in a bunk a few feet away and smoking a cigarette. YM2 Bradley Lewis had red hair and freckles. He blew smoke rings at the bunk above him. It was a casual habit he picked up out of boredom. Like most military campaigns, long periods of inactivity followed dangerous and brief action. Lewis was impeccably neat. He loved order. As a civilian, Lewis was a librarian. That's one reason he became a yeoman: He had access to files and books and information.

"A what?" asked Lewis.

"A Quasimodo. You know, a real bell ringer."

"Sorry, I don't get it."

"Somebody who makes a lot of noise to get your attention."

"He doesn't have to make noise to get our attention. He's the captain," replied Lewis.

"But still, he don't go into no detail, does he?"

"Well, he's not Victor Hugo."

"Who?" asked Philips.

"Victor Hugo."

"Never heard of him."

"Probably the greatest western writer of the 19th-century. Known for his descriptive detail. He wrote 'The Hunchback of Notre Dame.' It was about Quasimodo."

"Well, I'll be damned. Learn something new every day."

Lewis sat up. He put out the cigarette on the floor, picked up the butt, and brushed the ashes back and forth with his shoe. "Don't we all," he replied.

9 May 1944
0700 Hours
Wardroom, USS Osage

Two ship's stewards had just finished setting up a side table under one of the far portholes when LCDR Michaels entered the wardroom. The table held a large metal urn of fresh coffee and a row of white mugs, two small plastic pitchers of water and a dozen glasses.

"Good morning," said Michaels.

"Mornin', cap'n," replied SS2 Melvin Wilson, a light-skinned African American with a slender nose, high cheekbones, and round eyes. "Coffee's hot an' fresh." Pigeon-breasted, he had wide shoulders and very narrow hips. His previous billet was on an attack troop transport destroyed in Efaté by Japanese kamikaze pilots. Wilson and the other African-American stewards aboard the AKA were in Tulagi almost two weeks before they volunteered as a group for duty on the Osage.

"Ya, good. Thank you."

Michaels filled his cup and took his seat at the head of the wardroom table. Reading the notes from the officers' meeting the day before, he lifted the cup to his mouth, blew lightly, and sipped.

Wilson and the other steward, SS3 Rufus Hazelton, stepped aside at the hatch as the officers entered the wardroom. Hazelton had skin the color of chocolate and was Wilson's brother-in-law. Wilson kept him close because Hazelton had a bad attitude and a quick temper.

Officers greeted the captain and, after filling cups of coffee, quickly sat in the same seats they held the day before.

"Mr. Morton," began Michaels, "report."

"Yoeman Lewis and I prepared the chain of command and duty rosters for watches, fire drills, and abandon ship. Mr. Becker and I are still working on refueling details. We are trying to coordinate them with Mr. Clark and Mr. Jackson so we don't cross duties bringing on supplies with replenishment details. Might come the time when we have to do both at the same time. I'm waiting for Mr. Lycovec's assessment of our guns and gunners before we assign GQ stations."

"Good. Post the chain of command this morning." Michaels faced the supply officer. "Mr. Clark?"

"Lt. Jackson, Mr. Morton, and myself should have everything worked out today. Tomorrow at 0800 hours, a cargo ship pulls alongside. From then on, we are in the loop. And we start serving hot meals the day after tomorrow."

"Good. Mr. Lycovec?"

"I was ashore yesterday afternoon with Mr. Jackson. Before I left, I asked yeoman Lewis to give me a list of gunners. We have five, sir, including a gunner's mate first class. That gives us some experience but we still need pointers and trainers. I'll take a close look at the guns this morning. They're new so we shouldn't have any problems."

"Take gunners with you to look at guns. Mr. Jackson, Mr. Becker, ask for volunteers to be trainers and pointers. Ve need 12. I vant back-up for pointers and for trainers. Mr. Lycovec start to teach as soon as you have men."

All three officers responded, "Aye, sir."

"Mr. Jackson?"

"Good news, sir! Espiritu Santo has chipping hammers and red lead. I asked Mr. Clark to start the paperwork. The blue-gray paint is a different story. Scuttlebutt says there's a storage facility across the strait on Aore that stores plenty. But the supply officer is rather tightfisted. They say he wants to trade for whatever he gives out. Problem is, sir, we have nothing to trade."

"Ve need the paint, Mr. Jackson. Do vhat you must to get it."

"Excellent." Jackson continued. "Sir, Santo also stores plenty of base coat. It's an ugly red-brown but I can use it."

Michaels looked at Jackson and furrowed his brow but did not ask why he wanted the paint. "Mr. Clark, add base coat to requisition," commanded Michaels.

"Yes, sir," replied Clark.

"Thank you, captain," said Jackson. He smiled and slowly rubbed the palms of his hands back and forth.

"Mr. Becker, is Engineering ready?" asked Michaels.

"Engineering and propulsion are ready to get under-way. We'll keep a close watch on the couplers when the screw starts turning."

"Good." Michaels clicked his pen and slid it in his shirt pocket. "Tomorrow at 1300 hours ve sail for Espiritu Santo. Questions?"

No one spoke.

Michaels pushed his chair away from the table and stood. All officers did the same. "I vill be on the bridge. Dismissed."

Lewis sat at a small metal desk in the aft superstructure in a room, port side, not much bigger than an officer's bathroom. The office was adjacent to Clark's. His filing cabinets and typewriter arrived late the previous day with a shipment of canned goods, powdered eggs, and cooking utensils. He was arranging service files in alphabetic order when Morton entered. Lewis stood and saluted.

"At ease, Lewis," said Morton.

Lewis relaxed but remained standing.

44

"Chain of command ready?"

"Aye, sir. Here it is." Lewis lifted a sheet of typing paper from the desktop and handed it to Morton.

"It looks good, Lewis"

"You should read it, sir. Just to make sure there are no mistakes."

Chain of Command

Commanding Officer
LCDR Honas Michaels

Executive Officer
LT Donald Morton
QM1 Hal Emerson
YN2 Bradley Lewis

First Lieutenant
LTJG Rick Jackson
CBM John Stacek
BM1 Buck Williams
BM2 Billy Phillips

Engineering
LT Henry Becker
WO Mel Cook
CMM Bernard Edwards
MM2 Bill Kraft
MM3 Jay Conway

Fueling
LTJG Phillip Harkel
MM1 Earl Frederickson
GM3 Harold Booth

Gunnery
ENS Fritz Lycovec
GM1 John Tipton
GM3 Ted Sedgwick

Supply
LTJG Roger Clark
SK2 Harry Schneider
SS2 Melvin Wilson
SS3 Daryl Smith
SS3 Rufus Hazelton

Communications
ENS Pete Russell
PH1 George Gander
RM2 Ron Miller

"Good job, Lewis. Go ahead and post the chain of command, fore and aft."

"Aye, sir. What about the other documents?"

"I'll get back to you."

"Very well, sir," replied Lewis.

Morton turned, ducked out of the compartment, and started walking to the bridge. Morton looked amidship and saw Ensign Russell, on watch as the officer of the day, leaning over the side of the ship. When the ship was anchored or tied to a pier, the officer of the day stood watch with an enlisted man at the ladder bolted to the port hull. At anchor, the ladder provided access on and off the ship. In port, sailors, vendors, and guests used a thick wooden plank to leave and come aboard.

Russell said something to a couple of men in a longboat alongside the Osage. One man was the coxswain; the other, a warrant officer. The boat was filled with six large brown boxes. Another longboat, with a coxswain and six more large brown boxes, floated alongside it. The boats bobbed slowly in the tide like large heavy corks.

"Shoes," yelled the warrant officer. "They're deck shoes. Genuine leather."

Morton walked up to Russell. "What's going on?" he asked.

"He says he's got shoes for us, sir. But I don't have him or shoes on my list," replied Russell as he handed a clipboard to Morton. "I sent the watch to get Mr. Clark."

Morton did not take the clipboard. "Good. Have him come aboard, Mr. Russell."

"Aye, sir." Russell turned and yelled down, "Come aboard. We'll handle this up here."

The warrant officer turned to the coxswain and said something before he ascended the ladder. He stepped onto the deck of the Osage as Clark and the enlisted watch arrived. As was the custom for officers and enlisted coming aboard ship, the warrant officer saluted the flag on the fantail, turned, and saluted the officer on deck who returned his salute. Clark, Morton, and Russell introduced themselves. So did the warrant officer.

Warrant Officer Harry McVey was the supply officer aboard the USS Rigel, a cargo ship transporting clothes to the troops in the Solomons and New Hebrides. Resembling James Stewart, the actor, McVey was tall and slender. He could have passed for the actor's older brother.

"I understand you have a boson's mate first class, Buck Williams, aboard. Big fella," said McVey.

"Maybe," replied Morton slowly. "I'll have to check. Ship's company is rather new."

"You the CO?"

"No. I'm the XO, Lieutenant Donald Morton."

"I know you just got your crew, lieutenant. And

47

Williams is part of it. I checked."

"Has he done something wrong?" asked Morton.

"Gosh, no. He done something good. Saved me from a couple of thugs trying to shake me down. If not for him, I'd have been beat up bad and lost payroll for the Rigel."

"Where? Here in Tulagi?" asked Morton.

"No, sir. Noumea. A couple o' weeks ago," said McVey. "That Williams fella came up from behind 'em. He grabbed one by the collar and threw him to the side. That boy just ran off quick. Only thing I could see of him was asshole and elbows. The other, he smashed upside the head with his fist. That hooligan fell back a few feet and didn't get up. Lay there until the shore patrol dragged him away. Williams didn't want no formal thanks and left right away. I took it upon myself to find him out and thank him proper. When I found out he was attached to this here tanker, I reckoned a new crew might need some good deck shoes. Gets mighty hot in the South Pacific—'specially on a steel ship in the middle of the ocean. Don't slip neither! Got crepe soles. Sailors appreciate a good pair o' shoes on a weather deck. If he wouldn't let me thank him personally, I figured to let everybody on this ship thank Williams for me."

"Thank you, McVey." Morton was smiling. "I'll make sure Williams squirms with endless thanks from the crew. Can we swing the davit around and hoist those boxes up from the longboats?"

"You betcha," replied McVey. "You got 12 boxes with 12 pair o' shoes in each box. All sizes. Not many extra-wides, though. They're hard to come by."

"I'm sure what's here will be fine for all hands. Thanks, McVey." Morton extended his hand. McVey shook it vigorously.

Morton turned. "Mr. Clark, how soon can we distribute the shoes?"

"Just as soon as we get them aboard and logged, sir. Tomorrow, probably."

"Very well. See to it, Mr. Clark. I'll inform the captain."

"Aye, sir," he replied.

10 May 1944
0700 Hours
Tulagi Bay

All hands aboard the Osage were at general quarters. Michaels wanted the officers and crew to become familiar with their battle stations right away. The captain's orders were simple: After muster, all hands were to find their GQ billet and wait for the alarm to sound. Everyone had ample time to find how to get to their assigned station.

On the bridge, QM1 Emerson lifted the microphone from its cradle on the console. A long, thin grey cable connected the microphone to the console. The mike was metal and grey and fit in the palm of his hand like a square grenade with rounded edges. The quartermaster held it as if it were about to explode. He pressed a small square button on the side of the mike and spoke. "Now here this. Now here this. All hands, general quarters. This is a drill. All hands, general quarters. This is a drill."

Emerson set the mike back into the cradle and punched a large red button on the console. The loud, intermittent, bong—bong—bong rang through the 1MC, the ship's announcing system. He picked up the sound-powered headset, strapped it over his head, and twisted the plug into the outlet. The headset had two ear pieces connected by an adjustable head strap, and a microphone that rested on a small breastplate. To speak, the operator simply pressed the button on the microphone; to listen, release the button.

Sound-powered headsets connected all areas of the ship. The 1MC was the ship's public address system; headsets were the internal and emergency communications system. Information passed through the sound-powered system. When one station spoke, all other stations plugged into the circuit could hear everything said.

Major and secondary work spaces, watch stations, and control areas like the bridge had a sound-powered station. Each station had two outlets—one regular, one backup—and a station ID.

During drills, replenishments, refueling, entering port, leaving port, and general quarters, each station reported to the bridge when all hands were in place and at the ready. To report in, the sailor wearing the phones at his station called the bridge and said his station ID. The bridge acknowledged the caller, checked off each station and reported, to the commanding officer, the time it took for the entire ship to be at the ready. With all hands in place when the drill began, it took only a few minutes to report. Michaels wondered how long it would take when the drills came as a surprise during the work day or in the middle of the night.

0800 Hours

The Osage prepared to hoist anchor and leave Tulagi Bay for Espiritu Santo. Many, but not all hands, had specific tasks for entering and leaving port. Often, sailors manned the same station for entering and leaving port as they had for general quarters. Whatever the event, Michaels and Morton were on the bridge.

In the forecastle, 4-man work details—one port, one

starboard—were beside the big electric winches that raised the anchors. Each machine was almost twice as big as a good-sized metal desk. Each had a large gear shift on the side of the thin plate-metal housing. Both work details included a boatswain's mate at the start/stop button, an engineer watching the winch to make sure it ran smoothly, another boatswain's mate monitoring the chain, and an electrician on the sound-powered phones.

In the engine room, Becker and the black gang stood by. The huge diesel hummed stridently. As soon as the anchors were out of the water, they would engage the propeller and the Osage would be on its way.

On the bridge, Emerson stood at the helm. Another sailor, standing between the helm and the captain, manned the sound-powered phones. Michaels sat in his chair and Morton stood behind him. Michaels gave the order to raise the port anchor. The sailor with the phone relayed the order to the forecastle.

Rick Jackson watched BM1 Buck Williams push the large red button on the side of the winch. Jackson watched him carefully. He knew that Williams was powerful but lacked good coordination. A good-old boy from Florida, Williams weighed almost 250 pounds. He was 6 feet 4 inches tall and barrel-chested with arms and legs solid like tree trunks. One thick eyebrow ran across his brow and started down the bridge of his nose. Jackson thought that Williams must easily be the strongest man aboard.

The winch shuddered as it started and quickly settled into a loud 60-cycle hum. Using both hands, Williams grabbed the gear shift and pushed it forward. The port winch shuddered again. A sudden jerk and the winch slowly began to pull the huge metal grey chain out of the water. With a deafening scrape and clang as each link passed through the porthole, the chain crawled through the winch's housing into a large storage compartment below until, 5 minutes later, the top of the anchor rested at the porthole.

Williams locked the gear shift in place and turned off the winch.

Jackson ordered the electrician to tell the bridge that the port anchor was raised and secure.

Michaels received the news with a rare smile and patted the armrest with his right hand. With the port anchor up, the ship slowly turned with tide. To compensate, he told the helmsman to give him 5 degrees starboard rudder. The helmsman acknowledged and shifted the wheel in front of him. Michaels gave the order to raise the starboard anchor.

John Stacek stooped in the corner of the starboard forecastle and watched intently as Billy Phillips pushed the gear shift out of neutral and forward. The winch shuddered. The chain jerked and slowly moved up out of the water, into the forecastle with that same loud scrape and clang, through the housing, and into the compartment below.

Stacek smiled. He found it difficult to gauge how machinery would work until it was turned on. There were just too many things that could go wrong. And machines, like people, were temperamental. Most machines worked the way they should. But a few—even though they had all of the same parts in all of the same places as similar machines assembled by the same people at nearly the same time—didn't work exactly like their counterparts. Stacek couldn't explain it. He just knew it.

Jackson ducked into the compartment from the passageway. "How's everything going, chief?" asked Stacek.

"Fine, sir," he said. "Not a care."

No sooner were the words out of his mouth than the winch started pounding and hissing like an 800-pound cat. A small column of light blue smoke rose slowly from

52

the housing. Phillips grabbed the gear shift and pulled to bring it back into neutral. The lever wouldn't budge.

"Put your back into it, sailor!" shouted Stacek.

Phillips put his foot against the housing and pushed with his leg to give himself more leverage and power as he pulled again. Nothing. The winch still screamed and the blue smoke still rose in a thin, indifferent column. Stacek reached over and punched the red button. The winch ground to a halt and the chain stopped.

Jackson looked at Stacek but did not make eye contact. "Well, my winch worked fine."

Stacek ignored him. He told the electrician to report to the bridge that the winch was smoking and hissing and that he had shut it off.

Michaels glanced at Morton. "You have the bridge. I will be in foc's'l."

Morton replied, "Aye, sir."

Michaels jumped out of his chair. Morton watched him descend the stairwell and told the sailor with the phones to tell the forecastle that the captain was on his way.

When Michaels arrived, Jackson, Stacek, and Phillips stood behind two engineers kneeling on either side of the winch. The engineers had just finished unscrewing half a dozen metal plates of the housing so they could look at, and work on, the winch's motor.

Bill Kraft, senior engineer in the detail, had mopped up a puddle of dark brown oil with a rag. The other engineer was MM3 Jay Conway, barely in his twenties, blond hair cut in a flat top. His tool belt lay on the deck beside him. Conway was in the port forecastle sitting on the deck and waiting with the electrician for the detail to end when Chief Stacek ducked in and ordered him starboard.

"Captain on deck," called Jackson. Jackson and the enlisted men jumped to attention and saluted.

53

"As you vere. Vhat is problem?" Michaels looked directly at Kraft.

"We had some blue smoke, sir," replied Kraft. "Usually, that means a problem with oil."

Kraft reached in to find the dipstick. He pulled it up, wiped the tip with a rag, and reinserted it. Kraft held it in place for a moment and withdrew it again. He looked at the tip of the dipstick.

"She's pretty dry, sir," said Kraft. "When the motor is running, the oil circulates around the motor. When the motor stops, the oil flows down into the pan. Oil lubricates the pistons so they don't heat up from friction and expand in the cylinders. If that happens, the motor freezes. We got precious little oil in the pan." He lifted the dipstick to show Michaels. "We might have a problem with the pistons ... sir."

Bernard Edwards ducked into the overcrowded compartment.

He saluted Michaels. "Mr. Becker sent me, suh."

"This petty officer says vinch has oil problem. Maybe pistons too. How long to fix it?"

Edwards looked at Kraft.

"Five minutes after the winch started, we got blue smoke, chief. Then it froze quick," Kraft said. "When I opened the housing, I found a puddle of oil. I checked the oil pan and it was near dry. Might be a blown gasket."

Edwards turned back to Michaels. "Sounds like the pistons, suh. Prob'ly take half a day once we get the parts."

"Great Hamlet's ghost!" bellowed Michaels. "Can you use parts from port vinch?"

"Yes, suh. I reckon we can."

"Take parts from port vinch to repair starboard. You have two hours. Fix port vinch in Espiritu Santo" Michaels turned and stormed out of the forecastle.

Edwards looked at Conway. "Boy, double time it to engineering. Come back with Mr. Becker, Frederickson, and a double set of tools. Now, git!"

"Aye, sir." Conway jumped up and out of the forecastle.

Edwards turned to Kraft. "Let's start takin' this damned thing apart."

11 May 1944
1100 Hours
Coral Sea

Once underway, the tanker headed south-southeast at six knots toward Espiritu Santo, the largest and most mountainous island of the New Hebrides. At the southeastern tip of the island, the Allies constructed several large airstrips near the principal city, Santo. The airstrips were a major link in the Allied attack force and supply chain of the southwestern Pacific Ocean.

Santo sat at the head of a large natural harbor, perfect for large ships like aircraft carriers, battleships, and cruisers. Aore, a much smaller island a couple of miles to the southeast, boasted a large naval supply depot.

Like the day before, and the day before that, the sun smothered everything in the South Pacific with relentless, ever-present heat and humidity.

Michaels sat in the captain's chair on the bridge. His cap was pushed up on his forehead. Elbows propped on the arm rests, he looked straight ahead, out to sea, apparently at nothing in particular.

"Seventeen minutes, sir," said the quartermaster.

"Seventeen minutes." Michaels looked at the watch on his left forearm and shook his head. "Secure from general quarters. Ve try another drill at 1300 hours."

55

"Aye, sir," replied Morton.

1300 Hours

Michaels stood at the glass window on the bridge and watched the men on deck scramble to get to their assigned stations. Bong-bong-bong rang loud and clear through the ship's 1MC.

Four sailors, at the 3-inch-50 on the bow of the ship, rushed down the ladder to the deck and scattered like roaches in a sudden burst of light.

Directly below the bridge, at the base of the mast, five or six sailors turned—almost in unison—and started to run forward. One tripped and stumbled over a coiled rope. The two immediately behind slammed into him and all three fell to the deck in a sprawling mass of flesh, boots, hats, and rope.

Michaels threw his hands up in the air. "Ve are all dead!" His voice was loud. In the small confines of the bridge, it boomed.

He turned and addressed LT Morton. "Let them sit in this heat for an hour. Vhile they sit, devise plan to make GQ in four minutes. I vill be in my stateroom."

"Aye, sir," replied Morton.

16 May 1944
0900 Hours
Espiritu Santo

With the winch repaired, the Osage sat calmly a little southeast of Santo, just outside the harbor. The huge diesel hummed steadily in the engine room. Officers and crew were adjusting slowly, painfully, to the new shoes. The thick soles protected their feet from the tropical heat and hot metal weather decks, but created an equally insidious—albeit temporary— menace: blisters.

The naval air station was northwest of the tanker's anchorage. Occasionally, the roar of bombers and P-38s, landing and taking off, drowned the ceaseless noisy natter of hammers chipping paint and rust aboard ship. The crew worked in two-section duty: one day on, one day off. The ubiquitous heat and humidity soaked uniforms with sweat and dampened enthusiasm for the task at hand.

Less than a mile to the east was Aore. The navy storage depot covered a large section of the western end of the island. An 8-foot chain-link fence, topped with razor-sharp barbed wire, surrounded the almost exhaustive selection of supplies. Because of Aore's central location, The armed forces stored everything from abacuses to zinc ointments at the depot for distribution throughout the South Pacific.

A slender wooden guard box stood just inside the chain-link gate. A single heavy padlock kept the gates in place. One guard was on duty in the compound 24 hours a day. Every 4 hours, he walked the perimeter, checked the few small storage sheds, and returned to the guard box. The guard changed every 8 hours.

Jackson sat backwards on the chair in his stateroom. His chest leaned into the back; arms wrapped around it; hands clasped. He had company. Stacek and Williams sat on his bunk and faced him. Phillips stood near the door with his back to the passageway.

"We have 24 large cans of red-brown paint on the fantail that we don't want," he said. "Aore has 24 large cans of blue-grey paint that they don't need. I say we swap the paint. Chief, any thoughts?"

"How far is Aore from here?" asked Stacek.

"According to the harbor chart, 45 minutes—maybe an hour—if we use one of our powerboats."

57

"We'll need both boats. Those cans aren't that big, but they are heavy." Stacek looked to his left. "Can you handle 'em, Williams?"

"I can handle 'em. How much time will we have?"

"Two hours," said Jackson.

Phillips spoke up. "Sir, they have 24 cans and we have 24 cans. That's less than 3 minutes per can. We have to unload the old paint, load the new paint, and restack the cans like we found 'em—without any noise. Two hours ain't enough time."

All three enlisted men looked at Jackson.

"How about a dry run, lieutenant?" asked Stacek. "We can plan better if we see it firsthand."

"All right, chief. Ready the starboard powerboat at 2100. Everyone wears dungarees and ball caps. And blacken your faces with burnt cork or something."

2130 Hours

A half moon rose slowly in the sidereal blackness of the night sky. Jackson, Stacek, and Williams sat in the center of the powerboat skimming across the water. Phillips had the helm. The powerboat hummed as it rose and fell with the waves. A light breeze lifted saltwater spray into the boat. Jackson constantly mopped his face with a handkerchief. The others didn't seem to mind.

As they approached the island, Stacek pointed to a few small red lights. At night, the military used red lights instead of white. Even the smallest white light could be seen for miles on a clear night. Red lights did not carry as far.

As soon as the powerboat drifted into the island with the surf, Phillips cut the engine, swung the outboard motor out of the water, and locked it into place with a cotter pin. He brought the boat to shore just north of a long wooden pier. Williams hopped out of the boat. The water came to his knees. He grabbed the bow and lugged it up onto the beach.

Stacek, Jackson, and Phillips climbed out and helped drag the boat farther up on the sand to keep it from being pulled out to sea with the tide.

All four men set their watches with flashlights. It was 2150 hours. Jackson told Williams to head north and Stacek south toward the pier. He would go inland. Everyone had to be back at 2300 hours. Phillips stayed with the boat and alternately watched all three men disappear into the night.

2245 Hours

Stacek returned first. He carried a six-pack and was breathing heavily. Phillips started to ask him a question but the chief waved him off and sat on a rock next to the boat.

Williams arrived a few minutes later. "I found dry storage," he said and held up a box of crackers and a wedge of cheese.

At 2305, Jackson returned with flashlight in hand. "Let's shove off," he said. All four men grabbed the boat and slid it into the water. With the propellers of the outboard in the water, Phillips wound and yanked the cord. The small gasoline engine sputtered. He wound the cord again and yanked it. The engine started and the boat lurched into the surf.

Well out to sea, Jackson asked Williams and Stacek what they found.

"Not much," began Williams. "I went north but all I found was a barracks and a couple of storage sheds. Brought these along for the ride home." He nudged the crackers and cheese on his lap.

59

"Fine job," replied Jackson. "I worked up an appetite. Pass 'em around, Williams."

The large boatswain's mate opened the box and tore the waxed paper. He reached in, pulled out a handful of saltines, and passed the box to the lieutenant.

Jackson took the box and looked at Stacek. "Looks like you scored too, chief." He reached into the box and retrieved a handful of crackers. He passed the box to Phillips.

"The mess hall was closed but they didn't lock the walk-in. Security is pretty lax. I liberated this six-pack." He grabbed a can, pulled it off the plastic ring, and handed it to Jackson. He gave one to Williams and one to Phillips.

"Nothing like a beer to wash down cheese and crackers—even if it is lukewarm Budweiser," replied Jackson. He was the only one who laughed.

"Well, I found the compound on the other side of the inlet. Tall fence with barbed wire and a padlock on the gate. The fence is close to the water so we should be able to pull up close in boats. Chief, how are you with locks?" Jackson took a long gulp from the beer can.

Phillips interrupted. "I can grab the lock cutters from the boson's locker."

"That won't do at all, mister," replied Jackson. "We don't want them to know we swapped paint until we are long gone. That means no wire cutters either." Jackson turned to Stacek. "Chief?"

Stacek shook his head. "I cut 'em open or pry 'em open. I don't have the finesse to pick a lock. But I might know someone who does."

"Who, chief?" asked Jackson.

"Let me talk to him first, sir. I don't know the man that well."

"I'll leave it to you, chief."

"One other thing, lieutenant," continued Stacek.

"What is it, chief?"

"I'm not the man for this job. I got winded on the beach. You need strong, fast legs. If this other man takes the duty, let him replace me straightaway."

"Are you sure, chief?" asked Jackson.

"Yes, sir." Stacek nodded.

"Very well, chief." Jackson lifted his can of beer to the center of the group. "To success." he said.

The others lifted their beer cans. "To success."

17 May 1944
1000 Hours
Espiritu Santo

Lem Turkin was on his knees. He was hot and sticky and unhappy. With a chipping hammer, he pounded the rust on the afterdeck and wondered why he responded to that recruitment poster on the corner of 5th and Spruce. He was doing all right on the streets with a hell of a lot less effort than he was putting out now.

Turkin was stocky—thick shoulders and forearms. And he kept to himself. Some of the crew noticed that he surrounded his plate with his arms and leaned over his food when he ate. It was a routine practiced by more than one ex-con. He was still muttering to himself when Stacek walked up to him.

"Turkin?" asked Stacek.

"Yeah, I'm Turkin."

"Knock off for a while and come with me."

Now what, he wondered.

Turkin dropped the hammer and stood. Stacek led him to a compartment in the aft superstructure. Turkin quickly surveyed the room. It was small and empty.

61

Stacek noticed Turkin was uneasy. "I'm having the place redone," said the chief boatswain's mate. "All this grey is depressing." Stacek smiled. "Can I call you Lem?"

"Sure, chief."

"Lem, what kind of work did you do before you enlisted?"

"Odd Jobs."

"Like what?"

"Night watchman. Auto body shop. Stuff like that."

"Know anything about padlocks?"

"Why ask me, chief?"

"I need someone who can open a lock."

"Why don't you just cut it or pop it?"

"The lock I have needs a softer touch."

"Ah. What kind of lock?"

"Standard navy issue.

"Key or combination?

"Key."

"Aboard ship?"

Stacek shook his head. "Nope."

"What kind of tools do you have?"

"What kind of tools do I need?"

Turkin hesitated and looked Stacek in the eye. "Level with me, chief. What's the grift?"

"The lock's on a gate. I need the gate opened quick. No noise. No commotion. No talking later."

"Are you in, chief? Or are you just a front man?"

"I'm in deep but I'm not part of the work detail."

"Who else is in?"

"You'll find out when it's time."

"What's in it for me?"

Stacek took a deep breath. "What do you want?"

"Let's see," replied Turkin. He paced a few steps back and forth. "I want to be the gunner for that big gun on the bow."

"No way," replied the chief. "I might be able to get you on one of 20 millimeters, but not the 3-inch-50."

Turkin replied quickly. "Deal. I'll need a small, flat-head jeweler's screwdriver and a metal shim like the kind to set the gap in a spark plug. The shim's gotta be about a six-teenth inch wide. Thin but strong." Turkin held up his thumb and forefinger to show Stacek. "I'll also need a can of WD-40 and an oil can."

"You got it, Lem. One last thing. Can you keep your mouth shut?"

"I learned to do that a long time ago, chief."

"Good. At 2100 be at the starboard powerboat. Wear dungarees and blacken your face."

"Tonight?"

"Tonight. Now, back to the hammer."

2100 Hours

Jackson, Stacek, Williams, Phillips, and Turkin mustered at the starboard powerboat. All but Stacek walked back to the fantail to get the paint. The cans were black and more than twice the size of store-bought paint. Each lifted a can by the wooden grip in the center of a wire handle. They were so heavy that Williams was the only man who carry one in each hand.

After they loaded the red-brown paint into the two boats—12 cans in each boat—Jackson gave them instructions how to approach the compound. Jackson and Williams went in the starboard boat; Phillips and Turkin, in the port. Stacek remained aboard. He stayed by the davit on the tanker's deck to lift the paint when they returned.

The sky was partially overcast and, luckily, the sea was very calm. The boats sat low in the water from the heavy cans of paint. They would have sunk quickly in rougher water.

Because the fence was so close to the water, and they didn't know exactly where the guard would be on his rounds, Jackson had them again cut the engines early and drift in with the surf. The boats were so deep in the water that they ran aground five yards from shore. Williams and Turkin carried the cans ashore before Jackson and Phillips hauled in the boats and secured them.

In a few trips, the group brought all of the paint quietly down the beach. Williams and Turkin showed no signs of wear but Jackson and Phillips were winded. And Jackson's biceps were beginning to tighten. He stretched his arms and looked at his watch: 2230 hours.

Turkin held up his hand. He put his forefinger vertically across his mouth, pointed to himself and then to the gate. He loosened a large leather pouch tied to his belt, held it in his hand, and walked ten yards or so to the gate.

First, Turkin checked the gate and lock for wires and alarms. He found none. He lifted the WD-40 from the pouch and generously sprayed the keyhole of the padlock. Turkin replaced the WD-40 and pulled out the metal shim and jeweler's screwdriver. He inserted the shim into the keyhole. With the other hand he slipped in the small screwdriver next to the shim.

Slowly, Turkin twisted the screwdriver until he felt the tumbler. He pushed up and twisted again. The tumbler fell away and the padlock opened with a soft click.

Turkin put the hacker's tools back into the bag and pulled out the oil can. He oiled the hinges of the gate. He motioned to the others to start bringing the cans up the sand bank. Turkin kept a watchful eye for the guard. When all of the paint was at the foot of the entrance, Turkin pushed the gate. It slid silently open.

All four men rushed inside to the paint locker, grabbed a can, and carried it to the gate. The group emptied 24 cans from the locker and replaced them with the 24 they brought to the island. The navy had a habit of using black cans for every kind of paint. Before they left the Osage, Stacek notched each can of red-brown paint with a metal file. That way, they could identify the cans they swapped in against the ones they swapped out.

At 2345 hours, Jackson, Williams, Phillips, and Turkin stood outside the gate with 24 cans of blue-grey paint. They were sweaty and tired. Turkin wiped the lock and hinges with a rag. He closed the gate, secured the padlock, and brushed fresh sand on the entrance to cover the oil and WD-40 that dripped to the ground. Then all four picked up a can and walked up the beach to the powerboats. By the time they had the paint loaded in the powerboats, it was one o'clock in the morning.

They arrived at the Osage a few minutes before 0200 hours. One by one, Stacek pulled up the cans with the davit on the fantail. When the four came aboard, he had cold beer and sandwiches waiting. They ate quickly. After the meal, Jackson spoke.

"Great job, men. Sleep in. Your division officers and duty section officers have been notified that you will miss morning muster." Jackson stretched his arms. "Oh, and one last thing: This never happened."

Phillips yawned and said, "I don't know what you're talking about, lieutenant."

18 May 1944
0800 Hours
Aore Storage Facility, Enlisted Men's Barracks

Sergeant Keith Leonard marched into the barracks

and stood at the head of the row of bunks. Leonard was a marine, bitter because he had been relegated to guard a storage depot far from the front lines. He wanted to see action. But his age was cause for his superior officer to transfer him to Aore. He took out his bitterness on his subordinates.

"Who had the graveyard last night?" he barked.

Private First Class Joe Rodriguez jumped to attention. "Sergeant! I did!" he shouted back.

Rodriguez stood near his bunk halfway down the row. Leonard strode down the aisle and stood toe to toe with the private. Everyone in the barracks turned to watch.

"Did you check the paint locker, soldier?"

"Yes, sergeant! 2200 hours and 0200 hours!"

"Why is the grass trampled in front of the door?"

"Trampled, sir?"

"Trampled. It means smashed, flattened."

"Yes, sergeant, I know what . . ."

"Then if you're so damned smart, why is it flattened? Were your buddies out there smoking fags and keeping you company while you were on watch, private?"

"No, sir!"

"If I catch you smoking in the paint locker, I'm gonna kick your ass all the way to Guadalcanal. You got that, soldier?"

"Yes, sergeant!"

The sergeant turned and scanned the room. "And that goes for everyone here."

All of the other soldiers turned away and pretended to be busy with something in their lockers.

Leonard turned back to Rodriguez. "As you were, mister."

Rodriguez saluted and turned away from the sergeant.

66

Chapter 5
The Change

18 May 1944
1000 Hours
Espiritu Santo

Now that the paint chipping was nearly complete, the Osage had to be primed and painted—including the two 90-foot masts. The problem was finding someone to climb the masts. Almost all of the men were able. Few, if any, were willing. At morning muster, Jackson asked for volunteers.

Tony Fiore was a seaman apprentice, the lowest rank in the navy, but smart, talented, and agile. Before the war, he was a professional softball pitcher. Fiore had no problem advancing in rank. He had problems keeping rank. Fiore liked to drink when he had shore leave. And he often got busted for being drunk and disorderly.

Stacek, Buck Williams, and Billy Phillips stood at the foot of the forward mast. Williams and Phillips were looking up. Stacek watched Fiore walk up to the group.

"Chief, you lookin' for someone to paint the masts?" asked Fiore.

"No," replied Phillips. He pointed to the top of the mast. "But the sky hooks need to be calibrated."

"Zip it, Phillips," ordered Stacek. He turned to Fiore. "What's your name, sailor?"

"Tony Fiore."

"You got experience up high, Fiore?"

"Nope. Just rig me a good boson's chair, chief."

"A boson's chair? Sorry, Fiore. We can't rig a chair to the masts. They're too high and too narrow. You gotta wear

67

a vest. It kinda looks like a skinny parachute with clips at the ends of a couple of straps. You clip the vest to the toe rungs welded to the mast—like this." Stacek took an imaginary clip in his right hand and moved to the mast. He stepped on the bottom rung and hooked the imaginary clip to a rung, chest high." Clip, step … clip, step. It's slow goin' but safe enough."

"Just don't forget to clip. I saw one guy slip and fall 60 feet. Wasn't pretty," added Williams.

"Still interested?" asked Stacek.

"Sure. No problem. I'll do both masts."

"Good man!" replied Stacek. He turned to Phillips. "If Fiore needs anything, get it for him. If you have any problems, come straight to me. Got it?"

"Aye, sir. When do we start?"

"You're day on, day off, just like everyone else. And consider yourselves on duty, so get started," replied Stacek laughing as he and Williams walked away.

19 May 1944
0900 Hours
Espiritu Santo

In the ocean between Espiritu Santo and Aore—as all through the South Pacific—a bevy of islets dotted the seascape. None were big enough to put on maps and they were almost completely covered by sand. Some boasted a few palm trees. On one of the islets close to the Osage, the crew took turns on liberty. Every day, both powerboats shuttled men, food, beverages, and game gear between islet and ship.

Chipping and painting an entire ship was arduous, loud, and boring. Officers and enlisted men relished time away from the tanker. They read books, exercised, played softball, volleyball, and card games. Poker, hearts, and spades were very popular. From debris left on the islet by crews from other ships, and castoffs from the airbase on Espiritu Santo, they fashioned simple benches, tables, and whatever else they needed.

A group of the ships' company disembarked from one of the powerboats onto the islet. Six of them set up a game of poker. Two other sailors had books to read and claimed a seat beneath a weathered palm tree. Most stood ready to choose sides for a softball game. Softball and volleyball were usually played early—before the oppressive heat terminated physically strenuous activities.

Only one or two of the men had gloves and they were seldom shared with the opposing team. The owners referred to their selfish custody as "fair advantage". Fiore owned a glove. So did Billy Phillips. Tipton carried a duffel bag filled with bats and balls. Lewis and another sailor carried a cooler of beer, soda, and water to the makeshift field. Phillips called to him.

"Hey, Lewis, you're pretty smart. How did these little islands get here?"

Lewis set down his end of the cooler.

"Greek mythology claims that Poseidon, the god of the sea, wanted to marry Hestia, the first-born virgin goddess on Mount Olympus and patroness of the earth. She refused but he pursued her relentlessly. So she spit in his eye to insult him and stop his advances. The result is all of these little islets in the sea."

For a moment the group, not knowing if he was serious or teasing, was silent and waited for him to continue. One sailor nudged his buddy with an elbow and asked, "What the fuck is he talkin' about?"

Lewis' face remained laconic, expressionless, as he returned the gazes of the sailors around him.

69

"Okay," said Phillips breaking the silence, "we're playing softball on a sand spit. I'm choosing first and I take Fiore." He pointed to Fiore with his glove. "Who's captain of the other team? Choose your man."

Buck Williams stepped forward and pointed to a sailor. "Tipton." In a few minutes sides were chosen.

Phillips was a self-admitted smart-mouth. But he was no fool. Working with Fiore, Phillips discovered he was a pro softballer before being prompted to join the service. Apparently, Fiore had been arrested more than once for fighting and drunken public disturbances. The local judge reached the limit of his patience with Fiore and gave him an ultimatum: the armed forces or jail. He eagerly chose the Coast Guard.

What Phillips didn't know was that Fiore was a pitcher and the ball flew out of his hand like a rocket. One pitch into the game, Phillips had to surrender his glove to the catcher.

Fiore's delivery was unique. He always wound up before he released the ball. Most of the time he let go after one full rotation. Sometimes, however, he released after two rotations, so the batter really never knew when to expect the pitch.

Jackson sat on the bench of the opposing team. When he saw Fiore pitch, he smiled, rubbed his hands together, and muttered "excellent" under his breath. As the game progressed, a plan to field a team and play for stakes against other ships in the South Pacific slowly developed in his mind. He made mental notes of players, positions, and batting order.

23 May 1944
1700 Hours
Espiritu Santo

During a poker game on the sand spit, seaman Gil Fillmore drank too much beer and lost a lot of his pay. Two or three beers in the tropic heat could cloud a man's judgment. Serious card players drank soda and water. Fillmore had four beers.

Unhappy with his losses, Fillmore took a Swiss army knife out of his pocket and lunged at the sailor who held most of the day's winnings. Fortunately for the sailor, Fillmore was too drunk and slow to do much serious damage. He only cut the forearm of his intended victim.

With his knife in hand, the drunken sailor slowly backed away from the card game, grabbed two more beers, and went down to the beach to wait for the powerboat to take him back to the ship. On the ride back, the other sailors in the boat stayed clear of Fillmore who sat in the back.

Fillmore was the last to scale the ladder to the deck of the Osage. As he stepped on deck, ENS Russell, the officer on deck, challenged the sailor to stop and surrender the knife. Crew members who climbed the ladder before Fillmore were quick to tell the officer about the incident ashore. Russell wore a sidearm, a 45-caliber pistol. He placed his hand on the handle of the gun as he approached the drunken sailor. Russell was more than a little worried because his gun had no ammunition and everyone aboard ship knew it.

Fillmore refused and backed away toward the forward superstructure. He slowly waived the knife back and forth to keep the officer at bay.

Stacek pushed through the crowd watching the officer and enlisted man. He quickly sized up the situation and charged Fillmore.

"What the fuck are you doing?" he shouted. "Give me that goddamned knife."

Fillmore stepped back. When the chief was close, he

raised his hand quickly to strike down at his assailant. On the upswing, his wrist hit a stationary air vent. For a moment, he lost his grip on the knife and looked to see what he had hit.

Stacek saw his moment and lunged like a bear. He grabbed Fillmore's arms. Fillmore shouted and kicked Stacek's shin. Stacek held tight. As they struggled, other crew members grabbed the sailor. In a moment, he was subdued. Two men held Fillmore's arms as they and the officer of the day marched him to the brig, the ship's small one-room sjail in the 'tween decks.

The captain watched the commotion from the bridge. He was disheartened by the incident because he knew he had to send Fillmore to the stockade ashore after a formal captain's mast. Captain's mast is the navy's court at sea. The captain of the ship is the judge. An officer brings charges against the accused who defends himself. Sometimes other officers or fellow enlisted men speak on behalf of the accused. Michaels knew no one would speak on Fillmore's behalf.

28 May 1944
0900 Hours
The Sand Spit

The crew finished painting the tanker. From mast to waterline and bow to stern, she was scraped clean, covered with an undercoat of red lead, and brushed with a thick, fresh coat of blue-grey paint. The heat quickly dried the viscous paint and soon the ship sparkled in the summer tropical sun like a top-of-the-line tanker.

To celebrate the ship's new look, Michaels authorized an all-hands party on the sand spit. Stewards left the ship early to prepare a cookout for the afternoon meal. A handful of sailors built a large barbeque pit from barrels and pieces of an old chain-link fence.

Other crew members doubled the number of benches and tables to accommodate the entire crew. Electricians carried a generator to the islet and set up a movie projector for an evening movie. Boatswain's mates used bed sheets to rig a giant screen.

A couple of inventive swabbies rigged a makeshift shower so the crew could cool off. They dug a shallow pit under one of the palm trees and made a partition from sheets unused for the movie screen. Then, they ran a hose from the ocean to the pit and tied it to a metal rod hammered into the trunk of the tree. One of them took a large empty chili can and, with a screwdriver, poked holes in the bottom of the can to make a showerhead. He hung it from the metal rod with a piece of wire. The sailor sucked on the hose until siphoned water ran freely. He turned his head, spit salt water out of his mouth, and placed the end of the hose in the soup can. The ocean water slowly filled the can and fell out through the holes in the bottom. As he stepped into the shower pit, the sailor received a roar of approval from onlookers.

Half a dozen coolers were filled with beer and soda. As many jugs of water were also carried ashore. To prevent another Fillmore incident, Michaels ordered beer off limits until the afternoon. And each sailor had a three-beer limit.

Softball and volleyball games, checkers, chess games, and card games filled the morning. One sailor had a guitar; another, a harmonica. It wasn't long before someone grabbed an empty, discarded barrel and used it for a drum. The impromptu combo played songs by all of the big bands. A couple of sailors tried to sing along but they were soon booed—almost unanimously—into silence.

When the merciless heat forced the games to stop

just after noon, the crew prepared for the feast. Gamers showered. Chow lines were clearly marked with ropes. Tables were moved close so the entire crew sat together in camaraderie. Coolers, recently stocked with beer to chill, were placed strategically between tables.

After an hour or so, the meal began. More hot dogs and pork steaks than anyone cared to count, buns and bread, hard-boiled eggs, large bags of potato chips, mustard, and ketchup filled the improvised tables. Men shared pictures and stories of their families, told jokes (the raunchier—the better), cursed the Germans and Japanese, guessed where the top brass might send their ship next, and wondered about the course of the war.

When the meal ended, everyone just languished in the heat. Some returned to their card games. Some took naps. A few went to the shower. Some went for a swim. Late in the day, all hands helped the stewards clean up. Equipment brought ashore for the barbeque was carried to the beach and arranged near the powerboats. Only the movie projector remained in place.

Just before sunset, the officers rounded up the crew to assemble for a few words from the captain before the electricians powered up the projector. Michaels stepped in front of the provisional movie screen.

The XO stood at his table and shouted, "Company, atten ... hut!"

Officers and crew rose and stood at attention.

"As you vere," said Michaels loud enough for everyone to hear. All hands returned to their seats. "Vell, I thank each and every vone for job vell done. Ya, she vas a floating piss pot but she's a fine-looking lady now." The crew howled in agreement. Michaels smiled. "Tomorrow ve sail for Tulagi but now Mr. Jackson has a movie and I think it's a new vone." The crew applauded and shouted their approval. "Only vone more thing." Michaels paused. "Enjoy yourselves tonight because tomorrow ve go to var."

As Michaels took his seat for the movie, the crew stood and cheered their captain. When the electricians started the reel-to-reel and the credits of the movie began to flicker on the sheets, the chatter hushed and clapping quickly died.

After the movie, Michaels was in the first boatload back to the Osage. He sauntered up to his stateroom and left the door open so the heat radiating from the bulkheads would be carried away quicker on the evening breeze.

Michaels avoided drinking beer on the sand spit because he had to preside over captain's mast in the morning. Tonight, he had to prepare for the proceedings. Although he had only heard about what happened between Fillmore and Stahl after the poker game, he witnessed the knife threat to the officer of the day on the deck of his ship. That, in itself, was a punishable offense.

The Dane walked to the desk and picked up a ballpoint pen. He took off his cap and set it down. Then, Michaels lifted a pad of paper and walked to his bunk. As he sat, Michaels dropped the pen. It rolled under his bed as the ship listed gently to port in the ocean current.

"Great Hamlet's ghost!" he said. Irritated, Michaels threw the pad on the mattress and knelt beside his bunk. He bent over and looked beneath the bed. The pen started to roll back as the ship returned to an even keel and leaned to starboard. As the captain reached for the pen, he saw a metal box, more than a foot long, under the headboard. It was welded to the floor.

Michaels put the pen on the pad of paper and stretched out on the warm metal floor. He reached under, lifted the lid, and put his hand in the box. Michaels felt a glass bottle. He pulled it out and looked at an unopened

75

bottle of brandy. As he brushed off dirt and dust, he thought about how the bottle had survived a torpedo, floating adrift, repair and reconstruction, and the past month or so. Perhaps Commander Johns was right. Maybe this ship was a lucky lady.

Patting the label he said, "Thanks, old girl," as if she might answer.

Michaels stood and, with bottle in hand, walked into the head. He washed the bottle and wiped it dry with a towel. He went back to his bunk and tucked the bottle under his pillow.

2200 Hours

Jackson was sleeping soundly in his bunk. Normally, he was a light sleeper. But after hours of playing softball in the Pacific sun and a few beers during the movie, he slept hard. Jackson didn't hear the first knock. The second one woke him. He rolled out of his bunk and opened the door. "Who the f…" Jackson stopped in mid-sentence when he opened the door and his eyes focused on the commanding officer.

Michaels was to the point. "Mr. Jackson, I vant to see you and the other four who got the paint."

"Yes, sir." Jackson leaned against the door jam and yawned. "After muster in the morning?"

"Thirty minutes, my stateroom!"

Jackson rubbed his eyes in disbelief. "Sir?"

"Dress whites!" Michaels turned and left a bewildered lieutenant in the doorway.

Jackson closed the door. "Dress whites in the middle of the goddamned night. No wonder the Danes lost Denmark. They're fucking crazy."

76

2230 Hours

Jackson, Stacek, Williams, Phillips, and Turkin stood outside of the captain's stateroom. Jackson knocked. The captain opened the door and greeted them with a smile. He was in full dress uniform as well. "Ya, come in," he said.

When everyone was in the room, Jackson said, "Company, atten ... hut!" The group stood at attention.

Michaels walked to the head and returned seconds later. He carried a small tray laden with six glasses and a bottle of brandy. "At ease," he said.

Michaels strode across the room and placed the tray on the table. He broke the seal on the bottle and poured a finger of brandy in each glass. He handed one to each man in the room.

"You made me proud of this ship and you gave life to an old voman. You vorked above and beyond the call of duty. I salute you."

Michaels raised his glass and saluted the five men in front of him. He emptied the glass with one gulp. Each raised his glass and followed in kind. They set their glasses on the table. Michaels picked up the bottle of brandy and poured another finger into each glass.

"Vone more salute."

They picked up the glasses and held them ready for the toast.

"To Ellen," said Michaels, "an old sea whore but a fine-looking ship."

"To Ellen," the rest repeated. All six men emptied their glasses and set them on the table again.

"Ve have a long day tomorrow, gentlemen. Thank you and goodnight."

The five sailors left the captain's stateroom almost as quickly as they had arrived. Down the ladder to the deck,

Phillips asked to no one in particular, "Who the hell is Ellen?"

"Ellen Hagerman was the name of this ship before she was recommissioned," replied Jackson.

"Why'd they rename her?" asked Turkin.

"The navy rebuilt her after she was torpedoed a few years ago. The navy commissions tankers after rivers and lakes with American Indian names," said Jackson. "Osage fits the billet. Ellen Hagerman doesn't."

"Still," Williams said, "it was damned nice of the captain to bring us to his stateroom for a toast."

Jackson responded without hesitation. "Yeah, but it's damned near midnight! Why couldn't it wait until tomorrow? After supper or something."

"It's his way," replied Stacek. "Just enjoy the honor."

"I'd rather be enjoying some shuteye."

29 May 1944
0700 Hours
Espiritu Santo

Michaels sat at the head of the table in the officer's wardroom. Gil Fillmore sat at the other end of the table. His wrists were handcuffed. Two guards stood behind him—one on each side of the chair. Jackson stood behind the guards. Russell sat mid-table, his back to the bulkhead. Morton, on the other side of the table, stood with his back to the door. He faced Fillmore and held a clipboard in his right hand. Everyone wore dress whites.

Morton read a litany of charges against Fillmore. When he finished, he asked Fillmore how he wanted to plead.

"Not guilty," replied Fillmore.

Morton turned to the captain. "With your permission, sir."

"Proceed," said Michaels.

Morton opened the door and stepped into the passageway. He returned in less than a minute with Seaman George Stahl. Stahl was in his mid twenties—with short brown hair and big, brown, cow eyes. He held his hat at the waist with both hands and sat in the chair opposite Russell. Facing the captain, Morton stood between him and Fillmore.

"Tell us what happened on the islet, Mr. Stahl," Morton said.

"About half a dozen of us were playin' cards, sir," began Stahl. "Gil—Seaman Fillmore—had too many beers and was losin' bad. We told him to give it up but he wanted to keep playin'. So we stopped dealin' him in. He got mad and pulled the knife. Cut me 'cross the forearm." Stahl held his arm forward to show the bandage that covered his forearm. "Gave me 12 stitches."

Fillmore broke in. "That lyin' sack of shit was cheatin'." He pointed at Stahl.

Morton told him to remain quiet until it was his turn to speak.

"Vhy did he cut you and not someone else?" asked Michaels.

"I was holdin' the cards. I wouldn't deal him in."

"Why did you not deal cards to him?"

"Like I said, he was losin' bad. I was tryin' to cut his losses 'cause he wasn't thinkin' straight."

"You von some money, ya?"

"Yes, sir," replied Stahl. "It ain't often I win big. But I had some hot hands, for sure."

"Vere you cheating?"

"No, sir! Fillmore was drunk. No one else thought I was cheatin'."

79

Morton excused Stahl and told him to send in another sailor. All five sailors playing cards with Fillmore that day told roughly the same story. No one else thought Stahl had cheated during the card game. Russell next related the incidents on deck when Fillmore returned to the ship. Then Stacek was called in from the passageway to give his account of what happened on deck.

When Stacek left, Morton turned to Fillmore. "What do you have to say for yourself, mister?"

Fillmore looked down at the table. He knew nothing he could say that would change the verdict about to be read.

"Captain, it's true I had a couple of beers. But I could've swore Stahl was cheatin'. I wanted bad to hurt him for takin' my money. As for what happened on deck, I don't know. I just got caught up in somethin'. It's like I had no control. I was mad and I wanted to hurt someone and I didn't want no one messin' with me. Maybe I done a fool thing."

"Mr. Fillmore," began Michaels, "I find you guilty of assault with deadly weapon. Vhen you attack fellow sailor in time of war, it is punishable by death." Michaels paused and looked out the porthole to his right. Fillmore's eyes grew wide.

Michaels asked Jackson to step forward. "Mr. Jackson, is Fillmore good vorker?"

"I've never had a problem with him, sir. He's always on time for muster and works as hard as everyone else."

"Mr. Morton, change the charge against Seaman Fillmore. Make it dereliction of duty that caused bodily harm to another sailor. I don't know correct article in Uniform Code of Military Justice. Write it good, ya?"

"Yes, sir."

"Mr. Fillmore, you vill probably stay in stockade until end of var. I don't know vhat vill happen then. But thank God you are alive. Dismissed."

"Prison! But sir …"

Michaels cut him short. "Prison or firing squad. I give you the choice."

Fillmore was silent.

Michaels turned to the first lieutenant. "Mr. Jackson, escort Mr. Fillmore off ship to stockade at Espiritu Santo."

"Aye, sir."

"Mr. Morton, vhen they return, hoist anchor and set course for Tulagi Bay. I vill be in my stateroom."

"Aye, sir."

1 June 1944
1000 Hours
South Pacific

Before the Osage raised anchor to return to Tulagi Bay, Lycovec petitioned the captain to allot more time for gunnery practice and Michaels readily agreed. He ordered the helmsman to set a course for the Banks Islands just north of Espiritu Santo.

While he was chipping and painting, Gunner's Mate First Class John Tipton wondered when they'd be able to practice on the guns. Without practice, it would be well nigh impossible for a gun crew to coordinate and execute well enough to hit the broad side of a barn from the inside.

Tipton was an average guy: 5 feet 9 inches tall, 160 pounds, squinty blue eyes and thin lips. He parted his brown hair down the middle and kept it slicked down with an occasional handful of water. He didn't like hair creams. Tipton liked to exercise and the cream burned his eyes when it mixed with sweat and ran down his brow.

During one of the softball games on the sand spit, Tipton saw a pile of discarded metal oil drums. They might be a little small but if a gun team could hit one of those—or come relatively close—it could hit a plane. That would be a life-saving asset if the Japanese attacked their ship. He corked the holes in a few and brought them aboard the Osage.

Tipton had urged Lycovec to ask the captain for gunnery practice and showed him the drums he stowed in one of the holds. When Lycovec talked to Michaels, he took the captain to the hold where the drums were stored. The captain was easily persuaded to detour for practice. Michaels was curious to see how the gun crews would perform.

A drum was dropped into the water offshore of one of the small uninhabited islands. The Osage moved a few hundred yards away and made three passes, slowly back and forth. That way, the port and starboard gun tubs had 3 chances each to hit the floating target.

GM3 Ted Sedgwick was harnessed into the seat of the 20-mm gun forward, starboard side. He was just a kid, barely 20 years old, and more than a little intimidated to shoot first in front of almost the entire ship's company on deck to watch. Sailors bet on who would and would not hit the target, and on what pass the drum would be hit. They even bet on how long it would take the drum to sink.

With his foot on the deck, Sedgwick shifted his weight to the left and the gun swung right. He squeezed the trigger and held it. Ship's Steward BJ Owens fed the ammunition belt into the housing chamber from a pile on the deck. Although a bright cloudless morning, tracers clearly marked the flight of the 20-mm shells as they shot high over the mark.

As the ship slowly sailed past the drum, Sedgwick eased his weight to the right and the gun slid left. He wasted half a belt before he stopped. Not one hit! Dollar bills quickly changed hands between sailors to a chorus of jeers and cheers.

The gunners aft fared no better. The gunners port side missed as well. On the second pass, gunners and feeders changed positions so both men could practice firing the gun.

Like the first pass, no one hit the drum bobbing lazily in the ocean current. GM3 Dave Ritter was young, but confident and determined. His father was a lifer in the army and he grew up with guns. The 20-mm was, however, the largest piece of hardware he had ever handled. In the port gun tub aft, he came close to the target on the third pass but did not hit it.

Michaels ordered the ship to come about so the bow faced the island approximately three hundred yards from shore. The 3-inch-50 was much bigger than the anti-aircraft guns. The barrel moved up and down, and the housing moved left to right on a mesh of gears.
Instead of two men, the gun team was nine: gun captain, GM1 John Tipton; pointer, GM3 Harold Booth; trainer, SN Sam Chance; shell loader, SN Tom Raymond; 4 shell passers: SN Herb Pelk, SN Charlie Able, SN Tim Perkins, SN Fred Greer; and hot-shell man, SN Frank Elson.

Tipton sat in the seat that reminded Michaels of the tractor on his uncle's farm in Denmark. The pointer sat on the right side of the housing and the trainer sat on the left. Both had a sight glass with a line that ran through the center. The line on the pointer's glass was horizontal; vertical on the trainer's sight glass.

First, Booth lined the target in his sight. He grabbed the knob of a small wheel and spun it clockwise to slide the barrel in place. Then Chance did the same. The four shell passers were below the deck directly under the gun. They handed up a shell, man to man, to Raymond who shoved

83

the shell into the end of the barrel with his right hand. The spring-loaded hatch knocked his arm up and closed itself.

Tipton fired. The gun erupted with a fearful bang. Even with mufflers over the gun crews' ears, the noise was deafening. A puff of light blue smoke drifted from the tip of the barrel as the missile hurtled wide and long.

The hot shell self-ejected from the housing. Elson knelt waiting. He wore thick gloves and knocked the steaming metal carcass over the side of the bow. It hit the water with a hiss and a splash.

The crew reloaded. Booth and Chance re-aimed. Tipton fired again. The barrel was pointed in the right direction but the trainer had the barrel too high.

The third shot blew the oil drum out of the water. Everyone on deck cheered—in part because the deafening noise would stop, now that the target was hit—and more money changed hands. The captain curtailed gunnery practice and ordered gun crews to clean their weapons—after they cooled to the touch.

3 June 1944
2130 Hours
Officers' Wardroom

"Come on, deal!" said Cook. "We don't have all night."

"Lemme shuffle, Cook," replied Lycovec. "I need to change the spots on these cards. Lady Luck is givin' me the cold shoulder tonight." Lycovec split the deck and shuffled one half into the other. The stiff cards made a fluttering sound as they fell together.

"Where'd you learn to play hearts, Cook?" asked Jackson. "You gotta be patient with cards."

"Patience is for people who're still tryin' to figure out

how to play cards." Cook's reply was almost a sneer.

Lycovec dealt the cards: first, to Clark on his left then clockwise to Cook and Jackson. As he dealt, the three men picked up their cards and arranged them by suit. When he finished dealing, Lycovec picked up the 13 cards lying face down in a pile in front of him.

"Why can't we play teams?" asked Cook.

"Because every-man-for-himself builds character," said Lycovec. "That, and the way we're seated, you'd be my partner." Cook sneered. Lycovec and Jackson laughed; Clark smiled.

Each player pulled three cards from his hand, set them face down on the table, and slid them to the player on his left. They picked up the cards given to them and placed them in their hands.

"Who's got the two?" asked Cook.

Clark drew the two of clubs from his hand and placed it in the center of the table. "It begins again," he said.

Cook, Jackson, and Lycovec followed with a club. Lycovec's ace took the trick. He led the next trick with the seven of diamonds.

"Nice job with gunnery practice yesterday, Lycovec," said Jackson. "I made almost 50 bucks betting your gunners would miss the drum."

"You bet against the gunners?" asked Clark. "How droll."

"Common sense, Roger," replied Jackson. "First time they fired those things, they were bound to miss. Only a cockeyed optimist would have bet on them to hit it. Did you bet, Mr. Clark?"

"No. I was in my office."

"I sure as hell hope we have a few more times to practice before we really need them," said Lycovec.

Clark picked up the four cards and placed the trick neatly in front of him. He led a spade.

"The captain knows how important it is for your men to practice. I'd bet 50 bucks you get another practice round before we pull into Tulagi. Any takers?" Jackson laughed at his own joke as he threw the queen of spades on the trick pile.

Cook winced. "Damn! I got the bitch again."

The other three men laughed as he raked in the cards.

4 June 1944
0700 Hours
South Pacific

The Osage headed northwest at 8 knots. San Cristobal Island lay a few miles off the port bow. In the light of early morning, the island shone pink and brown and grey. The ship and crew were less than a day from Florida Island.

Pete Russell had the watch on the bridge. Standing on the port wing of the flying bridge, he saw the island appear with the rising sun. With the 7/50 binoculars that hung around his neck, he watched the island's morning shadows change shape like Melanesian specters taking cover from the light of day.

Russell turned, walked slowly into the bridge, and stood in front of the chronometer. He tapped the glass like he had seen the captain do. The needle did not move. Russell turned at the waist and asked the helmsman his course.

"Course zero-one-seven, sir."

"Steady as she goes."

"Aye aye, sir," replied the helmsman.

Russell ducked into the chart room to check the ship's position. A large flat map was pinned to a table in the center of the small room. Ship's course was 017. He picked up a set of calipers lying to the side and stepped off the distance the ship had traveled during his three hours on watch. A large pin marked the position of the ship on the map. Russell lifted it and stuck it into the map at Ellen's current position. He wanted everything up to date when he was relieved of the watch at 0800 hours.

As Russell poured a cup of coffee for himself, he asked the helmsman if he wanted a cup.

"No, sir," he replied. "Thank you."

Russell picked up the coffee and walked out onto the starboard wing of the flying bridge. The gold braid on the lip of his cap, cocked slightly to the side, sparkled a deep orange with the morning's red sun.

His mind drifted back through the past action-packed year of his life: a chief boatswain's mate working security in New York City; officer's candidate school in New London, CT; marrying the girl he met and dated in NYC; their honeymoon in upstate New York; the long train ride from Boston to San Francisco; and a longer ocean voyage from San Francisco to New Caledonia where he boarded the USS Osage.

His nostalgic reverie was suddenly interrupted. A heavy cruiser sped past Ellen off the port side. A couple of sailors, leaning against its starboard rail, pointed to the slow-moving tanker and laughed. Showoffs, thought Russell. You wouldn't be going anywhere without the oil we carry.

He thought back to the first time he saw the Osage: chipped paint—where there was paint—dirt, dust, and rust. He remembered the chipping and painting, and how the ship's carpenter cut a hook-door in the closet at the foot of his short bunk so he could stretch his long legs straight out while he slept.

Apparently, LT Jackson and a few others had managed to get the blue-grey paint denied them by the supply depot at Espiritu Santo—at least, that was the scuttlebutt. But rumors were as plentiful as big fish in the sea so it was hard to know what to believe.

Russell was brought back to the moment with a tap on his shoulder. He turned to see Jackson, holding a cup of coffee.

"I'm ready to relieve you," said Jackson.

"Course is still zero-one-seven at eight knots," replied Russell.

"Be sure to fill out the rough log. See you later, ensign."

"Aye, sir. See you later."

6 June 1944
0700 Hours
Tulagi Bay

Waiting for a civilian tanker to pull alongside, the Osage sat in anchorage 147 in Tulagi Bay. Bays and harbors were divided into lanes and anchorage berths. They were, basically, watery avenues and parking lots for ships at sea. Lanes and anchorages were assigned to ships much like runways and tarmacs are assigned to aircraft when they land, take off, and load or unload passengers and freight. Anchorage 147 was north and west of the mouth of the bay.

Harkel stood in front of the gauges on the console in the 'tween decks. The console sat between and perpendicular to the catwalks that ran fore and aft. In front of the console, a short metal ladder extended up from the deck to another catwalk that stretched athwartship, parallel to the console. On either side of the ladder, a 4-foot by 4-foot metal partition supported the catwalk across the ship.

The port and starboard catwalks gave access to the manual valves for the storage tanks. The tanker had 16 tanks—8 on each side of the ship—to hold 70,000 barrels of oil. Harkel checked fittings and valves on the fuel tanks. When Ellen took on oil, he had to fill the tanks evenly—port and starboard, fore and aft—or the ship could capsize.

Earl Frederickson knelt on deck between the starboard ladder and the aft superstructure. He pulled up eight metal plates and set them to the side. Beneath each plate was a hose folded and stored, nozzle up. At the bottom of the storage compartment, the hose attached to a valve that fed two storage tanks: one port, one starboard. They looked like a few of the fire hoses he saw stored in the hallways of buildings in Chicago when he worked on the tankers that sailed the Great Lakes. He stood and walked back to the first opening in the deck.

Frederickson knelt and signaled the davit operator to swing the boom and lower the hook. He let the hook fall to the deck with a couple of feet of slack in the line before he held his hand up. The operator stopped.
Frederickson grabbed the hook and slid it under a metal ring welded to a small cover behind the nozzle. He signaled the operator to raise the hook. Slowly, the slack in the line disappeared.

The davit lifted the hose out of storage until the nozzle was almost 10 feet above the deck. With another signal from Frederickson, the davit operator swung the boom across the ship. Frederickson guided the folded hose up and out until it stretched half way to port. He signaled the operator to stop.

Frederickson walked athwartship until he stood

beneath the nozzle. He signaled again and the nozzle slowly descended until it rested on deck. He unfastened the hook.

It took a little more than 30 minutes to pull all eight hoses from storage and stretch them across the deck. Frederickson and three other sailors checked each hose to make sure they did not have any kinks or holes, or tears where the hose was attached to the nozzle.

By 0800, he was satisfied the hoses were shipshape. Frederickson reported to Harkel and the bridge. The Osage was ready to take fuel.

At 0830, the civilian tanker pulled alongside. Michaels stood on the bridge with a pair of binoculars hanging from his neck. He lifted them and watched Frederickson send the first hose across 20 feet of sea that separated the two ships. When the hose reached the other tanker, he scrutinized the civilian crew attaching his hoses to theirs.

One by one, Michaels watched the davit lift the hoses off Ellen's deck and send them to the civilian tanker. The civilian crew worked like a Swiss clock, precise with no wasted motion. His crew was a little slow, he thought. But the Osage would get plenty of practice in the weeks to come. The crew will learn and get better.

Harkel, in the 'tween decks, monitored the incoming fuel from one tank to the next, and back and forth. He kept a steady balance of fuel, port and starboard, fore and aft.

By 1300, the Osage's tanks were topped. Empty, her deck sat 31 feet above the waterline. Fully laden, the deck was only 7 feet above the waterline.

7 June 1944
0800 Hours
Tulagi Bay

Still at anchorage 147, the Osage waited for a destroyer, the USS Reid DD369, to come alongside and refuel. As often as possible, ships refueled in the morning. The tropical heat and humidity were not as oppressive as later in the day.

All hands aboard the Osage were at their refueling stations when the destroyer came into view. Destroyers were named after distinguished officers and enlisted men in the navy and marine corps. The Reid was a Mahan Class destroyer commissioned in 1936. It was 340 feet long and 34 feet wide with 9 guns and 4 torpedo tubes. With a top speed of nearly 37 knots, it was one of the fastest destroyers in the South Pacific.

The Reid approached from the starboard side and it came quickly. Michaels watched the destroyer from the bridge. Only 100 yards away, it was still heading for the middle of the Osage at top speed. Michaels had seen this before in the Atlantic off the coast of Virginia. "Vell, it seems ve have a hot dog," he said to Morton and the helmsman. Both looked at the captain but didn't ask.

Ellen's crew was nervous. A destroyer was 80 yards away and quickly bearing down on them. A collision with another ship—especially at that speed—would be fatal for many. Certainly, the captain must be watching. Many wondered why he did not ring for general quarters on the 1MC. A few looked at the destroyer and then up at the bridge. Michaels stood at the glass but did not move.

The Reid was closing fast. 60 yards. 40 yards. Still at top speed. The destroyer was only 20 yards away. Ellen's crew was close enough to see the color of the eyes of the crew aboard the Reid and, still, it steamed even closer at full speed! Some of Ellen's crew began to back away from the side of the ship.

Suddenly, the ship swung starboard. It's engines

roared. The props swung into reverse and kicked up a fountain of white water. The destroyer reeled hard to port and rolled back to an even keel as its engines shut down completely. The USS Reid drifted to fewer than 5 yards away from Ellen, almost perfectly parallel to her starboard side and dead in the water.

The commanding officer, a young lieutenant, called out from the bridge. "Ahoy, USS Osage. We're ready to take on fuel."

Chapter 6
Action

12 June 1944
0800 Hours
Tulagi Bay

The summer tropical sun slowly rose above the horizon into a cloudless blue sky. The Osage's crew prepared to get underway as part of a four-ship convoy to Eniwetok, an atoll in Marshall Islands, a few hundred miles east of Guam. Jackson was in the forecastle with Stacek and Phillips. Harkel and Edwards stood near the diesel with Frederickson and Kraft. Michaels and Morton were on the bridge.

Tulagi Bay lay midway between Brisbane and the Marshalls. Between Tulagi and Eniwetok, a bevy of islands, islets, and atolls dotted the Pacific through Melanesia and Micronesia. The vast majority were too small to maintain a military presence. As a result, the Allies and Japanese used them to sneak in, strike quickly, slink away, and hide. With a lot of open sea, the run between the Solomon Islands and the Marshall Islands was long and dangerous.

Two destroyer escorts were assigned to guard the Osage, a gasoline tanker, and two supply ships. DEs were smaller and slower than destroyers, and they had less firepower. But they were fast enough to chase submarines and carried two racks of depth charges.

Leaving the safety and familiarity of Tulagi Bay, the Osage took its place in the convoy. The ships sailed due north in a straight line. First in the convoy was the gasoline tanker. Approximately 100 yards astern, the first supply ship followed. The second supply ship followed 100 yards behind it. The Osage brought up the rear, yet another 100 yards astern. One DE sailed 100 yards off the starboard side of the convoy between the first tanker and supply ship. The other DE sailed 100 yards off the port side between the tanker and the supply ship in front her.

13 June 1944
1000 Hours
South Pacific

The day began humid. Beneath the clear blue sky, no wind blew through midmorning. The only relief from the increasing heat was the breeze created on deck by the ship sailing north at eight knots.

The port and starboard rails were lined with officers and enlisted men alone, in pairs, or in groups. Many of those not on duty or working, took off their shirts and stood or sat shirtless. Everyone stared at the ocean. Few spoke.

From the bridge, Captain Michaels looked at the water. He had been a sailor most of his life, an old salt of the rough and unpredictable North Atlantic, but he had never seen the ocean like this. He gave the conn to Lieutenant Jackson and walked down to the port rail just forward of the ladder.

Michaels walked up behind three seamen and looked over their shoulders. One of the seamen turned around to see the ship's captain. He tapped his buddy on the shoulder and they stepped aside to let Michaels stand closer to the rail. Michaels nodded in appreciation and stepped forward. "Great Hamlet's ghost," he said under his breath.

Ellen sailed in the fading wake of the supply ship in front of her. The wake slowly opened out and melted into an ocean that looked like liquid glass—completely smooth.

The swells rolled gently into each other without a wave or a ripple. Half of the crew were veteran sailors. The other half were fresh out of boot camp or transferred from shore duty. Even among the vets, most had never seen an ocean so calm and peaceful, so pristine and effortless.

"How does the ocean do that, captain?" asked one of the men who stepped aside for Michaels.

"I don't know, sailor," replied Michaels. "But this is vhy it is called Pacific Ocean."

15 June 1944
1300 Hours
South Pacific

Still in Melanesia, and south of the equator, the convoy continued north at 8 knots. To the east was Nauru; to the west, New Ireland. Beyond New Ireland were the Bismarck Archipelago and the Admiralty Islands.

One of the lookouts on the mast spotted a lone plane flying southeast. He called down to the bridge on the sound-powered headset and gave them rough coordinates. The helmsman relayed the information to the captain. Everyone on the bridge, except thc hclmsman, stepped up to the windows and looked up at the plane. It was a Japanese "Betty".

The Betty was a large, slow aircraft used for surveillance. This far south and east, it was probably checking for ships of war, supply convoys, and troop transports carrying reinforcements to the battle that had just started at Saipan in the Marianas.

Tipton was at the 3-inch-50 with his gun crew. He called the bridge and asked Lycovec for permission to fire. Lycovec asked Michaels.

The captain realized it would be, literally, a long shot

for that gun to hit the Betty. But it would be a good opportunity for gunnery practice and provide some relief for the crew from the monotony of three days of nothing but open sea. Michaels consented.

Lycovec left the bridge to join Tipton and the gun crew on the bow. Like they practiced, Tipton sat in the tractor seat while Booth and Chance adjusted their sights on the Betty. The shell passers handed a shell up to Raymond who loaded the barrel and ducked out of the way. The gun crew covered their ears with the mufflers before Tipton fired. Elson dropped the hot shell over the side of the ship as the gun crew and the bridge followed the shot skyward. The shell exploded far short and off the mark to the right.

Lycovec stepped into the gun tub and increased the range. Booth and Chance readjusted their sights. When the barrel was loaded, Lycovec yelled, "Fire!"

Seamen from below decks arrived topside to see why the gun was firing without a call to battle stations. They were greeted with a deafening bang. The second shot fell short and to the left. Booth and Chance had overcompensated for their previous shot and sent the shell to the other side of the target.

Lycovec increased the range yet farther, and the pointer and trainer aligned their sights. The third shot was aligned perfectly but it exploded well short of the mark again.

The gunnery officer was determined to hit the Betty. He extended the range as far as it would go. Why not, he thought. Nothing to lose. The gun crew would have one, maybe two more shots before the surveillance plane was out of range.

Pelk, Able, Perkins, and Greer passed the shell up to Raymond who shoved it into the end of the barrel. When the spring-loaded hatch slammed shut, he patted it with his hand and said, "Find your way home, baby." Tipton sat ready. Booth and Chance zeroed in on the plane. Lycovec yelled, Fire!" Elson dropped the hot shell over the side and looked up.

A ball of fire erupted from the right wing of the plane. Smoke billowed behind it as the Betty began to slide to its right. Everyone on deck and on the bridge cheered. The gun crew jumped up and down. Elson threw down his gloves and danced. As the plane spiraled, two parachutes blossomed and floated down like autumn leaves bitten by the teeth of an early winter's frost.

The DE on Ellen's starboard side swung out to look for the pilots and confirm that the plane was down. An hour later it returned with confirmation. With a 3-inch-50, the Osage, an oil tanker, shot down an enemy plane!

When the DE returned with the good news, Lycovec was back on the bridge with Michaels and Morton. Michaels shook Lycovec's hand and congratulated him. Lycovec was modest. "It was a team effort," he said. "And a lucky shot."

2100 Hours

Raymond sat at one of the card tables in the crew's quarters aft. Three other seamen—Tex Akins, Art Hill, and Ray Hereford—sat at the table and waited for him to deal the cards for a game of spades.

"It wasn't until I patted the breech that we dropped that Betty," he said to the group as he slid a card in front of each player.

"Lucky shot," offered Hereford.

"Destiny ain't luck, brother," replied Raymond. He continued dealing.

"Destiny?" asked Akins in his West Texas drawl.

"What's destiny got to do with it?"

"We were destined to hit that plane. I knew it as soon as I loaded the fourth shell."

"That's crazy talk, Raymond," said Hill. "How can you know sumthin' before it happens?"

"Where'd you learn to deal, Raymond? The horse stables? This is a load of crap," said Akins.

"I'm savin' the good stuff for my hand," laughed Raymond.

The four players arranged the cards in their hands according to suit and rank. For a moment, they sat and looked at the hand dealt, and counted the tricks they could take.

The speaker in the crew's quarter keyed with a click. "Now hear this. Now hear this. The USS Osage is passing over the equator. We are now in the northern hemisphere."

"Does that mean it'll start gettin' cooler?" asked Akins. "I bid three."

"Hell, no," replied Hill. "It'll be a long time before we feel a cool autumn breeze like we get back in St. Louis. I bid three."

"Thought you hailed from Texas," said Hereford. "Ain't it hot there too? I bid four."

"Hotter'n hell on the Fourth of July," replied Akins. "But at least we got a cactus or two to crawl under fer some shade. Ain't nowheres ta go here. It's hot in the mornin'. It's hot in the evenin'. It's hot in middle of the damned 'tween decks. Shit, I'm liable to sweat my damned self to death."

"I bid three," said Raymond. "That's thirteen tricks, gentlemen. No room for mistakes or someone burns."

"Well, at least we can take off our shirts. The captain's good about that," said Hill.

"Yeah, but I'm still sweatin' my ass off below this here belt and I ain't droppin' my dungarees around you

98

buckaroos," laughed Akins.

"If you sweat your ass off," said Hereford, "you can always wait for replenishment detail and get one of them United Fruit boxes and tie it to your backside to take up the slack in your pants."

"The problem there," said Hill, "is that you take the chance of shittin' pears until your ass grows back."

Everyone at the table laughed.

"I was right," said Akins. "You're a bunch a god-damned buckaroos."

18 June 1944
1130 Hours
South Pacific, Southeast of Kolonia Island

Other than shooting down the Betty, the trip north was proving uneventful. Relentless heat and humidity were constant companions and dulled the senses of more than one man.

Michaels was looking over the smooth log in his state room.

Morton had the watch on the bridge. As he turned to speak to Emerson, the helmsman, an explosion—louder than the 3-inch-50—erupted somewhere in front of the Osage. Before he could turn back around, he heard another explosion. Great balls of red, orange, and white flames engulfed the middle of the gasoline tanker, first ship in the convoy. A third and fourth explosion followed before he could get the binoculars to his eyes.

"Sound general quarters!" he commanded.

Emerson punched the red button on the console and keyed the microphone for the 1MC. Bong-Bong-Bong rang though the Osage. As he called all hands to battle stations, Michaels stepped onto the bridge. He held a pair of binoculars. "Vhat happened?" he asked.

"The tanker exploded," replied Morton. "It sank like a rock. There's just debris and gas slicks on fire where it was just a moment ago. I don't see any survivors. It's unbelievable."

Michaels raised the glasses to his eyes and looked at the sea where the tanker had been only moments before. "Submarines," Michaels whispered.

Two enlisted men arrived on the bridge. One picked up a pair of binoculars on a shelf next to the hatch and began to search the sea, port to starboard. The second reached next to the binoculars for the sound-powered headset. He strapped it on.

"The DEs are heading hard to starboard sir," reported SN Barry Olsen, the enlisted man with the binoculars. "There's a Jap sub at two o'clock, 1200 yards. It's turning, sir."

Michaels turned. He found the small submarine quickly. It was not submerged. He lowered the binoculars. The DE on the starboard side of the convoy was chasing the sub. The port DE was following, cutting across the bow of the first supply ship. When Michaels saw the second DE in pursuit, he was so mad he began cursing in Danish and stomping on the deck.

"Lort! Kneppe! Bastard son of a shit-festered whore! NO, NO, NO!" He paused, pulled off his cap and wiped his brow with his shirt sleeve. Michaels put his cap back on and turned to SN Mel Hobbs, the sailor wearing the sound-powered phones. "Tell every station to secure all vatertight hatches on the double!" he ordered.

As Hobbs relayed the captain's order, an explosion rang out in front of the Osage. The second ship in line was hit with a torpedo. A few seconds later, another explosion rocked the supply ship. It quickly began to list to port.

"What happened?" asked Morton. "The sub is leaving."

"They vork in pairs, lieutenant," replied Michaels. "First sub hits and runs. Everyone sees it run and the convoy relaxes because destroyers chase it. The second sub vaits until destroyers commit."

"How'd they know we're here?"

"The Betty relayed information before ve shot her down."

Michaels turned to the watch. "Forget them," he said pointing to the DEs. "Scan ocean off port side. Look for periscope 1200 to 1800 yards out."

"Aye, sir," replied Olsen. He stepped quickly to the port side of the bridge and raised the binoculars to his eyes.

"Ve do not have much time, Mr. Morton. Next two torpedoes will hit ship in front of us. They are reloading tubes vone and two for us."

Michaels just finished speaking when the supply ship in front of them burst into flames with a loud explosion. Morton looked at Michaels. "Ve are on our own, lieutenant," said Michaels. "Pray to God for luck."

Another explosion rocked the ship in front of them. Morton closed his eyes and exhaled.

"Periscope at three o'clock. About 1400 yards," called Olsen.

Michaels and Morton stepped to the port side of the bridge and raised their binoculars.

"Hard port rudder!" ordered Michaels.

"Hard port rudder," repeated the helmsman. He spun the wheel to his left. The Osage slowly turned toward the Japanese submarine.

"Two torpedoes off the port bow. 1200 yards and closing," said Olsen.

"Keep rudder hard to port," ordered Michaels. He

watched the propellers of the torpedoes, just below the waterline, kick up white water as they headed toward the Osage.

"Rudder hard to port," replied the helmsman.

"Ve vill not give them easy target," Michaels said defiantly.

"800 yards," called the watch.

Realizing it left the port flank vulnerable, the second DE returned and was coming up the starboard bow. As it passed Ellen, everyone on the bridge followed it briefly.

"400 yards," called the watch.

Michaels turned to Hobbs. "Pass the word: Brace for impact," he said.

The sailor keyed the mike and relayed the message through the headset. Olsen turned from the glass, shut his eyes, and grabbed the console. Eyes wide, Morton looked around the bridge for something to cling to. Emerson squeezed the helm until his knuckles were white.

Michaels turned back around, and grabbed the bulkhead beneath the glass just in time to watch the first torpedo narrowly pass the bow of the ship without striking. He quickly found the second torpedo a few yards from the ship. It was going to hit. So much for luck, he thought.

The next torpedo hit the hull with a loud, lifeless thud just aft of the forward superstructure. For a moment, no one moved or exhaled.

"It's a dud!" cried Morton. Everyone on the bridge cheered.

"Maybe," said Michaels. He faced Hobbs. "Tell engine room all stop."

Hobbs relayed the captain's order.

"Get me damage report from 'tween decks."

Hobbs keyed the mike on the headset and called the port refueling station 'tween decks. There was no answer.

He told the captain.

"Call foc's'l. Tell Mr. Jackson to get a detail to 'tween decks."

"And do what, sir?" asked Hobbs.

"Great Hamlet's ghost! Get that goddamned torpedo off this ship!" he yelled.

Hobbs fumbled with the mike and relayed the orders.

The first lieutenant was in the forecastle with Stacek, Williams, and Phillips. "Chief, stay here with the watch. Williams, Phillips, with me—on the double." Jackson opened the hatch and stepped into the passageway. Williams and Phillips followed. Stacek secured the watertight hatch when they left.

The three men ran aft along the port bulkhead. Jackson opened the hatch to the 'tween decks and was greeted by the soft roar of a large continuous splash. He looked up and saw the torpedo wedged into a gaping hole in the hull. Three men stood on the catwalk near the torpedo. Water was pouring into the compartment and falling on the deck. They ducked inside and Phillips secured the hatch behind them.

Jackson ran up to the group of men. "What do we have here?" He yelled to be heard above the roar.

Harkel yelled back. "The torp hit us at an angle—not head on. Might be why it didn't explode. Could still be live."

"Damn! Are your phones working?"

"No. The torp broke the phone lines in the bulkhead." Harkel pointed to the connection box hanging by its wires to the right of the hole.

"Send a runner to the foc's'l with the damage report," ordered Jackson.

Harkel turned to SN Kirby Stinson who was wearing a pair of sound-powered phones plugged into the refueling console. "Sailor, report to Chief Stacek in the foc's'l. Give him the damage report. You are the designated runner until further notice."

"Aye, sir," replied Stinson. He took off the headset, turned forward, and quickly left the 'tween decks.

Harkel turned back around to face Jackson. "What are we going to do, Jackson?"

"Pry the son of a bitch out of the hole, patch'er up, and get this water outta here."

"Yeah, but how?"

"We need some pry bars, a 4-foot steel plate, some tar or pitch, and a rivet gun. And we need to dump fuel to raise the waterline."

"I can't dump fuel without the CO's permission," said Harkel.

"Get it when the runner returns," replied Jackson. "Meantime, we need to round up everything else."

Phillips spoke up. "I can get the pitch and the rivet gun, sir."

"Hurry!," replied Jackson.

Phillips ran aft down the catwalk.

"We got some pry bars in the engine room," said Frederickson. "I'll go get them."

"No," replied Jackson. "I'm gonna need you here." He turned to the fueling officer. "Mr. Harkel, send someone else."

Harkel nodded and turned to a third class petty officer standing on the starboard catwalk near the manual release valves for the storage tanks. He motioned for him to come over. "Conway," yelled Harkel when he stood next to him, "go aft to the engine room. Bring back three pry bars—on the double."

"Aye, sir," replied Conway. He ran aft down the catwalk.

Jackson pointed to the metal partitions that supported the catwalk in front of the console. "Do you absolutely need them?" he asked Harkel.

"We can take one side down. The other side should hold the catwalk."

"Good," replied Jackson. "Plus, the other side gives us a back-up just in case we do it wrong."

"Doin' it wrong is not an option. The longer we have a hole, the more water we take in."

"You're right, Harkel. Shut down everything electrical except the lights." We don't need any more problems to deal with."

Harkel stepped up to the console and began securing circuits and equipment.

Kirby returned and ran up to Jackson. "The skipper wants to know how long it's going to take to fix it."

"Tell the captain, about 2 hours—if everything falls in line. And tell him we need to dump some fuel after we knock the torpedo out. We have to raise the waterline a couple of feet to patch that hole."

"Aye, sir," replied the sailor. He returned to the forecastle.

Jackson pivoted and faced Williams and Frederickson. "You two take down one side of that partition." He pointed left of the ladder connected to the catwalk in front of the console. "And bring it over here." Jackson pointed to the bulkhead where the connection box hung.

On the bridge, Michaels stood at the glass and looked at the carnage in front of him. The supply ship was listing hard but was not sinking. The other supply ship was slowly breaking apart. It would probably sink in an hour or two. The gasoline tanker was gone. All that remained was debris, pockets of a gas fire on the water, and smoke.

With Jackson busy in the 'tween decks, Michaels told Morton to lower the longboats and pick up survivors of the first two ships in the convoy. He knew they would find few, if any, from the tanker. Before he arrived on the bridge for general quarters, it had already disintegrated in a series of quick, cataclysmic explosions.

Michaels was disappointed that he had to dump precious fuel. But at least he would have most of it when they arrived—if they arrived—in Eniwetok. And he would have his ship and crew. The ship was afloat; the crew was safe. Perhaps he had been rash about cursing his luck earlier.

Williams and Frederickson dismantled the wall of sheet metal and, with the help of Jackson and another sailor, hoisted it onto the catwalk and dragged it across the metal grate to the hole. Harkel stood at the console and monitored the release of oil into the open sea. He was surprised to see Jackson pitch in so readily. He thought the first lieutenant was a pretty boy and a smart-ass. It was good to see Jackson dig in when it counted. Maybe he wasn't all bad.

Slowly, Williams, Frederickson, and Phillips used the pry bars to lift and dump the unexploded torpedo from the hole in Ellen's port side. Phillips was the most nervous of the three. His hands were sweating so much that once he lost his grip on the bar and it tumbled to the catwalk with a clang. The torpedo shifted but did not fall in or out of the hole.

Fortunately, the water outside of the ship provided enough buoyancy that it did not affect the leverage. Still, everyone in the compartment was relieved to exhale and open their eyes.

Jackson, Williams, Frederickson, and Phillips used pipe wrenches to bend back the ripped metal that jutted into the compartment. As the waterline slowly rose, Conway applied the pitch around the perimeter of the hole.

He started at the top and worked down.

When he finished, the lieutenant and his three enlisted assistants raised the sheet to the hole. Conway propped the sheet with the pry bars and then drove rivets into the metal plate as the four men pushed it against the side of the ship. Then Conway liberally added more pitch around the perimeter of sheet. The rush of water halted to a trickle.

Jackson told the runner to tell the captain that they were ready for the pumps and hoses to drain the compartment of the water that had accumulated on the floor. Kirby again ran forward to forecastle.

27 June 1944
1600 Hours
Eniwetok

The four ships remaining were forced to crawl to Eniwetok. Although afloat, the supply ship could manage no better than 3 knots. The Osage and the DEs had to keep the slower pace. All four ships doubled watches until they arrived in Eniwetok late in the afternoon of June 27.

Original orders assigned the Osage to drop anchor at berth 87. Because the convoy arrived much later than expected, the harbormaster changed the tanker's anchorage to berth 125. It took another hour to drop anchor farther up the bay. It would take even longer for them to drop the longboats and ferry the survivors of the supply ship to the small naval station ashore. The Osage's crew grumbled at the new orders. They were tired and wanted to put the trip to rest.

29 June 1944
0830 Hours
Eniwetok

The Allies planned to invade Guam in the third week of July. In and around the island, almost 400 ships of war gathered. A small armada of tankers was busy refueling a flotilla of cruisers, battleships, destroyers, transports, and other ships to advance on the small, but strategic, island.

The Osage had just received permission to pull alongside a tender—a floating dry-dock—for repairs to the hull. Michaels was on the 1MC telling the crew they would spend 3 or 4 days alongside the repair ship when a giant explosion and fireball erupted a few miles down the bay. Two more explosions followed and dark grey smoke billowed into the air. Michaels turned to the radioman in the radio shack and told him to find out what happened.

Approximately 30 minutes later, the radioman received an answer. A light cruiser was refueling from a tanker in berth 87 when a kamikaze pilot dove into the cruiser. The explosions killed or wounded almost 100 men on the two ships.

Michaels picked up the 1MC, relayed the story to the crew, and asked for a minute of silence. After he hung up the mike on the console, he patted the helm and said, "Vell, Ellen, old girl, you really are a lucky lady. I vill not doubt you again."

Chapter 7
Chewing Guam

3 July 1944
0800 Hours
Eniwetok

Near the south edge of the fleet, the Osage tied up to the tender at the bow and stern. The tanker still had fuel in her tanks so the hole in her port side remained just above the water line. Captain Michaels told the Engineering and Deck officers to assign 20 sailors from their divisions to help repair the ship. Tenders had little more than a skeleton crew and, at sea, relied on a ship's crew to supplant the work force. The rest of Michaels' crew performed planned maintenance tasks on equipment to keep the ship operating at peak performance.

The ripped section of the hull was not the only thing that had to be replaced. Communication lines, electrical lines, pumps, gauges, hoses, and other equipment in the 'tween decks had to be replaced, refitted, and reconnected because of the torpedo and water damage. The commanding officer of the tender was quiet and soft spoken. He was not, however, timid and his eyes flashed the spark of a keen mind that missed very little. He estimated the repairs would take a week—give or take a day.

8 July 1944
1500 Hours
Eniwetok

Repairs on the tanker were finished. She pulled away from the tender a day under schedule and anchored just south and east of Eniwetok.

The battle fleet had already begun raids on Saipan, Tinian, Rota, and Guam. A constant stream of warships sailed from Eniwetok to the southern Marianas. Approximately 1000 miles west of Eniwetok, and 1400 miles east of the Philippines, the Marianas had a long history of foreign domination. They were claimed by the Spanish in the late 1500s. Spain ceded Guam to the United States after the Spanish-American War in 1898 and the rest of the archipelago was sold to Germany one year later.

The Japanese took the German-held Marianas during World War I and their occupation was ratified by the Treaty of Versailles. Even before Japan left the League of Nations in 1935, it had already begun to fortify the islands as a strategic defense around the Japanese empire. Japan captured Guam in December 1941.

Although no official orders had yet come through, Michaels reasoned the southern Marianas were the Osage's next destination. When they sailed depended on how long it took to soften Guam with naval artillery and air force bombing sorties, and how long it took the army and marines to land and establish a secure beachhead. Until then, it would be a monotonous—yet vital—cycle: give fuel to navy warships, take fuel from commercial tankers, give fuel to navy warships.

10 July 1944
1900 Hours
Crews' Quarters Forward

Playing a game of hearts, YN2 Bradley Lewis, BM2 Billy Phillips, SN Lev Holland, and SN Emmet Weston sat at one of the card tables. Lewis was the only one in his dungarees. The other three were in their skivvies.

"Ain't you warm in your dungarees, Lewis?" asked Weston. Weston was a third class petty officer who was busted down in rank a few months ago for sleeping on his watch. Since that episode, he eagerly volunteered for extra duty to help reclaim his petty officer status.

"Naw, he ain't warm," responded Holland. "He's a cool cat. He lets the heat go right around him." Holland threw down the 8 of diamonds to start another trick.

Lewis pulled the 6 of diamonds from his hands and slipped it under the 8. "Not a chance, Dutch. I'm not playing above that 8. Diamonds have gone around twice, the court cards have all been played, and I've still got a diamond in my hand."

Phillips looked at the cards that had been played. He looked at his hand, glanced at the other players, and looked at the cards again. As he drew a card, he began to whistle. Then he quickly slapped the queen of spades on top of the two cards lying in the center of the table.

"Gotcha, Dutch," laughed Phillips.

Holland frowned.

Weston grimaced as he lay the 10 of diamonds on the pile. "No, ya got me!" he said and pulled the cards toward him.

"You got a lucky split this time," said Lewis.

"Maybe it's luck, and maybe it ain't," replied Holland.

Weston led the next trick with the 3 of hearts. "How'd you know to go under the 8?" he asked Lewis.

"Elementary, my dear Weston," replied Lewis and he laughed aloud at his own joke.

"What's so funny? I don't get it," said Weston. He lay down the 4 of hearts.

"Elementary, my dear Weston. Elementary, my dear Watson. Arthur Conan Doyle."

"I still don't get it."

"Have you never heard of Sherlock Holmes?" Lewis played the 2 of hearts.

"Sure, but who's Watson? This is Weston," said Phillips. He took the trick with the ace of hearts.

"Dr. Watson was Holmes' partner in most of Doyle's stories about his fictional detective, Sherlock Holmes," answered Lewis.

Phillips quickly placed the 6 on the table to continue play in the same suit. "Someone else can eat this trick," he said grudgingly.

"Told ya Lewis was a cool cat," said Holland. "He was probably a teacher or a scholar or somethin' before the war."

"I was a librarian at a university."

"A librarian. Now, there's a beefy job. All that climbing and lifting," Phillips said sarcastically.

"Exercise for the mind is just as important as exercise for the body," countered Lewis.

"Did you meet a lot of smart women, Bradley?" asked Weston.

"Yes, I met a lot of smart women."

"Were they rich?"

"No doubt, some had money," said Lewis.

"How about pretty?"

"A lot of very attractive women go to the library, Emmet."

"That's the woman for me—smart, rich, and pretty," said Phillips.

"Yeah, but you're not the man for her. A woman like that needs a real man," said Holland. Everyone laughed.

"What did you do before the war, Billy?" asked Weston.

"I was on the Escobar out of San Francisco," he

replied. "High seas and high tides. Seein' the world through a porthole, no worries, and a girl in every port. That's the good life."

Lewis looked up from his hand at Phillips.

"You was in the navy?" asked Weston.

"I was in the navy when ships were wood and men were steel," answered Phillips.

"Don't be impressed, Emmet," Lewis added. "The Escobar is not a US Navy ship. It's the ferry that runs between San Francisco and Oakland." Phillips' mouth opened wide as he glared at Lewis. "No doubt, at some point, while Phillips was stationed in San Francisco, he was on the ferry that crossed the bay to Oakland—probably because he was two-timing his girlfriend."

"Man, how do you know all this shit?" asked Phillips.

"Elementary, my dear Weston," replied Lewis and everyone at the table groaned. "Hey!" he said. "You gave me the straight line."

15 July 1944
1730 Hours
Officers' Wardroom

The officers arrived for dinner in the wardroom. Captain Michaels sat at the head of the table with his back to the bow of the ship. LT Morton was to his right. The chair next to Morton was vacant because LT Clark had the watch on the bridge. LTJG Jackson and WO Cook filled out the side. To Michaels' left, sat LT Becker, LTJG Harkel, ENS Lycovec, and ENS Russell.

They sat in descending rank away from the captain—not from any direct order or conscious decision. It was just the way seating fell into place. Officers usually took the same seat for dinner and meetings. For informal gatherings, like card games and chit chat, seating was open.

"An awful lot of ships moved out this morning," said Harkel. He picked up his knife and cut the potato on his plate.

"We must be getting ready to take Guam," said Morton.

"Can you imagine all that firepower concentrated on one little island?" said Harkel.

"The Japs won't have a chance," Jackson said.

"Maybe not, but they won't just roll over and hand it over. They haven't done it on any other island and they won't do it on Guam," said Lycovec

"When it falls, it'll sure take a bite out of the Japanese defenses," Becker said.

"Let the emperor masticate on that for a while," said Jackson. He stabbed a couple of overcooked green beans with his fork and put them in his mouth.

"If he does masticate on it, shouldn't we change the name of the island?" asked Russell.

"To what?" asked Cook.

"Chewing Guam."

Michaels put down his cup of coffee and smiled. Almost everyone else at the table groaned at the pun. Russell grinned like a grade-schooler who brought home the first A on his report card.

Jackson swallowed. "I hope you're not writing that kind of drivel in the smooth log, ensign," he said. "It's an official Navy document."

"Masticate. Drivel. Lieutenant, that's two big words in past couple of minutes. Have you been reading again?" asked Lycovec.

"Crotch novels don't have big words, Fritz," said Morton.

"A good vocabulary can be an excellent tool or

weapon," responded Jackson.

"If he can't kill them with flattery, he can always bore the Japanese to death," said Cook. Everyone laughed.

"Why, Mr. Cook," said Jackson, "I believe that's a joke coming from your thin little lips."

"And a good one," added Becker who had just finished a drink of water. "I salute you." He raised his glass to eye level.

The other officers followed his lead and muttered, "Here, here."

Conversation paused as the officers finished dinner and the stewards arrived with bus tubs on thin metal carts to take away the plates, silverware, and glasses.

"Mr. Harkel, do we have more refueling details?" asked Michaels.

"Just one, sir. On the nineteenth, we're taking on fuel from a commercial tanker."

"Then, ve sail soon for Guam," Michaels said. He softly slapped the table top with the palm of his hand.

"It's good to know that we're going, sir" Morton said.

"Ya, sure, Mr. Morton. Knowing helps. But vaiting is hell."

"Especially for the boys hittin' the beach," said Lycovec.

19 July 1944
1100 Hours
Eniwetok

Thirty-four miles long and five to nine miles wide, Guam was the largest island of the Marianas. It had hilly shoreline cliffs, many caves, sharp rises, and deep ravines. The thick vegetation made it look like a floating jungle. The

18,500 Japanese defenders represented a considerable force on the small, well-fortified island.

The United States started the attack with the heaviest softening-up bombing to date in the war. Day and night, gunfire from 6 battleships, 9 cruisers, a dozen destroyers, and rocket-launching gunboats bombarded the Japanese. Army B-24s dropped tons of bombs and Navy carrier-based fighter squadrons relentlessly strafed island fortifications.

The American strategy was to first take the Orote Peninsula, a rocky finger of land off the southwest coast. The plan was for the marines to land and secure the peninsula. Then, the Seabees would build an airstrip to fly in troops and supplies to help take the rest of the island.

RM2 Ron Miller stepped out of the radio shack on the bridge and handed a note to the officer of the day, Ensign Lycovec.

"Better take it to the captain, Miller. He's in his stateroom."

"Aye, sir," answered Miller.

Miller left the bridge and stepped down the metal staircase to Captain Michaels' stateroom. The hatch was closed. He knocked.

"Ya, come in."

Miller opened the hatch and stepped in. He did not close the hatch. A warm breeze blew against his back. He felt the wet shirt sticking to his skin—as if he needed another reminder of the tropical heat. Without a word, Miller handed Michaels the message he deciphered in the radio shack.

Michaels took the note and read slowly. He looked up and said, "Thank you. Dismissed."

Miller replied, "Aye, sir," and returned to the radio shack.

Before Miller arrived, Michaels was sitting and reading the smooth log. Amazing, all of the things that had happened to the ship in just three months. At once, it seemed longer and shorter than three months. A lot had happened but it happened really fast.

Now, the Osage received orders for Guam—right into the heart of the war. Michaels wondered if their luck would hold.

21 July 1944
0600 Hours
Eniwetok

The Osage joined eight other ships en route to Guam. The 9-ship convoy—2 hospital ships, 2 tankers, 3 supply ships, and 2 cargo ships—left Eniwetok with 6 destroyer escorts, the 2 DEs that sailed with the Osage from Tulagi Bay and 4 others.

27 July 1944
1800 Hours
Orote Peninsula, Guam

Despite heavy shelling, Japanese resistance to American landing parites on the peninsula was ferocious. The Osage sailed into Agat Bay to refuel the USS Boyd DD544 guarding the southern flank of the peninsula. Small-arms fire hit the decks of both ships so the detail was canceled. The tanker sailed a few miles down the coast and waited for another time to refuel the destroyer.

28 July 1944
0900 Hours
Agat Bay

The Osage lay in a cove between the USS Iowa BB61 and the Orote Peninsula. The Iowa was a massive ship: almost 900 feet long and more than 100 feet wide. It boasted nine 16-inch guns and twenty 5-inch guns.

When the battleship fired at Japanese positions on the island, the huge shells flew over the tanker and a few other ships anchored nearby. The noise was deafening. Fireballs shot 150 feet from the ends of each of the 16-inchers. At night, they lit up the bay brighter than any Fourth-of-July celebration back in the States.

The cliffs of the peninsula exploded with each shell. Explosions belched lumps of earth, construction, and humanity skyward. They fell onto the beach and into the water. It was as if the gods of lightning and thunder combined their might and wrath to punish—whether through death or deafness—all of those involved in this deadly game. Ellen's crew prayed for it stop. Not only was it loud, the concussion from the noise rocked the tanker back and forth with every salvo.

A squadron of fighters was returning to its aircraft carrier after a strafing run. Smoke began to billow from the tail of one of the planes as it crossed the peninsula. Then, it rolled over and quickly plunged into the ocean. Ellen's crew, who watched from her deck, realized this was no game.

29 July 1944
1300 Hours
Agat Bay

The marines made substantial progress on the Orote Peninsula so the Osage moved up the coast and refueled the USS Boyd and a few other ships. With the exception of the engine room, where the huge diesel droned its 60-cyle hum that filled everyone's ears, the crew could still hear artillery and small-arms fire on the peninsula.

That night, during a card game in the crews' quarters forward, Lewis was quick to point out the difference between the sounds a Japanese rifle made when fired and the sounds from an American Browning. The next day, a half dozen of the deck crew, on deck during lunch, listened to the skirmishes on the island. Though the heat smothered the deck like a heavy woolen blanket, they sat patiently and tried to identify the shots—either Japanese or American—based on Lewis' descriptions.

1 August 1944
0800 Hours
Agat Bay

The Osage moved back down the coast. Several cargo ships steamed into the bay and unloaded their rolling stock: bulldozers, tanks, jeeps, trucks. The airstrip on Orote was nearly finished.

The tanker gave much of her fuel to other ships in the fleet. In return, she received a number of stories about the fighting on Guam. As the lines were hooked up and fuel passed from its fuel tanks to the tanks of destroyers, destroyer escorts, and gunboats, sailors shouted the stories to Ellen's crew across the narrow strip of water that separated the two ships. In two days, everyone aboard the Osage heard every story more than once.

One story told how a group of Japanese soldiers walked up to the American GIs. The Japanese in the front line walked with their hands in the air as if to surrender. As soon as the Americans relaxed their guard, the front line fell to the ground with machine guns strapped to their backs. The men behind dropped to their knees at the same time, grabbed the machine guns and opened fire.

Another story said the Japanese booby-trapped their dead comrades left behind on the battle field. When the GIs tried to lift them to bury them, the traps exploded. Other stories said the Japanese booby-trapped bayonets, hats, rifles, and pistols. When GIs tried to pick them up for souvenirs, they triggered mines and hand grenades buried just beneath.

9 August 1944
1130 Hours
Agat Bay

The Osage hoisted anchor and sailed around Orote Peninsula to Apra Harbor. Apra was the main town on the island. It lay at the edge of a large natural harbor. Marines had already pushed the Japanese farther inland so the tanker's crew heard very little small-arms fire. What they did hear was faint, like firecrackers going off at the far end of the next city block down the street. The noise from the battleships, cruisers, and destroyers could still be heard but it more resembled distant thunder.

12 August 1944
0800 Hours
Apra Harbor

Jackson, Harkel, and Russell climbed down the ladder into a longboat waiting in the water on the port side of the ship. The coxswain shoved off and headed for Apra. The gentle sea breeze carried the smell of salt and fish— not the sound of artillery and gunfire. They ceased four days previous. Although a few Japanese were still straggling into American camps to surrender, the main army was defeated. Those who were not killed were under armed guard in hastily constructed—but secure—stockades.

Halfway to shore, Harkel pointed to a squadron of Marine F4Us returning from a raid on Tinian, still in Japanese hands, just to the north. The planes flew low. With their landing gear down, they approached the airstrip near Agana on the Orote Peninsula. One of the fighter pilots apparently dropped a little too low on a strafing pass over his target because he had a full-sized coconut wedged between the lower cylinders on his engine.

As the longboat slipped closer to Apra, Russell concentrated on the town. He found it difficult to focus with the sun glaring off the water. Apra was more village than town. Tall, slender palm trees and coconut trees towered above the simple huts and mud-brick buildings. Many seemed to be covered with a steep, thatched roof. Not a single road was paved. They were single lane, bare, packed earth. Following the road with eyes, Russell noticed the town seemed to slowly melt into the ravines that snaked up into the hills behind it.

The longboat pulled alongside the wooden pier which stretched 30 yards from the sand into the bay. It was an old pier, weathered wood that creaked with each wave that washed up against it. Russell wondered how long the pier had been here and how many sailors had walked down the pier to come ashore and trade for fresh coconuts, breadfruit, and pineapples.

The three officers walked through the center of town and kicked up a small cloud of dust behind them. Few of the Chamorro natives were in the streets. Many of the men were hired as guides for the US Army and Marine Corps. Gradually, the rest of the town returned home from the safety of deep caves.

At the end of town they approached a checkpoint

with two marine guards. The marines warned them about nonsecured areas delineated by strips of red cloth. Red flags also marked specific items thought to be unsafe. The Japanese set numerous booby traps around potential war souvenirs.

Harkel, Jackson, and Russell continued up the road. It rose into the hills surrounding Apra. On either side the vegetation grew increasingly thick. A half mile out of town, Jackson stopped and turned to his right. A footpath, heading northeast, cut through the jungle. The path was wide enough for two soldiers to walk side by side. "Let's go this way," he said, and led the other two officers into the tropical forest.

"Lieutenant, shouldn't we stay on the road," asked Harkel. It wasn't really a question.

"God, no. We'd be ducks in a pond on the first day of hunting season.

Harkel looked at Russell who just shrugged his shoulders and followed Jackson.

After ten minutes, they walked up to a stack of Japanese rifles tagged with a piece of red cloth. Carefully, vigilantly looking left and right, they stepped around it.

"What's that smell?" asked Harkel. He waved his hand in front of his face in a vain attempt to dismiss the pungent odor.

"I smell it too," said Russell.

"I don't know," said Jackson, "but I don't like it either."

A few yards more, Jackson stopped. Harkel and Russell stopped right behind him. The path emptied into a broad clearing. A green and khaki tent full of small round holes stood to their left. A Japanese soldier lay face up in the entrance. His rifle was broken, bayonet on the ground beside it. Another tent, a few yards away, had fallen to the ground. Between them, a bunker of sand bags protected a machine gun that faced the path. The belt of the machine gun was still in the chamber. The gunner was dead. He lay over the bags, helmet on the ground by his hand.

More bodies littered the compound. A faint buzz filled the air. Large green flies swarmed over the bodies.

Harkel gagged. Russell reached into his pocket for a handkerchief. He pulled the thin white cloth over his nose and tied it behind his neck.

Jackson cautiously took a couple of steps into the clearing. "I don't see any red flags," he said.

"No one could stomach the stench long enough to flag anything here," answered Harkel.

Russell walked over to the machine gun and reached for the ammunition belt.

"Be careful, Pete," Jackson said.

"I just want one bullet," replied Russell. "They wouldn't booby trap one shell. They'd rig the whole belt." He slowly pulled a cartridge out of the belt. Russell held it between his thumb and forefinger and looked at it before he slid it into his pocket.

Harkel walked over to the tent where the Japanese soldier lay. He reached for the bayonet.

"Hold it," said Russell. "A bayonet on the ground might be booby trapped."

Russell walked over to the tent. He pulled some string out of his back pocket and unwound it. He handed one end to the Engineering officer. "Tie one end to the shaft."

Harkel slipped the string under the shaft and tied it. He and Russell backed away to the path and crouched behind a tree. Jackson ducked behind a wall of sandbags on the other side of the camp as Russell pulled the string. The bayonet inched toward the two men behind the tree.

123

"It's clean, Phil."

"Thanks, Pete," said a delighted Harkel. He walked back to the tent and picked up the bayonet.

Jackson stood. His attention focused on the sound of a twig snapping behind him. He turned to see a Japanese soldier standing half behind a tree at the edge of the clearing. The soldier leaned on the butt of his rifle that he used as a crutch. The barrel was down in the dry, dusty earth. The right sleeve of shirt was torn off at the shoulder. The wounded soldier tied the cloth above his right knee to stop the bleeding of a gunshot wound. The dark red stain of dried blood covered his pant leg.

"Ohayô gozaimasu." Leaning on his rifle, the soldier stiffly bowed.

Jackson returned the bow. "Ohayô gozaimasu. Watakushi wa Rick Jackson desu."

"No Hyodo Ito desu."

"Hajimemashite Hyodo-san. Shitsurei desu ga … do you speak English, Mr. Hyodo?" asked Jackson.

"Only little," replied Hyodo.

Russell and Harkel looked over when they heard Jackson speak. They did not see the soldier in the shadows of the tropical foliage.

"Who are you talking to?" asked Harkel.

Jackson turned. "Mr. Hyodo."

Harkel and Russell looked at each other.

Jackson faced Hyodo. "Shiken wa itsu desu ka?" He pointed to Hyodo's leg.

"Hai, okagesama de." Hyodo smiled and limped into the light of the clearing.

Harkel and Russell quickly drew their service revolvers.

"Atsui desu nee," said Hyodo.

"Sô desu nee."

"What did he say, Jackson?" asked Harkel. He and Russell moved slowly closer.

"He said it was hot. I agreed."

Harkel and Russell looked at each other again.

Hyodo spoke again. "Anáta wa Nihongo ga totemo jozú na n desu ne.

"Máda hetá na n desu."

"What did he say now?" asked Harkel.

"He complimented my Japanese but I brushed it off. Now, if you please, I'm trying to talk with this man." Jackson was rather curt.

"But he's Japanese!" exclaimed Harkel.

"First and foremost, he is a human being," snapped Jackson. "And he's wounded." Jackson turned to Hyodo and addressed the soldier. "Hyodo-san, please speak English. My friends are nervous."

"Hai, Jackson-san." Hyodo used his rifle to ease himself down and sit on a sandbag. "I surrender. No food. No water. Very tired."

"I understand, Hyodo-san. Can you walk?" asked Jackson.

"Hai. Rest often, please, Jackson-san."

"No problem. Where did you learn English"

"Wife translator before war. Teach me. Where learn Japanese?"

"My father owns a fishery in San Francisco. I knew many Portuguese and Japanese fishermen."

"You never mentioned that," said Harkel.

"It never came up," replied Jackson. He turned to Russell. "Ensign, go back to Apra. See if you can get some transportation for this soldier. And find out which compound, exactly, we escort him to."

"Yes, sir." Russell jogged across the clearing to the path and disappeared into the jungle.

125

"Harkel, stay with us."

"Aye, sir."

Hyodo pushed himself to his feet and slowly hobbled across the clearing. Jackson walked next to him. Harkel trailed behind, still carrying the service revolver in his hand.

13 August 1944
1600 Hours
Apra Harbor

The crew gathered in the mess hall for mail call. Everyone was excited. No one had received mail since they left Eniwetok. Ensign Russell received 47 letters from his wife and a bevy of cat calls from his shipmates.

The biggest story passed around the ship, however, was started by Harkel. Harkel was quick to tell the other officers at breakfast in the wardroom about how Jackson talked a Japanese soldier into surrendering. At first, the officers thought it was just a yarn to rib Jackson. But Russell verified much of the story. It didn't take long for the story to spread throughout the ship.

15 August 1944
0800 Hours
Apra Harbor

As part of a six-ship convoy, the Osage left Guam and sailed for Eniwetok. With the shipping lanes between Guam and Eniwetok secure, the convoy had no destroyer escorts.

1930 Hours
Aft Crews' Quarters
South Pacific, between Guam and Eniwetok

A few enlisted men were playing cards at a couple of the tables. Some answered letters received at mail call earlier in the week. A couple were coming back from the head after taking a shower and others, already in their bunk, read old letters or books.

A nearly constant stream of music from the Big Bands fed the speakers of the ship's 1MC. The radiomen picked up short wave radio broadcasts from naval bases in the South Pacific and channeled them into the ship's announcing system after 1700 hours. Many programs contained popular music, new releases, news about the war, events in the United States, and commentaries.

The music stopped and a sweet, throaty female voice said in flawless English, "Good evening, boneheads. This is your favorite enemy, Ann. How are all of you orphans of the South Pacific? Are you enjoying yourselves while your wives and sweethearts are running around with the 4Fs back in the States? How do feel now that the Imperial Japanese Navy has sunk so many of your weak and inadequate ships? How will you get home? Here's another record to remind you of what you are missing." Immediately, "In a Little Gypsy Tea Room" followed her diatribe.

"Thank you, Tokyo Rose," said Kraft. "We can always count on you to bring our spirits down."

"Why'd you call her Tokyo Rose?" asked Conway. "She said her name was Ann."

"It's a nickname that GIs gave her, Jay," answered Kraft. "Tokyo Rose rhymes. Sounds better than Yokohama Ann."

"She's always on the radio. When does she sleep?" said Conway.

Chief Edwards answered. "Well, uh course thez mo' than one of'em. Probly a dozen or so on shifts. That way they have a constant stream of insults tuh grace our ears."

His southern drawl drew a sharp contrast to the soft feminine voice a moment ago.

"Why can't Miller find something better on his short wave? I don't like listening to her. She always talkin' about home," complained Kraft.

"It's jus' propaganda, Kraft. Don't pay it no never mind," replied Edwards. "Else go an' talk tuh Millah and ask'em tuh find somethin' bettuh. But ya ain't gonna find it. They play the best music so y'all will listen."

22 August 1944
1030 Hours
Eniwetok

The Osage arrived at Eniwetok and received her anchorage berth. To reach the berth, the tanker had to navigate past 10 aircraft carriers at anchor in the bay. The larger ships—carriers, battleships, cruisers—used a different, richer fuel than the kind the Osage held in her tanks. The tanker usually refueled only the smaller, lighter ships of the fleet.

24 August 1944
1500 Hours
Eniwetok

Michaels received orders for the ship to sail to Guadalcanal so the Osage could receive new radar equipment. He called the officers to the wardroom and told them to prepare to get underway at first light.

29 August 1944
1300 Hours
South Pacific

"Now hear this. Now here this," blared from the ship's 1MC. "We are now crossing the equator. All polliwogs muster on deck. All polliwogs muster on deck."

The US Navy had a time-honored tradition. Sailors who never crossed the equator were considered polliwogs. Sailors who had crossed the equator were shellbacks. Crossing the equator was only the first step in the initiation to become a shellback. The second, and final, step was the ritual.

Two and a half months ago, as part of a four-ship convoy in unsecured waters, the crew was not allowed to initiate the polliwogs. Now that the Japanese were driven back to the Philippines, shipping lanes from the Marshall Islands to the Solomon Islands were not nearly as dangerous.

Roughly half of the ship's company were shellbacks. For two days, they met and planned the ritual. Shellbacks manned all of the duty stations. Michaels was on the bridge with Emerson and Miller. Becker was in the engine room with Cook and Kraft. Those not on duty administered the initiation. With everyone at muster between the superstructures, Morton took roll call to make sure all of the polliwogs were present and accounted for.

The wogs were grouped in threes and led by a handler. There were 15 groups. First, each handler led his group to the ships' barber to make the wogs presentable to Davey Jones, master of the briny deep. The barber sat in a chair near the 3-inch-50 at the bow of the ship. Handlers presented each wog to the ship's barber who cut a shock of hair from each head. Then the hair was pasted to the man's chest because real men have hair on their chest.

Then each group of polliwogs was led aft to the starboard side of the ship between the superstructures where shellbacks created a mock Davey Jones' locker. SK2 Harry

Schneider was a large man but not very tall. He resembled the Pillsbury Dough Boy, large and soft. Schneider sat on a bench, shirt off, back to the ocean. He wore a pair of shorts, no shoes, and had a white cloth tied around his head. Axle grease was liberally applied to his stomach. Two men, one on each side, stood next to him and fanned palm branches over his head.

Each handler brought his polliwogs to Davey Jones locker so they could "kiss the baby." Each polliwog had to kiss Schneider's greased belly. When they puckered and were about to kiss his stomach, Schneider grabbed them by the ears and rubbed their faces in the axle grease. As the axle grease rubbed off, one of the palm-waving attendants reapplied the grease liberally.

After visiting Davey Jones' locker, Jackson led Lycovec, Russell, and Clark to port side of the ship. Three enlisted men—Tex Akins, Mel Hobbs, and Emmet Weston—knelt on the deck. Jay Conway, their handler, stood behind them. In front of them, 3 fifteen-foot lanes were drawn in chalk on the deck. A raw egg lay before each sailor.

"Get down on all fours," Jackson told his wogs. "I am going to treat you to a little entertainment and lunch." The officers knelt.

Conway addressed his wogs. "Here's the deal. You have to roll the egg with your nose to the end of the lane. And here's your incentive. The winner does not have to eat the egg."

Lycovec, Russell, and Clark smiled. "I'm going to enjoy watching this," said Clark.

Conway blew a whistle and the three men scrambled forward pushing the raw eggs with their noses. Hobbs, in the left lane, quickly rolled his egg out of bounds. He reached for it but, before he touched it, Conway yelled,

"With your nose, mister!" Hobbs crawled after the egg.

In the center lane, Weston nosed his egg forward and jumped out in front. Akins, to his right, was pushing his egg almost as quickly. He picked up speed and nosed his egg across the finish line a second before his rival. Akins grabbed the egg, knelt, and thrust his hand into the air. "I don' haffa eat the egg!" he cried.

Conway was nonchalant. "That's right, Akins. You don't have to eat it. Give me the egg."

Akins gave the egg to his handler.

"Take off your hat," said Conway.

The sailor grabbed his ball cap and slowly pulled it off his head. Conway cracked the egg and broke over the Akins' head. "You have to wear it." The yolk broke immediately and followed the raw, clear albumen down the side of his face.

Conway turned to Hobbs and Weston. "Get crackin' boys."

Both sailors cracked the eggs on the deck, threw their heads back, and emptied the shells into their mouths. Weston swallowed hard. Hobbs gagged and vomited on the deck.

Lycovec, Russell, and Clark could not contain their laughter. Jackson pulled them to the side. "Hope you enjoyed the show, fellas. Time for lunch." He led them to the officers' wardroom. Melvin Wilson waited. He stood on the other side of the table.

"Mr. Wilson," began Jackson, "these are three hungry polliwogs. Got anything to fill their miserable polliwog stomachs?"

"Aye, suh," replied Wilson. "Come 'round the table."

The officers walked around the table. Wilson opened a can of oysters packed in olive oil and set it on the cart. Then, he picked up a ball of string and cut 3 three-foot lengths. Wilson tied a slimy oyster to the end of each piece of string. He gave them to Jackson.

Jackson told Clark to step forward. As he approached, Lycovec whispered to Russell, "Im going to enjoy watching this."

Clark opened his mouth and tilted his head back. Jackson raised the string and lowered the oyster into Clark's mouth. "Swallow," commanded Jackson.

Clark swallowed the oyster but Jackson held onto the string.

"Now, keep your mouth open and relax your throat."

Jackson slowly pulled the string. Inch by inch, the string grew longer until Clark gagged and the oyster popped out of his mouth. "Seconds, Roger?"

"I fear I've lost my appetite," replied Clark. He wiped his mouth.

"No doubt."

Lycovec was next. "You know the drill, Fritz," said Jackson. "Open wide." Lycovec opened his mouth and Jackson dropped the second slimy mollusk down his throat. Before Jackson could retrieve the oyster, Lycovec bent over and heaved.

Clark leaned over and whispered to Russell. "I enjoyed watching that."

Wilson reached under the shelf of the cart and threw some towels on the floor. He looked at Jackson and smiled. "I thought somethin' like this might happen." Jackson returned his smile.

"Pete, my good man, I think we will have to improvise," said Jackson. He was not a small man but Russell stood about a head taller. Jackson stepped onto a chair and dangled the oyster in front of Russell.

132

Chapter 8
R & R

30 August 1944
1400 Hours
South Pacific, East of Bougainville Island

The captain stood at the glass window on the bridge when a change of orders—to continue straight to Espiritu Santo—came through the short-wave. The Osage could stop at Guadalcanal only for supplies and fuel, if needed. Michaels walked into the chartroom and looked at the map. He decided to change course and steer clear of Guadalcanal. The sooner they arrived at Espiritu Santo, the better. He told the helmsman to head south-southeast on a course that took them just west of the Santa Cruz Islands. From there they headed due south.

2 September 1944
1800 Hours
South Pacific, East of the Solomon Islands

Phillips, Fiore, and Turkin stood on the fantail. Fiore invented a game using a case of empty soda bottles. One person threw an empty bottle high in the air over the ocean. Then, two others each threw an empty soda bottle and tried to hit the first. He called it "soda pop", and was very happy with himself that he came up with the name. Best out of five won a dollar for each hit more than the other player. Hits were low. So was the amount of money won. Still, nobody wanted to throw against Fiore—much less bet against him.

133

9 September 1944
0730 Hours
Espiritu Santo

The Osage arrived in Segong Channel but no docking berth was available. Michaels ordered the helmsman to set a course and drop anchor close to where they anchored last time they were in the New Hebrides.

With the holding tanks empty, the crew could not refuel other ships. To prepare for the new radar, they completed almost all planned and preventative maintenance on existing equipment during the voyage from Eniwetok. Work on the Osage was minimal so Michaels granted shore leave to officers and men not in the duty section of the day.

13 September 1944
1145 Hours
Espiritu Santo

In the days following their arrival at Espiritu Santo, those who went ashore visited the clubs, spent time on the beach, and organized softball games against other ships in the area. Those who stayed aboard ship played cards—poker, hearts, spades—or craps.

Seaman Fred Hook was a young man from southern Georgia. He had a wide-eyed innocence and pollyannic optimism that was as irritating to some as it was infectious to others. His cheerful acceptance of life, as it presented itself, earned him friends and a good deal of teasing. He also attributed his amazing luck to his unbridled joie de vie.

Hook reported to the bridge for the watch. Sailors arrived at duty stations 15 minutes before the watch actually started. That gave the off-going watch time to update the on-coming watch about orders and issues of the day. When

Hook stepped onto the bridge, he commanded everyone's attention. It wasn't that he was a big man. He was waving $1800 in cash won at craps and cards.

"Hoo-oo-ey," Hook cried. "I got more money than Carter has liver pills."

Lycovec was the officer on duty on the bridge. "That's a lot of money, sailor. You want me to talk to the captain about storing it in the ship's safe?"

Hook gracefully refused. "That jes' wouldn' be fair, sir. Gotta let the boys try ta git their money back." He threw his head back, laughed, and stepped lightly across the bridge to take Mel Hobbs' place on watch.

15 September 1944
1545 Hours
Espiritu Santo

Morton was the officer on duty when Hook arrived to relieve the watch. Hook walked up to Hobbs who handed him the sound-powered phones.

"Well, Hook," said Morton, "still carrying a wad of cash?"

"Gawd no, lieutenant. I'm stoned broke. Lost it quicker 'n I won it." He threw his head back and laughed.

16 September 1944
0800 Hours
Espiritu Santo

The Osage left Segong Channel and tied up to Pier 3 at the naval base. At 0900, an installation team crossed over the plank to mount and set up the radar equipment on the flying wing. Another team came aboard to refit navigation equipment on the bridge and in the engine room.

The radar was mounted on the starboard flying wing midway between the bridge and the 20-mm anti-aircraft gun. It was round, approximately 40 inches in diameter. The steel-grey dish was welded on top of a 4-foot pole and sat parallel to the deck. A 20-inch arm extended from the center to the end of the dish. Like the second-hand of a clock, it spun clockwise—only faster.

For the first time since spring, the temperature did not break 90°F.

18 September
1900 Hours
Espiritu Santo

Rick Jackson reputation's as a wheeler-dealer grew quickly because of all the new movies he brought aboard the Osage. Books were plentiful. So was beer—during off-duty hours. Beer cans were packed singly in cases. They had no pull tabs. To open the cans, the sailors used short, metal can openers that fit in their hands. Beer was stored warm and iced down in plastic or metal tubs. Cliques of sailors met in favorite spots to drink a few cold ones, tell jokes, and swap stories.

Stacek and Edwards often met with the junior officers in Lycovec's stateroom. Stacek usually brought the beer; Russell brought ice; Edwards, the tub; Jackson, a few extra metal folding chairs.

Stacek had a propensity for long-winded stories. He had a habit of reaching into the tub for a beer, leaning over, and setting it between his feet before he opened it. It was a routine the group recognized. And, occasionally, they teased him about it. In fairness, no one in the group was safe from the harmless barbs and pranks traded among friends far from home.

The group had been together about an hour when Jackson nodded to Russell sitting next to Stacek. Russell knocked over his beer onto Stacek's deck shoes. While everyone cleaned up the mess, Jackson vigorously shook up a warm beer and slipped it into the tub of ice close to Stacek.

A few minutes after the cleanup, Stacek was ready for another beer. He reached into the tub, pulled out a can, and set it between his feet. Edwards handed him the opener. Stacek leaned down and slipped the hook of the opener under the lip of the can. He lifted and the metal tip punctured the can of beer. With a sudden hiss, warm beer sprayed all over his arms, hands, legs, and face. Although the foam hit almost everyone, Stacek bore the brunt of the fermented explosion.

Everyone, Stacek included, howled with laughter. "Paybacks are a bitch, gentlemen. And I use the term 'gentlemen' loosely."

22 September 1944
0800 Hours
Espiritu Santo

Michaels received orders to sail for Samoa and hook up to a commercial tanker for a full load of oil. Samoa was discovered by Jacob Roggeveen, a Dutch navigator, in the 1720s. In 1879, Germany and the United States divided the group of atolls between them. New Zealand took over Germany's half of the Samoan Islands in 1914.

The US Navy established a base on Tutuila, one of the principal Samoan Islands, in 1900 because of it's magnificent natural harbor, Pago Pago. Japan never controlled Samoa during WWII. Roughly 2000 miles east of the New Hebrides, it was an important, strategic base during the war.

The Osage pulled up anchor, left Segong Channel, and headed east for the 8-day journey.

24 September 1944
1400 Hours
South-Central Pacific Ocean

With cooler weather and the rainy season approaching, the tanker sailed into a mild storm. The swells did not reach the weather deck but Michaels had the boatswain's mates rig life lines fore to aft.

Most ships of the line had railings that ran around the weather deck. Tankers did not. They had a removable chain draped from a series of waist-high poles around the edge of the ship's deck. The life lines ran port and starboard from the bow to the stern and were tied to eyehooks on the gun tub forward, the masts, superstructures, deck, and fantail. They usually remained up throughout the rainy season—until March.

27 September 1944
1330 Hours
South-Central Pacific

Emerson had the watch at the helm. Russell was the officer on deck. He stood on the port wing of the flying bridge and had a pair of binoculars up to his eyes scanning the ocean ahead. Michaels stood at the window at the front of the bridge. He had just come out of the chart room after reviewing the system of natural coral reefs surrounding the atolls and islands in the area.

Michaels turned to the helmsman. "Vhat's course heading?" he asked.

"Zero-zero-four, sir," answered Emerson.

"Change course to zero-zero-seven," ordered Michaels.

"Aye, sir." Emerson turned the wheel as he confirmed the skipper's order. "Coming about to zero-zero-seven."

Michaels turned back to face the glass.

Russell felt the change in the ship's heading. He let the binoculars hang from his shoulders by the strap around his neck and walked inside.

"What's going on, Emerson? I didn't give you a course change."

"The captain gave the order, Mr. Russell." He nodded toward Michaels at the window.

Russell walked up to the window and stood next to Michaels.

"Sir, why are we changing course? Did our orders change?"

"No, Mr. Russell."

"Did I miss something on the charts, sir?"

"You are doing everything by the book. But charts are old and never change. The sea is alive. She alvays changes. Reefs are alive too. Change like the sea."

"But why the course change here? Sagi Island is miles away."

"Just a feeling. Some people call it intuition. Some call it hunch. I have no name for it but I listen to small voice inside. But vhen ve anchor at Apia, go ashore and make sure ve have most recent charts."

Twelve minutes later, Michaels told Emerson to come back to course zero-zero-four.

30 September 1944
0900 Hours
Pago Pago, Tutuila, American Samoa

As the Osage pulled into the harbor at Pago Pago, a dozen outriggers paddled out to meet it. Each boat was filled with tanned, dark-haired, native Samoans. Muscled men smoothly paddled while young women enthusiastically waved to the ship's crew on deck. Slowly, the tanker slid next to one of the piers at the naval base. It was still followed by the small flotilla of outriggers.

Word quickly spread through the ship about the native welcoming committee. By the time the duty section finished tying up the starboard side to the pier, almost the entire crew stood at the port rail. Michaels and Morton stood on the bridge. Emerson was at the helm and Olsen manned the sound-powered phones.

With so many men on the port side, and nothing to balance the starboard side, the Osage started to list. The ropes that tied the tanker to the pier pulled taught. Boards on the pier started to creak from the strain. A rope handler on the pier yelled to a roper on the Osage. He waved to the bridge. Olsen saw him.

"Captain, a roper on the forward deck is trying to get our attention."

Michaels looked down. The roper on the pier was pointing to the lines. Michaels immediately recognized what was happening.

"Emerson, get on the von-MC," ordered Michaels. "Tell crew to back away from railing and stand amidship."

Emerson picked up the microphone on the console and spoke. "Now hear this. Now hear this. Ship's crew back away from the port rail and stand amidship. I repeat, back away from the port rail and stand amidship." Emerson replaced the microphone in its cradle.

Some of the crew continued to wave as they slowly backed away. Some, curious, looked up at the bridge but they did not move.

140

Michaels walked over to the console and picked up the microphone. He keyed the mike. "This is Captain Michaels. All hands move away from rail or no liberty in Samoa." Without hesitation, everyone backed away. The ship rolled back to an even keel and tension on the ropes eased.

1100 Hours

Russell and Clark were the first to go ashore in one of the longboats. Clark was checking available supplies and Russell had to go to the naval station chart house. The ensign carried the ship's map rolled and stuffed into a cardboard tube.

New charts were created and approved at Pearl Harbor and shipped to Samoa for distribution to the Pacific fleets. With its rounded roof, drab navy-gray color, and rows of small windows on either side of the building, the chart house looked like a small airplane hangar. Russell opened the front door and stepped inside. He took off his cap and looked around.

Directly ahead, a three-and-a-half-foot counter divided the room. Behind the counter, four enlisted men examined maps at drafting tables. Another sailor paged through files in a drawer of an oversized file cabinet. At the counter, a sixth stood writing in a legal-sized ledger. To the left, half a dozen tables were placed in two rows. Each table had four chairs. More than half of the chairs were occupied by sailors—some enlisted, some officers—filling out forms. To the right, another six tables were arranged in two rows. Almost all of the chairs were occupied. Russell walked forward to the counter.

"Excuse me," began Russell, "how can I get a chart?"

The sailor, a second class petty officer, did not look up. "I'll be right with ya."

When the sailor finished writing, he closed the ledger. "What are you looking for, sir?"

"I have our ship's chart and I want to make sure we have the most recent edition."

"What kind of chart?" asked the petty officer. The corners of his mouth turned up slightly. "Different charts have different kinds of information like stereographic projection, geometric perspective, parallels and meridians."

"I want the most recent copy of this." Russell put the tube on the counter.

The enlisted man pulled out the chart and unrolled it on the counter. "Ah, you want a navigation chart, mercator projection, South Pacific." He looked in the lower right-hand corner and copied a set of numbers onto a piece of paper. "Looks like this chart was created in 1927. I'm sure we have a more recent edition."

The petty officer reached beneath the counter and set a stack of papers in front of Russell. "You have to fill these out. There aren't that many but I need them in triplicate."

"Do you have any carbon paper?" asked Russell.

"Carbon paper?"

"You know, the pressure-sensitive black paper you put between pages with the matte side down. It creates copies of what you write, when you write it."

The petty officer laughed. "Touché, ensign. Sorry, sir, but I need originals. Those are my orders—from Pearl. You can have a seat at any of the tables."

Russell picked up the forms and walked to a table near the counter. He picked up a pen on the table and started filling out the paperwork. When he was finished—more than an hour later—he took the forms back to the petty officer behind the counter.

"Thank you, sir." The sailor turned and walked to a file cabinet near the far wall. He opened a drawer and paged through it until he found the folder he was looking for. He lifted it and closed the drawer. The petty officer returned and set it on the counter. "There you are, ensign. Thanks for the witty banter. Most who come in here don't have a sense of humor."

"Well, I know the difference between humor and odor," replied Russell.

"What's that, sir?" asked the enlisted man.

"Humor is a shift of wit," said Russell.

The petty officer cocked his head and lowered his eyebrows in a puzzled look. Russell picked up the tube and folder, and turned. Almost to the door, he heard the enlisted man laugh out loud.

1400 Hours

With charts in hand, Russell stepped through the hatch and entered the bridge. Lycovec had duty. He pointed to the bundles carried by Russell. "Hey, Pete. Whatcha got there?"

"New navigation chart, mercator projection, South Pacific. Picked it up on the island."

"Sounds like you have a serious case of fancy-word. Did you pick that up on the island too?"

Both men laughed aloud.

Russell walked into the chart room, taped the old chart to the bulkhead, and spread the new chart on the table. He anchored the four corners with clips. Before Russell went ashore, he marked the old chart where Michaels changed course near Sagi Island. He found his mark on the old chart and compared it with the new chart.

Where the old chart showed open sea, the new chart revealed a coral reef charted within the past 7 years.

Russell said aloud to himself, "Either this is the luckiest damned ship in the navy or Michaels' intuition really paid off."

1 October 1944
1200 Hours
Pago Pago, Tutuila, American Samoa

SS2 Melvin Wilson and SS3 Rufus Hazelton went ashore to see what they could buy to top off the officers' kitchen storeroom. Wilson didn't want to take Hazelton with him because his brother-in-law was the only other rated ship's steward onboard. But he had a knack for getting into trouble with officers and Wilson promised he would keep an eye on his sister's husband.

The two stewards walked down a dry, dusty dirt road toward the PX, the storehouse for perishable goods on the American naval base. The base was surrounded by a 6-foot chain-link fence. The PX was a wide, one-story white building just inside the front gate, a quarter of a mile from the pier.

As they passed the gate, the ship's stewards noticed one Anglo boy and three Samoan boys playing marbles on the other side of the fence. They stopped for a moment to watch.

The boys marked a 3-foot circle in the dirt and knelt just outside the perimeter. Inside the circle lay the swarm of marbles. The blonde-haired Anglo boy was getting ready for his turn. He held his shooter in his curved right forefinger. He set his knuckle on the ground and flicked it out with his thumb. The marble shot out of his hand and clacked against an orange cat's eye which spun out of the circle. The boy jumped up and retrieved the marbles.

A short, thin Samoan knelt outside the circle. Instead of holding his shooter in his right hand like the Anglo boy, he held it in his curved left forefinger. And he did not put his knuckle to the ground when he shot. He held it chest high, palm down. With his right forefinger, the Samoan snapped the marble into the circle. It careened off a solid blue marble into a green one and sent them out of the circle. The boy whistled, jumped up, and gathered up all three marbles.

"Did you see that li'l boy shoot them marbles?" said Hazelton. "He gotta hard shot. How'd he do that with both hands, Melvin?"

"Don't know, Rufus. Practice, I guess."

Hazelton held his hand up like the Samoan boy and imitated the snap with his right forefinger.

"You can't play marbles with the boys," laughed Wilson. "We got men's work."

"Man, I don't wanna play marbles."

"Careful now, Rufus, or I'll tell my sister you was eyein' young boys. An' you know she got a mouth that don't keep no secrets. When we get home, everyone in Detroit will give you shit fer it."

"Man, that ain't cool. You gotta mean way 'bout you."

Getting drunk and talking back to people of authority wasn't out of the ordinary for Hazelton. It was almost expected. Knowing his penchant for getting into trouble, Wilson's sister still married Hazelton—even though Melvin argued his disapproval two days before their wedding. When the war began, Hazelton enlisted because he didn't have a job. Wilson's sister implored Melvin to enlist to keep an eye on him but he didn't want to go. He had a good job—as good as most black men could find in Michigan—

and a boss who didn't look at the color of a man's skin to determine his worth as a human being. But he gave in and enlisted.

For the most part, his tour as a steward for the ship's officers saw no action. He was ashore in Efaté when a kamikaze pilot dove into the troop transport he was assigned to. His most hair-raising moments were intervening when Hazelton got drunk and disorderly or talked back to a white officer who had racial attitude.

Finally, he had something to keep Hazelton in line. Wilson just looked at Hazelton and smiled.

1600 Hours

Clark, Lycovec, and Becker walked down the plank that stretched over the water between the pier and ship. The tide lapped against the piles and struts in rhythmic waves under a blue tropical sky peppered with wispy cirrostratus clouds.

The walk from the pier to the officers' club was short but it sat on top of a steep hill. From the dirt road, stone steps with a simple bamboo handrail serpentined up through short, scruffy palm trees and tufts of thin, straw-colored grass. For Clark and Lycovec, the steps were no problem. For Becker, they were an obstacle. He was seriously overweight. Because his weight kept him from exercise and sports, Becker's legs struggled with each step.

Lycovec and Clark noticed Becker struggling halfway up. They slowed their pace. Lycovec stopped and picked up a discarded beer can alongside the steps—not so much to beautify the hill, but to generate a little extra time for Becker.

At the top of the hill, Becker leaned on the rail and breathed heavily. He wiped the sweat from his brow with a small grey handkerchief. Clark created a little more time for Becker. "Look at the horizon," he said. The sun seemed to dip into the water. The high, thin clouds were a mix of crimson and orange surrounded by an ever-deepening indigo. "Red sky at night, sailor's delight."

Lycovec completed the centuries-old maxim embraced by sailors worldwide. "Red sky at morning, sailor's warning."

"I'm ready for a cold one," puffed Becker.

Clark and Lycovec nodded. Clark opened the door and the three men walked inside.

The club was open and spacious. A bamboo-and-cane bar stood near the wall to their right. Rattan tables and chairs formed rows in a semicircle around the bar. Ceiling fans circled the warm, humid air. More tables and chairs were informally arranged on an exterior wooden deck, to their left, which covered a small ravine overgrown with tall grass and weeds. Planters filled with flowering plants separated the deck from the interior of the club.

Two dark-skinned Samoan waitresses stood at the cocktail station. Each wore a grass skirt with a multicolored bikini top that accentuated cleavage and exposed a bare midriff. And each had a delicate white hibiscus pinned to her hair over the left ear. The bartender was also Samoan, short and stocky. He wore black pants and a tuxedo shirt open at the collar, sleeves rolled half way up his thick, hairless forearms.

More than half of the tables were occupied by two, three, or four officers. One table had six men squeezed around it. Four more stood chatting at the bar. Clark, Lycovec, and Becker took an empty table inside, close to the deck, next to three junior Marine officers nursing glasses of cold beer.

One of the waitresses walked up to the table. She

held a small, round cocktail tray in her left hand. The waitress slipped a white paper cocktail napkin on the table in front of each man as she asked, "Good evening, boys. Thirsty?" She looked at each of them and flashed a big smile with pearly white teeth.

Before Clark, Jackson, or Becker could answer, one of the marines at the table next to them yelled, "Hey, sweetface, we could use another round over here."

She looked over but her smile vanished and her dark brown eyes narrowed. "I'll be right with you."

She returned her attention and smile to the officers of the Osage.

"Trouble?" asked Jackson quietly.

"Nothing I can't handle," she answered softly but defiantly. "Just a little too much to drink."

"Draft beer, please," said Becker wiping his brow.

"Me too," said Jackson.

"I'll have a bourbon and 7," said Clark.

Jackson and Becker looked at Clark. He answered their looks brashly. "I've had enough beer for a while. I want a real drink. Not as cultured as the British gin and tonic, perhaps, but certainly more American—and drinkable. Whoever came up with idea of putting juniper berries in a highball?"

The waitress pointed to each man as she repeated their order, "draft, draft, bourbon and 7." She nodded and walked over to the table of three marines. The waitress picked up two empty glasses from the table, balanced them on the center of her tray, and said, "Another round, gentlemen?"

"Yeah, baby," said the one who yelled moments earlier. He reached for her hand but she withdrew it behind her back. He was a lieutenant with broad shoulders and a wide chin. Sparse, thin black hair masked his upper lip. It looked like he was straining to grow a moustache without reaching full puberty. "How about joining us for a drink?"

"Now that's original." She laughed and walked away.

The marine pushed his chair back and stood. "Hey, you could be a bit more friendly."

Clark looked at the marine. "And you could have a modicum of respect," he said.

The marine faced Clark. "Pipe down, swab. No one's talkin' to you."

Clark turned to Jackson. "Say, Rick, why do they call marines 'jarheads'? With those tiny square heads, it seems almost impossible to screw their caps on tight."

The other two marines stood and pushed their chairs back.

Jackson and Clark stood and faced the marines. Still sitting, Becker looked up. "Now guys," he said, "this is a little friendly R&R. Let's just sit, have some cold beer, and save the attitude for the Japs."

"Just keep sittin', fat boy, and you won't get hurt," said the second marine. He was a junior grade lieutenant, slender with lots of freckles and short red hair. He pounded one fist into the open palm of his other hand.

The first marine swung his fist at Clark. Clark ducked, brought his right fist up, and jabbed twice with his left. Both scored hits on the marine's face. Jackson swung at the second marine who blocked it. The third marine stepped behind Jackson and grabbed his arms. The second marine hit Jackson in the stomach. Becker slid his chair back, reached down, and grabbed the ankles of the third marine. He pulled hard. The marine's feet came out from under him. He lost his grip on Jackson and fell. His chin hit the floor and he was knocked out.

As the marine fell, he pulled Jackson down—far enough so that the next punch from the second marine

149

glanced off Jackson's forehead instead of falling squarely on his chin. Jackson straightened up and landed a right uppercut on the marine who stumbled back against one of the planters and fell over it onto the outdoor deck. Jackson rushed him and held him face down.

Meanwhile, Clark continued to box his opponent. The first marine was unprepared for Clark's skill. Clark landed jab after jab and kept the marine at bay. Frustrated and angry, the marine picked up a rattan chair. Clark backed up quickly. The marine rushed Clark but Becker stuck out his foot and tripped him. Clark jumped forward and landed a hard right cross that sent the marine unconscious to the floor.

When the fracas began, the cocktail waitresses huddled at the bar, the other patrons quickly scuttled away from the commotion, and the bartender called the shore patrol.

By the time the shore patrol arrived, the Osage's officers had straightened up their area of the bar and helped the marines into chairs. The SPs interrogated Clark, Jackson, Becker, the employees, and other patrons in the bar. Because the marines threw the first punch, the SPs led them out of the club.

The waitress came over to the table. "Draft, draft, and a bourbon and 7," she said. "Thanks, boys."

3 October 1944
1000 Hours
Apia, Upolu, New Zealand Samoa

The Osage sailed half a day from US-controlled Samoa to New Zealand Samoa. The harbor for Apia was not as big or deep as Pago Pago but the water was crystal clear because it did not see nearly as much traffic. In the middle of the harbor, approximately 100 yards from shore, the bow and stern of an old merchant ship—wrecked decades earlier—stuck out of the water like a half-submerged V.

The capitol, Apia, was just a sliver of a village that hugged the crescent coast of the harbor. A small mountain range, not much more than large hills, formed the spine of the island and cradled Apia. Two main roads ran parallel to the shore. They were connected by short roads a block apart. Although German and New Zealand architectural influences were prevalent on the island, many of the buildings were huts with thatched roofs. The largest building was a 19th-century colonial-style church with two square white spires that towered over the town. For the week they were in Apia, Michaels granted 12-hour leave—9 a.m. to 9 p.m.—to the crew, day on, day off.

Seamen Lem Turkin, Hal Roach, Sam Chance, and Barry Olsen stepped off the longboat and walked up the short pier into Apia. A small crowd of the ship's crew followed. Once off the pier, the crowd split into cliques that went their separate ways to discover what the town had to offer.

Turkin, Roach, Chance, and Olsen turned left and walked until they came to the first cross road. They turned right and walked inland. At the next block, on the corner opposite from where they stood, they saw something very unexpected: an ice cream shop.

The shop was one story, more oval than round, and had no walls. Three thick wooden supports, made from palm tree trunks, on each side of the shop held up a thatched roof with exposed beams made from smaller palm trunks. Two more supports in front framed an entrance. A painted wooden sign, Ice Cream Shoppe, hung high by a chain between the two front supports. Six black wire tables—three on each side of the lobby—with black wire chairs separated the counter from the entrance. The back of the shop was enclosed by white walls.

Outside, a wrought-iron fence and gate marked an informal patio. A dozen more wire tables with chairs were in the patio. A Samoan man straightened the tables and chairs in the patio. He wore shorts beneath a grass skirt, no shirt, and a shell necklace. The Samoan was about fifty years old and moved with the grace and ease of a man half his age. Another Samoan man, younger than the one outside, opened a door that led from the back of the shop and stepped into the lobby. He closed the door behind him and walked behind the counter.

The four sailors stood for a moment in the side street and watched the men get ready for business.

"Ice cream," said Turkin flatly.

"Ice cream," repeated Chance.

"Let's see what time they open," said Olsen.

The four men walked up to the gate. The elder Samoan looked up and saw the American sailors heading toward his store. At the gate, a small wooden sign detailed the hours of operation. The shop opened at 11 a.m.

Roach looked at his wristwatch. "It opens in about 45 minutes."

"What do we do until then?" asked Chance.

"I doubt we find much to do just after 10 in the morning on this island," answered Olsen.

"Let's ask if we can wait." Turkin pointed to one of the wire tables just inside the gate.

Olsen spoke up and addressed the Samoan outside "Excuse me, sir. Can we sit at one of these tables and wait for you to open?"

The Samoan nodded.

Turkin opened the gate and the four men sat at a table.

"How many flavors do you think they have?" asked Chance.

"Don't know, don't care," said Turkin. "My favorite is vanilla. They got to have vanilla."

"Vanilla!" replied Roach. "That's pretty boring, Lem."

"What's your favorite, Hal?" asked Olsen.

"Strawberry," he replied.

"Just as boring," said Chance.

"Oh yeah? What's your favorite, Sam?" asked Olsen.

"Chicken ripple," answered Chance. "Yum!" He licked his lips.

The other three men grunted their revulsion and Roach was quick to add, "What kind of a mind even thinks of something like that?"

4 October 1944
1930 Hours
Apia

The harvest moon rose slowly above the horizon. A noisy flock of seagulls flew over the center of Apia to roost for the night in the trees beyond the town.

Half of Ellen's crew sat quietly in the middle of the main street. Chairs, arranged in rows, faced a small stage near the church. They were waiting for a performance by the residents. The show included music, juggling, singing, and the traditional ceremonial dance called the Civa. The night before, the Samoans put on the same show for the other half of the crew.

Off stage, musicians played ukuleles, drums, and reeds. Three men began the performance. They jumped on stage from the street and juggled balls—three, at first, then four. After the balls, they juggled batons.

153

When they finished, half a dozen young girls danced from one side of the stage to the other. Hair down around their shoulders, they wore grass skirts and multicolored bikini tops with leis of fresh flowers around their necks. They waggled their hips and waved their arms in a routine that resembled a Hawaiian hula dance.

When the young girls reached center stage, a group of women in their teens and early 20s entered from the other side of the stage. They were dressed like and danced like their younger counterparts.

As part of the finale, two men with batons ran to the center—one from each side of the stage. A young girl held a torch and walked up to them. Each man lit the end of his three batons and then juggled them—low at first, then gradually higher until the flaming batons were spinning eight or nine feet in the air. The audience applauded loudly as the men caught and held each of the batons to end the show.

Some of the crew stayed to talk to the musicians and performers. Some went to the ice cream shop which stayed open late for the crew on the nights of the town's show. Some went back to the ship. Fiore, Phillips, Miller, and Conway took a wrong turn down a side street and discovered a local tavern.

Like the ice cream shop, the building was oval. The bar's thatched roof and exposed beams were supported by palm trunks. Outside, an informal patio harbored a few black wire tables and chairs. Unlike the ice cream shop, the tavern had a bamboo-and-cane door and thatched walls.

Almost everyone on the island walked barefoot except the Lutheran minister from New Zealand; his wife and sister; the German merchant who owned the general store; and John Newton, a New Zealander who owned most of the island. Shoes were as unnatural to Samoans as steaks to vegetarians. When the sailors opened the door and walked—in their deck shoes—across the wooden floor to the bar, the native patrons turned to see who made so much noise.

Phillips stood at the bar. "What's the house specialty?"

The bartender reached behind him, picked up a bottle on the back-bar, and set it in front of Phillips. The bottle was filled with a clear viscous liquid. Wedges of pineapple lay at the bottom. "We have bush gin," he said.

"We'll have four," said Fiore. He patted the top of the bar with his open palm.

"Each?" asked the bartender. His eyes narrowed as he half-smiled at the American sailors.

Conway answered. "One each. Four total."

The bartender turned around and picked up four short glasses. He set them on the bar, filled them half full with the bush gin, and slid a glass in front of each of the Americans.

Miller picked up the glass and smelled the drink. He wrinkled his nose and pulled back quickly. "What is this stuff? It smells sweet."

"Fruit juice—mostly mango, papaya, and pineapple. Fermented twice," replied the bartender.

Fiore raised his glass and drank. He exhaled hard, shook his head, and set the glass on the bar. "Whew! It's got a kick."

Phillips and Conway took a drink. Conway coughed. Phillips hit the top of the bar with his fist. "Aagghh!" he gasped.

Miller laughed at them. "You guys are idiots. No one else in the bar is drinking this stuff." He called to the bartender. "Excuse me, can I get a beer?"

"Can I have yours, Ron?" asked Fiore.

155

"Help yourself," replied Miller.

Fiore took Miller's glass and emptied it into his. Then he raised his glass and offered a toast. "To the U S of A."

Phillips, Miller, and Conway responded in kind. "To the U S of A," they repeated. All four took a drink. Each sailor took his turn giving a toast. After 4 toasts, only Miller did not feel the effects of the bush gin.

Anybody heard any good jokes, lately?" asked Conway.

Phillips set his glass on the bar. "You guys ever heard of limericks?"

"They're poems, right?" offered Conway.

"Kind of," replied Phillips. "Some say the French started them. Some say they are based on old Irish folk songs from the Middle Ages. One theory says Irish mercenaries taught French soldiers some of their folk songs during a war against the English. Then the French developed the current limerick form. Edward Lear was first to publish limericks in a book in the middle of the 19th century."

"How do you know so much about them?" asked Miller.

"Read a book about them and got hooked. The first limericks were clean but sometime around the Civil War, they got really bawdy. It seems that the dirtier and ruder they are, the funnier they are."

"Really," said Fiore. It was more comment than question.

"I'll show you. Here's a clean one.
A lovely young woman in pink
asked her mom for something to drink.
But she said, 'O my daughter,
there is nothing but water,'
which vexed the young woman in pink."

His audience smiled. "That was okay," critiqued Conway.

"Now here's a dirty one.

A hot-tempered girl of Caracas
was wed to a horny old jackass.
When he started to cheat her
with a dark señorita
she kicked him hard in the maracas."

They all laughed. "You're right. Much better than the first," said Miller.

"Another," said Fiore.

"Clean or dirty?"

"Dirty," said Fiore, Conway, and Miller in unison. Fiore took a big drink and grit his teeth as he swallowed hard.

"Okay." Phillips took a sip and cleared his throat.

"There was a young man of Devizes
Whose testes were two different sizes.
The one was so small
it was no ball at all.
But the other has won several prizes."

All four men laughed.

Miller looked at his wristwatch. "Hey, guys, it's getting' close to curfew. We ought to get back to the ship. The chief will have our hides if we're late."

"One more lim'rick," said Fiore who took another drink.

"Hey," said Miller, "slow down, Tony. You're drinkin' that stuff pretty fast."

"I have twice as much as you guys." Fiore didn't look at Miller when he answered. He stared into his glass and waited for Phillips.

"One more," said Phillips. He looked at Miller who nodded. "Then we gotta shove off. We'll get keel-hauled if we get back to the ship late.

There was a young man from Berlin
whose prick was the size of a pin.
Said his girl with a laugh
as she fondled his shaft
Well, this won't be much of a sin."

Laughing, Conway slapped his knee. "How do you remember them all?"

Fiore laughed, stood and set his empty glass on the bar. He was the only one who finished his cocktail. Miller, Conway, and Phillips stood with him. Fiore sat down quickly and put his hands to his head. "Whoa!" he said.

"Now you know why no one else in the bar is drinkin' this," said Miller. "Come on, Tony. Get up."

Fiore stood and steadied himself using a chair. Chair after chair, he slowly made his way to the door. Outside, Phillips walked up to Fiore's right side. Conway walked up to his left. Fiore threw his arms over his friends' shoulders and they started toward the pier.

5 October 1944
1300 Hours
Apia

Reading the smooth log, Captain Michaels sat at the small wooden table in his stateroom. The hatch and portholes were open. This far south, and so close to the rainy season, the temperature remained warm but not nearly as oppressive as the summer months when the ship hugged the equator. He looked up when he heard a knock on the hatch. "Enter."

Seaman Mel Hobbs ducked into the stateroom. He held an envelope. "I have a letter for you sir."

"From?"

"I don't know, sir. It's sealed. A couple of native Samoans rowed out in an outrigger. One climbed the ladder and asked the OOD to give this to you."

Michaels waved him closer. Hobbs walked across the room and handed him the letter.

"Thank you Mr. Hobbs. That vill be all."

"Aye, sir." Hobbs turned and returned to his watch with the officer on deck.

Michaels tore the edge of the envelope and pulled out the letter. It was an invitation for dinner. John Newton, the largest landowner in Samoa, was asking Michaels and the executive officer to come to his plantation the following evening. Newton would send a driver to pick them up at the pier at 7 p.m.

6 October 1944
1900 Hours
Apia

Wearing dress whites, Michaels and Morton climbed out of the longboat and walked to the end of the pier. A Samoan stood next to a drab, olive-green jeep. He was barefoot and wore the traditional grass skirt of the island. His chest and shoulders were thick and tanned. "Captain Michaels?" he asked.

"Ya, I am Captain Michaels."

"Mr. Newton welcomes you to Upolu," said the driver. He pointed to the jeep. "Please …"

Michaels and Morton clambered into the jeep— Michaels in front, Morton in back. The driver started the jeep, shoved it into gear, and let out the clutch. The jeep lurched forward and kicked up a puff of dust behind them.

The driver did not speak as he wheeled through town to a road that led up into the hills. At first, the grade was low but grew steeper quickly. Half a mile out of Apia, the jeep slowed. On the right, a dirt road split a pair of old palm trees that stretched up and seemed to support the cloudless evening sky.

The driver turned onto the road. Lined with palms thicker and shorter than the two at the entrance, it snaked up the middle of a cleft in the hill. After a mile it emptied onto a large, flat grassy hummock. In the center sat a single-story, ranch-style home. It was a sharp contrast to the meager, oval thatched homes scattered throughout Apia and the rest of the island. The walls were white, the roof tiled. Wide bay windows flanked wooden double doors under a white canopy at the end of the driveway. A wooden outdoor deck extended from the rear of the house to the left.

"Great Hamlet's ghost!" exclaimed Michaels viewing the tropical mansion.

As the jeep stopped in front of the house, the front door opened. A tall, lanky man stepped outside. John Newton was a New Zealander near 50 years old with short brown hair. His dark green eyes were set deep under thick, dark-brown eyebrows. He wore a short-sleeved white shirt with tan slacks and canvas sandals.

Michaels climbed out of the jeep. Morton followed. Newton walked up to them and extended his hand to Michaels. "Welcome, captain." he said.

Michaels shook his hand and replied, "My pleasure, Mr. Newton. Ve appreciate your hospitality."

"Call me John, captain."

"Please call me Honas."

Newton extended his hand to Morton. "You must be the XO."

"Lieutenant Donald Morton at your service." He shook the New Zealander's hand.

160

"Please come inside, gentlemen." Newton turned and walked into the house. The Osage's senior officers followed.

Inside, a wrought-iron candle chandelier hung from the ceiling of the foyer. To the right, a mahogany table and chairs—with six place settings—rested in the middle of the dining room. As the naval officers viewed the room, a green gecko climbed out of the large earthen pot on the floor near the bay window. Against the far wall in the dining room, a mahogany hutch held rows of white plates, cups, saucers, and glasses made of crystal. Another gecko squirmed across the top of it.

A Persian runner stretched the length of the hallway from the foyer to the kitchen. "Had this custom made," said Newton pointing to the floor. "Cost a pretty penny, it did."

Michaels and Morton nodded.

"Please excuse the geckos," continued Newton. "The damned things are all over the place. It's impossible to get rid of them so we have accustomed ourselves to their company. Quite harmless, they are."

Newton led Michaels and Morton to the left. Two large, ruby-red leather armchairs had their backs to the bay window. A matching leather couch faced them. Between them rested a low, rectangular mahogany coffee table. In the center of the table, a gecko lay flat facing the humans. A portrait of two young girls in native dress hung on the far wall.

"Please, gentlemen, have a seat."

Newton sat in one of the chairs. Michaels took the other chair and Morton sat on the couch. A small mahogany side table separated the chairs. A short, wrought-iron candle holder and a smoky-glass ashtray lay on the side table.

A middle-aged Samoan woman entered the room

from the kitchen behind Morton. Two younger women followed her. Unlike most women on the island, Newton's wife seldom wore the traditional Samoan grass skirt. She wore a pale-yellow sundress patterned with large yellow and orange sunflowers. Her black hair was pulled up into a bun and her wide mouth and thick lips brandished a broad smile.

One of the younger women carried a tray that held a pitcher of iced tea and three filled glasses. She was seventeen years old with her mother's black hair and her father's green eyes. The other woman—with light brown hair and green eyes but a darker complexion and fuller lips—was two years older than her sister. She carried a platter of mangoes, papaya, bananas, and copra.

Tuai was the daughter of a local chief. When she married John Newton, her father gave her husband most of the land they now owned. Newton was a shrewd businessman. To date, he nearly doubled the size of the plantation and shipped coconut, papaya, mangoes, and bananas to New Zealand, Australia, and Borneo. Newton's latest economic adventure was looking into the rubber industry. In their first five years of marriage, Tuai gave Newton two daughters named for the months in which they were born.

All three men stood to greet the hostess and her daughters.

"Tuai, this is Captain Michaels and Lieutenant Morton from the USS Osage," said Newton.

"Of course they're from the Osage, dear," replied Tuai. "Pleased to meet you, captain, lieutenant. These are our daughters, May and June." Tuai stepped to the side. Her daughters stepped forward.

"Would you like some iced tea, captain?" May held the tray out to him. He took a glass.

"Ya, thank you, Miss Newton," said Michaels.

May turned to Morton. "Lieutenant?" She looked into his eyes.

"Yes, ma'am. Thank you." Morton took a glass and returned her gaze.

"Oh, please don't call me 'ma'am'. I am not 'ma'am' age yet. My mother is. I am not." Tuai smiled at her daughter and Morton chuckled lightly.

May set the tray on the coffee table.

"How long will your ship be in Apia, captain?" asked June.

"Ve leave in 3 days."

"What a shame you won't be staying longer." She looked at the executive officer, brushed the gecko off the coffee table, and set down the bowl of fruit. Morton raised his eyebrows and took a drink from his glass of iced tea. It was cold and sweet. Then he brushed each hand—one at a time—against the inside of a trouser pocket. He wasn't completely certain that all of the water on his hands came from the condensation on the glass because the girls made him nervous.

"If you'll excuse us, gentlemen, we must see to dinner." Tuai tugged the blouses of her daughters and the three Samoan women returned to the kitchen.

2130 Hours

Dinner was simple: baked fish with a mango relish, roasted yams, and fried bananas with lemon grass and coconut milk. The girls were first to push their chairs back from the dinner table. Each started to collect plates from the guests and their parents.

"That vas a great meal, Tuai," said Michaels. "Thank you."

"Yes. It was delicious," echoed Morton. "Thank

163

you."

"Thank you, gentlemen," said Tuai, "but the girls cooked dinner."

"Pretty and talented. You've raised two amazing girls, Mrs. Newton," said Morton.

"You think I'm … we're pretty?" asked May. With hands full of dirty dishes, she stood across the table from Morton. June stood behind her father.

"Sure I do. Both of you have eyes as green and sweet as the ocean is salt and blue."

May smiled and looked down. "Thank you." She took the dishes into the kitchen.

"This town has shown vonderful hospitality to my crew and me," said Michaels. "I vish I could repay in some vay."

"Some of the people in town said they were curious about your ship," said June. She picked a gecko off the leg of the table and set it on the windowsill. "Perhaps you could have an open house. Or, should I say, an open boat." She smiled.

"That's a great idea, sir," added Morton. He turned to his commanding officer. "Tomorrow's too soon and Monday we leave. Has to be Sunday."

"May and I could go into Apia tomorrow and tell everyone," said June. "Perhaps we could have lunch, lieutenant." She looked at Morton. "You, May, and me."

"Sorry, June. I have duty tomorrow. I have to help get the ship and crew ready."

"It would be very wonderful, Honas," said Tuai. "Everyone in Apia has enjoyed your visit. It will be the talk for a long time."

"It seems ve vill have company on Sunday." Michaels removed the cloth napkin from his lap and set it on the table.

164

8 October 1944
0900 Hours
Apia

For the open house, Michaels thought it a good idea to offer something genuinely American to their South Pacific hosts. Clark had a few hundred hotdogs in cold storage and so he organized a cookout.

On Saturday, the crew cleaned the weather deck and spaces civilians might like to see: the wardroom, bridge, and engine room. Crew's quarters were off limits. Makeshift grills, used on the sand spits in Espiritu Santo, were stored in holds below the main deck. Details set them up on the fantail. Others went ashore for charcoal and firewood.

Another detail placed half-barrels around the weather deck. Early Sunday morning, they filled the barrels with ice and sodas. Stewards and cooks lit the grills. A dozen volunteers—6 port, 6 starboard—stood at the embarkation ladders to be tour guides for the Samoan visitors. Another half dozen men around the deck wore sound-powered headsets. Their job was to report any problems to the bridge so Morton, the officer of the day, could quickly dispatch remedies and supplies.

By 9 a.m. the Osage was ready to receive visitors. Soft grey smoke from the grills on the fantail curled skyward. Tables of hotdogs and mustard stood ready next to the grills. Jackson double-checked each barrel to make sure the sodas were cold. Sailors stood proudly by their stations and waited.

At 9:15, one of the lookouts called to the bridge and told Morton that 2 outriggers were approaching the ship. The executive officer picked up a pair of binoculars and looked. John and Tuai Newton sat in the center of one outrigger. One man sat at the bow and paddled; another, aft. May, June, and two paddlers were in the other outrigger. Morton sent the watch to Michaels' stateroom to tell the captain the Newtons were on their way.

By the time the Newtons arrived, Michaels waited for them portside. He personally escorted them for a tour of ship. When they reached the bridge, the girls walked up to Morton to say hello. Morton fidgeted with his binoculars with the uneasiness of a man uncomfortable but doesn't know why he's uncomfortable.

While Michaels and the Newtons were on the bridge, a small armada of outriggers began to arrive at the port and starboard embarkation ladders. One by one, the curious Samoans climbed the ladders to stand on the tanker's metal deck. In an hour or so, nearly 200 civilians were aboard. As the sun rose higher in the cloudless South Pacific sky, the temperature also rose. The Americans were quick to note that the barefooted Samoans seemed unaffected by the hot metal deck.

Douglas Apoa was a big-shouldered Samoan who liked to smoke cigars. He picked up the habit from the German shopkeeper who gave him cigars in exchange for light work around the general store. Apoa carried a small leather pouch hanging from the belt of his grass skirt. In it he kept a few cigars, a cutter, and some matches. Like almost everyone else on the island, he walked barefoot.

Just after noon, Apoa stood on the fantail and faced the ocean. He pulled a cigar from his pouch, clipped the tip, and struck a match. As he puffed to light the cylinder of hand-rolled tobacco, one of the cooks walked up to him.

"Sir, I'm sorry but you can't smoke here. This is an oil tanker and we are restricted to smoke in designated spaces."

"Oh, I'm sorry. Can you tell me where I can

smoke?"

"I can take you there but you have to put out the cigar first, sir."

"Of course." Apoa took the cigar out of his mouth. He lifted his leg, bent his knee, and ground the glowing ash into the heel of his foot. The sailor watched with his eyes wide and his mouth open.

"There," said Apoa. "Now, where can I smoke?"

Chapter 9
The Tow

9 October 1944
0600 Hours
Apia

At the end of the open house Sunday, the captain and crew of the USS Osage bid farewell to their Samoan friends. John Newton shook Michaels' hand. Tuai gave him a hug. May and June gave Morton their address and told him to write. He simply wiped his palms on his pants and smiled.

After all of the civilians left the ship, details disassembled the tables, grills, and barrels. Clark noticed that few of the hotdogs had been eaten. He asked the cooks and stewards why they had so many leftovers. Only one, they said, finished his: Douglas Apoa. He ate four without the buns or mustard. Plucked them right off the grill with his hand. That night, Ellen's officers and crew ate hotdogs, fried potatoes, and coleslaw for dinner.

Monday morning, a flotilla of outriggers escorted the Osage easing out of the harbor to sail to Espiritu Santo. Sailors and Samoans waved to each other until Michaels ordered full speed ahead, and the tanker left the outriggers in its wake.

11 October 1944
1700 Hours
South Pacific Ocean, North of Fiji

Lycovec had the watch on the bridge. With binoculars in hand, he stood silently on the bridge near the port flying wing. Emerson stood at the helm and Hobbs wore the sound-powered phones on the other side of the bridge. He was watching the radar monitor.

To his right, Hobbs saw a flock of black-footed albatross flying about ten yards from the ship. With black bills and foreheads, brownish-grey cheeks and chests, they had a wing span of nearly six feet.

One of the birds broke away from the flock and gracefully glided directly above the newly installed radar. The albatross cocked his head and seemed to watch the arm rotating clockwise around the disc. He swooped down and tried to land on the arm. As soon as his feet touched the metal rod, he tried to fold his wings. But the rod kept spinning and the bird was forced to take flight.

The albatross circled and returned. He cocked his head like before and tried to ease onto the arm. Again, the bird flew off—unable to get a solid perch. For almost twenty minutes, the albatross tried to roost on the circling arm. Each time he was forced to take flight. Everyone on the bridge and a few sailors on deck watched the bird's futile attempts to perch on the radar. Finally, the bird settled on the arm. An impromptu cheer erupted from his audience as the bird spun around and around.

His glory lasted only a few moments. The albatross soon became dizzy and fell to the deck. He tried to stand but staggered like a drunken sailor.

Eventually the albatross regained his equilibrium. He had no fear of men. He sat on the deck next to sailors and took pieces of bread from their hands. A couple of men tossed bits of cookies over the side to watch their new feathered friend dive after them—sometimes into the water.

So close to the equator, some of the crew often set up a cot or pulled their thin, navy-issued mattress up onto the weather deck to sleep. The albatross didn't want to sleep. It wanted to play with the sailors. The bird waddled up to the end of cots and nipped at the sleeping men's feet. One sailor got so mad he grabbed the bird and threw him overboard. The albatross seemed to enjoy that game, too, because he flew back and stood, with wings outstretched, in front the man who grabbed him.

Close to 2200 hours the bird waddled to the forward gun tub. The unusual diet offered by the ship's crew did not set well with the albatross. To repay his hosts, the bird dirtied the gun, the housing, and the deck. He flew off and did not return.

12 October 1944
0800 Hours
Pearl Harbor, Hawaii

Because the supply chain in the South Pacific was so reliable and vital, Andrew Johns had recently been promoted from commander to captain. Now that Allied forces were so close to Japan, the Naval Planning Board met in Pearl Harbor to discuss the invasions of the Philippine Islands, Iwo Jima, Taiwan, and Okinawa. Johns attended the meeting to provide details of existing and potential supply chains.

Johns walked into the large, sound-proofed war room. Like oversized tapestries, huge maps hung on the white, windowless walls. A dozen large tables were spread around the room. Each table displayed a scale, topographical map of an area of the South Pacific. Tiny ships, army men, tanks, planes, and other vehicles dotted each miniature landscape. American and Allied forces were green; Japanese forces were faded khaki. Clipboards hanging from the side of each table listed units, unit strength, and commanding officers for opposing forces. Looking like a ten-year-old's candy store, they were part of a deadly serious game of war played there.

A group of top military brass sat at a table on a podium in the center of the room. From their table they could survey all of the hanging maps and topographical maps around them. Carrying his cap under his arm, Johns joined the group: two admirals, a Marine general and captain, two Army generals, and two Air Force generals.

"Good morning, gentlemen," said Johns.

Each returned his greeting as he took a chair next to the Marine captain who was short but stocky with thick eyebrows and a David Niven mustache.

"MacArthur's itching to retake the Philippines," said one of the Army generals. "But he needs more support—especially fuel." His hair line receded far back from his forehead. Although Johns knew him to be a tall man, the general was high-waisted and sat relatively low in the chair.

"And he'll get it, Frank," replied Admiral Walther. Walther sat at the head of the table. He was as even-tempered as a man could be. His deep-set brown eyes never betrayed a hint of emotion. Walther seldom lost at cards.

"Andrew," began Walther, "we have an issue that needs to be resolved and I think you might have the solution. It's important."

"What is it, Henry?" Johns was not a man to take flattery well. He believed it meant someone wanted to use you. He was usually right. Johns had known Walther long enough, however, to know that the admiral didn't try to cover a pile of excrement with sugary words.

"Carriers are raiding Taiwan: airstrips, bunkers, the works. They're using a lot of fuel. We're hitting the beach in the Philippines next week and I'm afraid we won't take it as quickly as Guam. MacArthur is going to need a lot of fuel—for three or four months. But we just don't have

171

enough tankers to cover hundreds of miles of sea for both theatres of operation. We have two floating concrete oil bunkers in Ulithi but we'll need more for an extended campaign. There are three in Tulagi. I've got two ocean-going tugs that I'm bringing up from Brisbane, but I need another tug for the third bunker. Can you help?"

Johns sat quietly for a moment. "Does it have to be a tug?" he asked.

"It could be a goddamned horse turd, captain," said the other Army general. Bill Fielding was big and loud. When he was a younger officer, Fielding boxed light heavyweight and had his nose broken twice in the ring. He fidgeted with a cigarette in his left hand. "If it can tow a 6,000-ton concrete barge from Tulagi to Ulithi, we'll take it."

"A couple of things you should know, Andrew," said Walther. "The ship will need a powerful engine. And it'll have to pass through hundreds of miles of Japanese-controlled waters."

"We won't be able to provide any air cover," said General Herb Fischman. "Your ship will be on its own." He was almost apologetic.

"The captain will have to be the smartest or luckiest man in the navy," said the Marine captain who sat with his hands folded on the edge of the table—as if praying.

"I have a ship in mind. It's a tanker."

"Perhaps you weren't listening, captain," said Fielding. "We need something to tow a concrete tanker. We do not need a tanker. Those damned turbines will burn up before they leave Tulagi Bay."

"I heard you, general," replied Johns curtly. "The tanker I have in mind can do the job. It's an old Standard Oil rig that I had refit in Sydney. Leeder dropped a diesel in it and added some guns. And she's got a reputation for being lucky."

"Pray to God you're right, Andrew," said Walther. "She'll need it."

17 October 1944
0930 Hours
Espiritu Santo

Ellen arrived mid-morning in Espiritu Santo. The harbormaster sent word that 14 bags of mail waited to be picked up at the federal post office on base. Jackson had no problem finding volunteers to go ashore and bring the mail back to the ship.

19 October 1944
0800 Hours
Espiritu Santo

Ellen's crew took on a full load of oil. For the next few weeks, the ship and crew took on fuel and refueled warships ships in the New Hebrides and New Caledonia. Many of them had sailed north from Australia and New Zealand to join the American forces retaking the Philippine Islands.

6 November 1944
1100 Hours
Noumea, New Caledonia

Next to the pier where Ellen tied up, a cargo ship was off-loading supplies with its crane. The inexperienced crane operator swung the boom too quickly and the line holding a large, heavy crate jumped off track and became wedged between the pulley and the upper housing of the crane's arm. The ship's crane repairman had a broken arm and could not work on it so the dock foreman sent runners to the ships nearby to see if anyone could lend a hand. Stacek volunteered Buck Williams, Billy Phillips, and Tony Fiore to help.

When they arrived, a small army of sailors and civilians were gawking at the crate hanging in the air. Fiore was quick to jump into the cab of the crane. As he started to crawl up the arm, Phillips called him back.

"What's up?" asked Williams.

"He doesn't have to climb up there," answered Phillips.

"How's he going to get up there?"

"We're not going to the problem, Buck. We're bringing the problem to us."

Phillips walked up to the crane operator and spoke to him for minute. The operator shifted the levers in his hands and the crane arm descended until the crate was on the deck of the ship and the line was just a tangled skein.

"Now, it's all yours, gentlemen," Phillips said to Fiore and Williams. With enough slack to pull and push on the rope and pulley, Fiore and Williams were quick to unbind the snag. Phillips signaled the operator to raise the crane. Williams held the rope taught so it would stay in the track of the pulley until the weight of the crate held the rope in place.

As the crate slowly rose, the crowd cheered. The operator swung the boom much slower this time and placed the crate easily on the dock.

Part of ship's cargo was beer—hundreds of cases. Gratefully, the skipper of the cargo ship sent 6 cases of beer to the Osage to thank them for their help.

12 November 1944
1500 Hours
Vila, Efaté, New Hebrides

Efaté was one of the southernmost islands of the New Hebrides. Vila, on its south end, was the principal town and, like many of the South Pacific islands, it had a good natural harbor. One of Vila's primary attractions was a large, immaculate, softball field. The dirt infield was raked between games and the outfield's thick, green grass never was allowed to grow higher than an inch and a half.

Softball games among ships were popular in the South Pacific during WWII. Each ship fielded its best team to play against the teams of other ships. Often, captains wagered work details, cases of beer, supplies, and other cargo on the outcome of the game. Side bets between crews of opposing ships were as common as grains of sand on the islands along the equator.

Jackson managed the Osage's team and organized all of the side bets. Like all good bookies, he never mentioned his betting strength: that he had a ringer who pitched professional softball before the war. But Jackson knew his secret would not remain undercover for long. Once word spread that the Osage had a fireball on the mound, good bets would be very hard to find. So Jackson built high stakes before the game and cut the losers some slack—if they promised not to tell other ships about Tony Fiore. Although the take on bets at individual games wasn't as great as it could have been, the prospect for long-term winnings, against a wider field of unsuspecting adversaries, looked good.

Without Fiore, the tanker still had a good team. Russell played first base. Clark was at second base. Harkel played short stop and Lycovec was at third. Williams, Stacek, Frederickson, and Emerson filled in the outfield. Tipton was behind the plate. Phillips, Booth, Chance, and Hobbs started the game on the bench. It was a strong team that was a good match for any ship in the South Pacific—

175

except, perhaps, the battleships and carriers who had thousands of men in their crews.

The tanker played the team from a light cruiser. The sky overhead was clear but a stiff breeze blew in a line of grey and white clouds from the southwest. The Osage led 4-1 in the fifth inning. The team from the light cruiser was at bat.

Suddenly, the ground shook violently. The backstop rattled. Tubs of ice and beer, grills, and tables of food collapsed in disheveled heaps. Unable to stand, wide-eyed players fell to the trembling ground.

The earthquake endured for less than a minute. When the dust settled, ballplayers brushed off the dirt and looked at each other. No one seemed to know what to expect next. After a moment, they began to clean up. The first thing righted were the beer tubs. With them returned to order, both teams agreed to end the game in a draw, drink beer, and just hang out. It was the only softball game the Osage did not win in the South Pacific.

23 November 1944
1300 Hours
Vila

Now in the rainy season, seldom a day passed that was not, at least, partly cloudy. Most days were overcast and wet. Waves crashed over the low lying deck—especially when the Osage carried a full load of oil. Rain pelted the weather decks. Duty watches wore pullover slicks to keep them dry. Sometimes, however, bracing winds drove the rain beneath the slicks and soaked the watches to the bone.

For Thanksgiving Day, the cooks and stewards prepared a sumptuous meal: roasted turkey and stuffing, mashed potatoes and gravy, baked ham with a honey-and-clove glaze, cranberry relish, carrots, asparagus, bread pudding, and pumpkin pie. It was one of two times in the year when officers and crew ate together in the enlisted men's mess hall.

Although well prepared, the lavish dinner offered little emotional support to the men aboard the Osage. Almost everyone aboard was homesick for the amity and comfort of family and friends during the holiday season. Morale began to ebb like a coastal tide.

3 December 1944
0700 Hours
Vila

During the previous night, the sky cleared. By noon, a stiff breeze grew from the northwest. With more dark clouds, the horizon held a promise of added rain in the late afternoon.

Well aware of the change in morale, Morton petitioned Michaels at breakfast for shore leave for the crew. Morton wanted to organize a party for the ship's stewards and cooks who had prepared such a great meal at Thanksgiving. He planned to rotate the watch sections so everyone could spend time ashore. Michaels consented, but only after Harkel reminded the captain there were no refueling ops scheduled on this first Sunday of December.

The other officers vowed to recruit help from their departments. Becker volunteered his men to set up the grills and cook. Clark promised to unlock the beer storage. Jackson said the deck hands would set up and ice down the barrels for beer and soda.

Jackson organized a softball game. Engineering and Deck fielded teams. Both sides boasted players from the ship's team. Electricians and machinist mates placed bets with boatswain's mates and gunners.

Before the game, Ensign Russell and RM2 Miller set up a portable microphone so Michaels could say a few words to the crew. Michaels was brief. He praised the cooks and stewards, and thanked everyone who pitched in to give them a well-deserved break.

By 1000 hours, everything was set up at the softball field. The game started at 1100 hours. Fiore did not pitch for Deck Division. Jackson wanted to rest him for the really important games against other ships. With the star pitcher not on the mound, the game turned into a slug fest. Deck beat Engineering 18-15.

Michaels was very diplomatic during the game. Not wanting to take sides, he cheered every run scored and scolded every error. Michaels even drank a couple of beers—something he had not done previously in front of the crew. Realizing how important morale is to the health and safety of a ship at sea in a war zone, he let his crew see him—albeit briefly—as a regular guy. After the game, Michaels returned to the ship.

By 1600 hours, the sky was dark with clouds. Morton ordered everyone to clean up. In less than two hours, everything and everyone was back aboard ship. No sooner had the ship's routine returned to normal than thick drops of rain began to fall in widely spaced drops.

25 December 1944
1000 Hours
Vila

Mail calls for the two weeks previous to Christmas were bountiful. Christmas cards and pictures were taped to bunks. Three fourths of the crew received packages from home. Cookies and fruit cakes were plentiful, and recipients shared them eagerly with shipmates. A nostalgic melancholy again began to settle on the crew so Morton called the first lieutenant to his stateroom.

"Rick," began the executive officer, "we have a morale problem."

"I know, sir. It's the holiday season back home and the guys are homesick. Plus, we haven't seen any action. Refueling ships is all very fine, but our duty right now is pretty anticlimactic. The crew is bound to get a little down."

"Can't afford it, Rick. We have to stay sharp or we're dead in the water. I mean that figuratively and literally."

"Right. I don't think another outing or softball game will turn it around. Do you have anything in mind?

"No. But we need something to lift spirits."

"How about if we decorate the ship for Christmas?" asked Jackson.

"I don't think the captain will go for that. Too many lights at sea."

"What if we just do up the inside of the mess hall and wardroom?"

"I'll run it by Michaels. But if he torpedoes the idea, we gotta come up with something else."

"Okay. But at least run it by him."

The week before Christmas, deck hands rigged running lights around the mess hall and wardroom. Phillips, Williams, Stacek, and Turkin went ashore and dug up a small palm tree. They placed it in a barrel and set it in a corner of the enlisted men's mess hall. Crew members decorated it with paper ornaments made aboard ship. Clark requisitioned popping corn and the stewards made popped-corn garlands to wrap around the palm.

Christmas Day passed much like Thanksgiving. Officers and crew ate in the enlisted men's mess hall and Michaels offered a few words before dinner. The camaraderie helped ease the depression but it did not lift it completely.

10 January 1945
1000 Hours
Noumea, New Caledonia

With the relatively mild excitement of the end-of-the-year holidays behind them, the officers and crew of the Osage settled into the familiar—if not monotonous—routine of taking on fuel and dispensing it to ships of the line in New Caledonia and the New Hebrides. Today, the tanker was in the calm harbor of Noumea under a partly blue sky. She waited to receive fuel from a commercial tanker scheduled to come alongside at 1100 hours.

The crew had just taken their refueling stations and were checking pumps, hoses, gauges, and valves. Jackson had the watch on the bridge.

"Sir," said Hobbs, who manned the sound-powered phones, "a powerboat is coming up on our port side. The port watch said it looks like a navy captain is aboard."

Jackson turned to port and raised his binoculars. Sure enough, a blue and white powerboat was nearly alongside. A navy captain stood next to the helm. Jackson thought it odd that a navy captain would pay a surprise visit to a tanker far from the front and that he stood next to the helm instead of sitting under the canopy, like most navy brass, at the rear of the boat.

Jackson left the bridge and double-timed it to Michaels' stateroom. The hatch was open and secured to the latch inside. Jackson knocked.

Michaels looked up from the book he was reading. "Enter, Mr. Jackson."

"We have company, sir. A navy captain is nearly

alongside. Is this an inspection?"

"Great Hamlet's ghost, I hope not. Usually I am notified before. But I received no notice." Michaels paused. Jackson waited. "Go to main deck. Bring the captain to the bridge. I vill be there."

"Aye, sir." Jackson turned and left.

Michaels slipped on his shoes, tied the laces, grabbed his cap, and walked up to the bridge. Ten minutes later, Captain Andrew Johns stepped onto the bridge. Jackson followed.

"Honas," said Johns, "it's good to see you." Johns held his hand out to Michaels who shook it firmly.

"Ya, and you as vell, Captain Johns," said Michaels with a wide smile.

"Drop the title, Honas. Call me Andrew. I got promoted because men like you and your crew are doing a whiz-bang job."

"Is this an inspection?" asked Michaels.

"No, no. But it's not a social call, Honas. Can we go somewhere to talk?"

"Ya, sure. Ve can go to my stateroom." Michaels turned to Jackson. "Tell the stewards to bring coffee and sandviches to my stateroom. You have the bridge."

"Aye, sir," replied Jackson.

Michaels turned and led Johns to his stateroom.

Once inside, Michaels shut the hatch and offered Johns one of the chairs next to his reading table. As he sat, Johns picked up the smooth log that Michaels kept on the table. He felt the cover and spine with his hands but did not open the book.

"I hear you have quite the lucky ship, Honas."

"Ya, it's true. Ve have been very lucky."

"How's that diesel holding up?" Johns put the book on the table.

181

"It has been no problem. Even with all the extra fittings and couplers she runs fine. Not fast, but very smooth."

"I'd like to take a look at it—if you don't mind."

Michaels started to push himself up out of the chair. "Shall ve go now?"

"No, no. It can wait. First, I want to talk to you about your next set of orders."

Michaels relaxed back into the chair. "Vhere are ve going?"

"It's not so much where you will be going. It's what you will be doing. This is an unusual assignment, Honas—especially for a tanker."

Michaels sat quietly waiting for Johns to continue. Before Johns could speak again, there was a knock on the hatch.

"Enter," called Michaels.

The hatch opened and Wilson, the ship's senior steward, stepped inside. He turned back and lifted a four-wheeled serving cart into the stateroom. A plate of finger sandwiches rested on the top shelf of the cart. Hazelton followed with a pot of coffee and 2 sets of cups and saucers. He set them on the cart and poured two cups of coffee. Wilson handed a cup to Johns. "Milk or sugar, sir?" he asked.

"No thanks."

Wilson poured a little milk into the other cup and handed it to Michaels.

"On my uncle's farm in Lokken, ve used milk straight from the cow."

"I'll bet that was a treat," replied Johns who lifted the cup to his mouth and blew on the coffee before he took a sip.

Michaels looked at the stewards. "That vill be all.

You can leave the cart."

"Aye, sir," replied Wilson, and they left.

Johns set the cup and saucer on the table. "Honas, MacArthur is knee deep in the Philippines and he needs oil for heavy equipment and support ships. We just don't have enough tankers to go around. But we do have hollow concrete tanks that can float offshore. They hold roughly 1500 tons of heavy oil. We had three in Tulagi. I sent two ocean-tugs to tow two of them. I need you to tow the third."

"Vhy this ship?"

Johns picked up one of the small sandwiches and took a bite before he answered. "The diesel. It's big and powerful. And we don't have any other tugs available."

"Ve vill tow it to Ulithi?"

"Yes."

"How much does cargo veigh?"

"It's flat and shaped like a regular tanker: 375 feet long and about 56 feet across at its widest. Draft is 28 feet. Full of oil, it's about 6500 tons."

"Great Hamlet's ghost! That is heavy. Ve vill not be able to sail at top speed."

"You'll be lucky to sustain four knots."

"Vhat vill be our route?"

"It's pretty straight forward, Honas. From Tulagi, you'll sail northwest to Manus in the Admiralty Islands. Then due north to Ulithi."

Michaels paused for a moment. "Vhat are you not telling me, Andrew?"

Johns smiled. "I knew you were the right man for the job." He pulled a thin white handkerchief from his back pocket and wiped his mouth. "The first half of the trip will be relatively safe. It will give you time to get to know your cargo and how best to handle it. The second half will be through a lot of open water still partially controlled by the

Japanese. You'll be alone, Honas. We can't give you air cover or an escort."

"Did the tugs make it through?"

"One did," replied Johns.

Michaels' brow furrowed. "How soon do ve start?"

"The day after tomorrow morning, you sail to Tulagi. You only have two weeks in Tulagi to get refit and learn how to handle the towlines. Can you handle it?"

"Ya, I'm sure ve can."

"Good. I knew I could count on you." Johns finished the sandwich. "Now, let's take a look at the old girl. The Navy spent a lot of money on her and I'd like to see what we got for it."

The two officers stood and walked toward the hatch.

Johns hesitated just before he stepped out. "One more thing, Honas. I'm sending you a pharmacist mate, petty officer first class. He comes aboard this afternoon with enough supplies for a basic sickbay."

"I vill tell Lieutenant Jackson and Lieutenant Clark to find space and help him set up."

"I pray to God you won't need his medical skills. And I'm betting you still have some of that luck I've heard so much about."

"Ya, me too." Michaels took a deep breath and exhaled slowly.

1400 Hours

After a tour of the engine room, Johns ate lunch with Michaels in his stateroom. Michaels sent for Jackson and told him to find a space big enough for the new pharmacist mate.

By the time PH1 George Gander arrived with his equipment and meds, Johns had left the ship. Jackson and a

184

detail cleared a room 10 feet by 10 feet. Perhaps not as large as most sickbays in the fleet but it was all the Osage could muster.

Gander was 30 years old, 5 feet 9 inches tall, and 160 lean pounds. He had hazel eyes and high cheekbones. His slender hands looked delicate but they belied a precision and agility matched by few in his field.

Once aboard ship, Gander reported to the officer on watch on the bridge. Lycovec took his paperwork and called for a deck hand to show Gander to his quarters.

"If you don't mind, sir, first I'd like to make sure the meds and equipment get to sickbay. Then, I'll bunk down," said Gander.

"As you wish, sailor," replied Lycovec. "I believe the first lieutenant has a couple of men waiting to help stow your gear. I'll have them meet you on the main deck near the davit. Do you know where that is?"

"Yes, sir. Saw it on the way up here. Thank you." The pharmacist mate saluted and left the bridge.

Gander made sure all of his equipment and supplies were aboard before he and the other two sailors moved them. As each item was placed on the weather deck, he checked it off a list he had folded in his shirt pocket. Satisfied that he had everything, the three men moved boxes, a couple of crates, a gurney, and two cots into the new sickbay.

11 January 1945
0700 Hours
Officers' Wardroom

Michaels sat at the head of the dining table. All of Ellen's officers sat at the table. There were few times when the captain insisted all of the officers—including the scheduled watch for the bridge—show up in the wardroom for breakfast after morning muster. This was one of those times.

The stewards were still serving coffee when Michaels addressed his subordinates. Because stewards frequently served food and beverages at officers' meetings, they had information about work details and orders before the rest of the crew. Occasionally, they traded inside information for things they needed in the officers' mess. If a rumor spread aboard the Osage, it probably originated with the stewards. It was no secret among the officers that stewards leaked information for favors. Once in a while, officers used it to their advantage.

"As you know, ve had visitor yesterday. He vas old friend. I met him before I took command of this ship. In fact, Captain Johns gave me this command."
Michaels had the officers' attention. They knew precious little about their commanding officer because Michaels was reticent to speak about himself. Even direct questions were answered with few words. Now, it seemed to them that Michaels was going to reveal a bit about his past.

"He vas impressed vith the ship and crew. You have done fine job." Michaels finished his cup of coffee before he continued. Wilson refilled it and added a spot of milk.

"But that is not vhy you are all here this morning. Ve have new orders." The officers glanced at each other before they returned their attention to Michaels.

"Tomorrow morning, ve sail for Tulagi. Our cargo is YO Class cement oil barge. Ve vill tow it to Ulithi, just south and west of Guam."

"Sir, that's about 2000 miles," said Becker. "And those cement barges are heavy. It will put a big strain on the engine and those jury-rigged fittings. Our top speed will be around four knots."

"Ya, it is true."

"What's our route, sir?" asked Russell.

"From Tulagi, ve sail to Manus. Then northvest to Ulithi."

"Don't the Japanese still control a lot of the water between the Admiralty Islands and Guam, captain?" asked Harkel.

"Ya, they do."

"What kind of escort will we have?" asked Lycovec.

"Ve vill have no escort." Michaels' face was expressionless.

The room became silent.

Harkel soon broke the silence. "No escort! That's crazy!" He sat forward in his chair.

"Ve vill be going too slow for our navy to provide escort."

"Too slow for our navy? But not too slow for the goddamned Japanese navy," continued Harkel. "They'll blow us out of the goddamned water like ducks in a pond!" He held his arms in front of himself as if he were holding a rifle. Then he jerked his arms slightly up and back to imitate the recoil of his imaginary rifle.

"Mr. Harkel, you are out of line," said Morton quickly. The executive officer slapped the table top with his hand and gave him a stern look.

The other officers looked at Morton. They had never seen the XO lose his composure.

"Let him speak, Mr. Morton," said Michaels.

"Captain, I am no coward—but I'm no idiot either. With no escort, this is a fool's mission," said Harkel.

"Vell, it might be fool's mission but ve are only ship available."

"Damn!" said Harkel. "Double damn!" He sat back in his chair.

187

"I understand your concern, lieutenant. But ve cannot choose vhat to do and vhat not to do. The army and marines who storm the beaches cannot choose vether to go or not."

"I know, sir. I just think that if we have to do this, then we deserve an escort."

"Ya, ve deserve escort. But ve do not get vone." Michaels took a deep breath. "Mr. Lycovec, ve need to schedule time for gunners to train. Come to my stateroom vith schedule today, 1300 hours. Ve vill discuss it."

"Aye, sir," replied Lycovec.

"Mr. Russell, vhen ve reach Tulagi, make sure ve have spare parts for radio and short vave. And visit harbormaster for most recent charts between New Guinea and Ulithi."

"Yes, sir."

"Mr. Jackson, Deck vill have most of the responsibility for towlines. If possible, see if you can get extra towline to store in case ve have problems."

"Yes, sir."

"Mr. Becker, make sure you have extra fittings and couplers. Ve cannot have problems vith propulsion. But if ve do have problems, ve need fast solutions."

"Aye, sir." Becker nodded and scribbled something on a pad of paper in front of him.

"Mr. Morton, schedule drills for general quarters. Come to my stateroom today, 1300 hours."

"Aye, sir."

"Mr. Harkel, bring schedule of remaining refueling details to my stateroom today, 1300 hours."

"Yes, sir."

"I vill address ship's company at morning muster. If you have no questions, you are dismissed."

12 January 1945
0600 Hours
Noumea

Low-lying grey clouds, a light mist, and stiff breeze from the north and west brought a chill to morning muster. A few enlisted men shuffled their feet and rubbed their hands. Cliques of sailors discussed whether the current scuttlebutt was true. Rumors said the Osage was going to Japanese occupied Malaysia.

Michaels spoke to his crew and outlined the orders given to him by Captain Johns. A deafening silence spread over the weather deck between the superstructures. To break the silence, Michaels invited questions.

One sailor from Engineering asked about the rumors he heard the night before. The captain denied Malaysia was ever a destination, but the trip in front of the Osage was daunting enough—especially with no escort. Michaels emphasized that all hands had to be extra vigilant on watch. Everyone had to take great care to make sure only red lights were used at night. Even garbage not weighted properly, when thrown over the side, might give away their position. One mistake could sink their ship. They would get no second chance. The relative ease and monotony of the past few months had just come to an abrupt end.

14 January 1945
1400 Hours
Coral Sea, West of Efaté

The first GQ drill took the crew by surprise. At first, no one knew if it was a drill or the real thing. Like the very first drill only seven months ago, men scrambled in disarray to get to their stations. Michaels watched from the bridge. When the watch reported 12 minutes for all stations to be manned and ready, he simply shook his head and, with raised eyebrows, looked at the executive officer.

"We have another drill scheduled in six hours," Morton said.

"Two drills every day until ve reach general quarters in less than five minutes," ordered Michaels.

"Yes, sir," replied Morton.

16 January 1945
1000 Hours
Torres Islands, Coral Sea

The Osage was a day and a half south of Tulagi Bay. Lycovec, Tipton, and Sedgwick took one of the longboats and dropped a few barrels into the water near a sand spit. Then, rigging an old sheet between a couple of palm trees, they set up a makeshift target.

Booth, Chance, Raymond, Pelk, Able, Perkins, Greer, and Elson waited at the 3-inch-50 for Tipton to return. Owens waited for Sedgwick at the 20-mm anti-aircraft gun tub forward, starboard side. Turkin and Eggers were in the starboard aft gun tub. Forward, port side, Stinson and Kincaid were prepping their 20-mm for target practice. Ritter and his belt feeder, Weston, were ready in the port aft gun tub.

On deck, sailors who did not have the watch stood well back from the huge gun on the bow of the ship. With fists full of cash waving in the air like banners, they bet on who would and would not hit the targets.

Emerson carried out Michaels' orders to pass the barrels and sand spit so the port gunners shot first. The return pass gave starboard guns a turn to sink the targets.

Finally, the 3-inch-50 would have the opportunity to fire.

The 20-mm anti-aircraft guns quickly found their marks. Two barrels were sunk by the time Turkin and Eggers, the last gun crew to practice, could fire. Turkin planted his feet firmly on the deck and gripped the handles. Eggers held the ammo belt ready. But when Turkin squeezed the trigger, only a few rounds fired before the belt feeder jammed.

Lycovec was with Michaels and Morton on the bridge. When he noticed Turkin and Eggers had problems firing the gun, he asked the captain for permission to join his gun crew. Michaels consented and told Lycovec he wanted a full report.

18 January 1945
1000 Hours
Tulagi Bay, Florida Island

Under a rare clear sky in the rainy season, the Osage pulled into Tulagi. Stacek, Williams, and eight other sailors were soon dispatched to an ocean-going tug to learn how to handle towlines. Nearly a year ago, the tug had been relegated to harbor duty because its diesel was too old and broke down too often for the open sea.

Morton and Jackson took Edwards, Phillips and another eight sailors to look at their future tow at anchor not far from the Osage.

The barge resembled a regular tanker: roughly the same length and width, pointed bow, rounded stern, low-lying weather deck. YO317 was painted on both sides of the bow. But the barge was made of concrete, not steel. Because steel was needed for war materials, the Maritime Commission recommended construction of a fleet of concrete barges. This was one of 22 concrete oil barges used by the Navy in World War II.

She had no superstructures or smoke stack on the weather deck—only a one-room shack amidship and a narrow deckhouse over the crews' quarters, which slept 12, under the fantail.

Two small, 45-horsepower diesel engines—for pumps, electricity, winches, and steering controls—were in the midship shack and a single, short antennae protruded through its roof. The shack also had a short-wave radio.

On each side of the ship, the barge had 4 fuel hoses connected to 8 storage tanks below the main deck. There was no engine or propeller—only a single rudder.

25 January 1945
0800 Hours
Tulagi Bay

During the week, Stacek and his detail were aboard the tug, workmen from the base installed a pair of towing chocks and cleats on Ellen's stern. When the chief boatswain's mate returned from his tour on the tug, his detail knew how to tow the concrete barge. With the exception of the executive officer, the detail that first inspected the barge returned each day to look over the equipment and repair any problems or malfunctions.

At the end of the week, Michaels, Morton, Jackson, Becker, Stacek, Edwards, and Williams met in the officers' wardroom to discuss how best to tow the concrete barge 2000 miles to Ulithi.

Morton proposed two towing teams of ten men each: one aboard the Osage and one on the barge. The men assigned to the barge would live in the crews' quarters. It would be much simpler and easier for duty and watch changes. The teams would rotate: one week on the barge, one week off the barge. That way, each team stayed relatively fresh and would not feel confined or exiled to the barge.

The first team was Chief Edwards, BM1 Buck Williams, QM2 Al Silvonic, MM3 Jay Conway, SS BJ Owens, SN Anthony March, SN Tex Akins, SN Arnie Paulson, SN Bert Caldwell, and SN Roy Kenmore; the second team: Chief Stacek, MM1 Earl Frederickson, QM1 Hal Emerson, BM3 Fred Reasoner, SS3 Rufus Hazelton, SN Jerry Kleck, SN Lev Holland, SN Zed Haggard, SN Harry Iverson, and SN Tony Fiore. Edwards and Frederickson would ensure there were no problems with engineering and refueling equipment. Stacek and Williams would supervise the deck hands working with the towlines. Emerson and Silvonic would man the helm and train 3 seamen on each team to control the barge's rudder. Each team also had a ship's steward to prepare meals.

Michaels liked the idea. He told his crew to implement Morton's plan immediately. The Osage had one week remaining before they left Tulagi and Michaels wanted to be shipshape for the long, slow haul north.

27 January 1945
1100 Hours
Tulagi Bay

Phillips sat next to the outboard motor in the back of the longboat. Rolling gently in the tide, the boat was tied up to the access ladder, port side, in the center of the barge. The sky was filled with thick, dark-grey clouds and a stiff breeze carried the smell of rain.

At the bow, the davit on an ocean-going tug held one end of the cable that Ellen would use to tow the barge. The towline was thick strands of wire cord twisted together to form one heavy cable almost 10 inches thick. The other end of the towline was already attached to the chock and cleat on Ellen's stern. Between Ellen and the barge—approximately 30 yards—the cable dipped deep into the water.

On the bow of the barge, Stacek stood behind Williams, Frederickson, and eight other men from the barge teams. Frederickson had just finished tying a lead rope to the hawser of the towline. Williams fed the lead rope through the chock on the bow and under the cleat. The cleat was, basically, a huge metal clamp with sharp teeth that grabbed and secured ropes and cables. Then, he pulled the lead rope until the hawser passed through the chock and cleat. The cable was ready to be hauled through by the men standing in front of the chief boatswain's mate.

The group of sailors grabbed the hawser and pulled. The cable inched through the chock and cleat with the loud scrape of metal against metal. When 12 feet of cable rested on the bow of the barge, they stopped and held it in place. Williams and Frederickson clamped the cleat down onto the cable and locked it.

Stacek signaled the bridge that the towline was secured and ready. Via sound-powered phones, Michaels called down to the engine room and told Becker to engage the engine ahead slow. The huge propeller turned slowly in the water and the Osage inched forward. The towline rose out of the water and grew taut. As the Osage continued forward, the cable vibrated and began to whine. Suddenly, with a loud bang, the cable snapped close to the bow of the barge and whipped back toward the Osage. Workers on the tanker's stern scrambled for cover as the huge cable flogged the rear of the tanker and fell into the bay.

"Great Hamlet's ghost!" cried Michaels watching from the bridge, "ve are lucky no vone vas hurt."

"What are we going to do if this happens in the open sea, captain?" asked Morton.

"Pray ve do not have to, Mr. Morton."

The tug puttered back to the Osage and retrieved the spare cable. It took four hours to remove the old cable and replace it with the spare.

After locking the cable in placed again, the tanker tried to pull the barge. This time the cable held and the Osage lugged the barge to the other side of the bay. Michaels ordered Stacek to splice the first cable and keep it for a spare.

For the rest of the week, the Osage pulled the barge around the north end of the harbor. Because they had to maintain radio silence in Japanese infested waters north of New Guinea, Ron Miller taught both teams basic signals using hand flags. That way, the tanker and barge could communicate course changes and exchange other vital information without using a radio. With Miller as trainer and guide, the teams practiced hand signals while they sailed in the harbor.

1 February 1945
0600 Hours
Tulagi Bay

Under a partly cloudy sky, the Osage slowly got underway. Michaels ordered the engines ahead at their lowest speed. Slowly the thick wire cable rose out of the water and grew taut. Michaels then ordered Becker to slowly increase speed to 1 knot. The cable creaked but did not give or snap and the barge was in tow.

Once out of the harbor, the captain told the engine room to bring ship's speed up to 2 knots. By noon, Florida Island was not much more than a speck on the horizon behind the Osage sailing at 4 knots.

3 February 1945
0700 Hours
Melanesia, South of Bougainville Island

The sky dawned a vivid crimson and orange so Michaels had his crew double check lifelines on the Osage and rig lifelines on the barge. Gradually, the winds shifted from the east to the northwest and, just before 1100 hours, rain pelted the tanker and barge amid peals of thunder and lightning. Swells rose to more than 10 feet.

Rising and falling with the high swells put a strain on the towline. The cable frequently gave up slack then quickly snapped taut when one ship suddenly dropped on the back of a swell and rose on the front of another. To prevent the two ships from colliding, Michaels ordered the barge to release the cable from its cleat.

Wearing lifejackets and belts hooked to the lifeline, Williams, Conway, and Kenmore walked forward in the storm on the barge's deck. Once on the bow, they pried the cleat open with crow bars. The cable slipped out and fell into the sea.

For two days, the barge and tanker drifted in the storm. The helmsmen on both ships used the rudders to stay within sight of each other.

5 February 1945
1200 Hours
Melanesia, South of Bougainville Island

Using the davit on the Osage and a winch on the barge, the teams retrieved the cable from the water and reconnected the towline. It took nearly 4 hours before they were underway again.

14 February 1945
1400 Hours
Manus, Admiralty Islands

The Osage chugged into Seadler Harbor three days behind schedule. The principal city of the Admiralty Islands, Lorengau, sat at the head of the harbor. The US Fifth Fleet established a major administrative center here after Manus was recaptured from the Japanese in 1944. Michaels told Clark to use the base's resources to restore the ship's supplies. Morton asked a navy tender to come alongside and check the chocks and cleats to make sure they weren't damaged during the storm. Welders reinforced the chocks and cleats to the decks of both ships.

16 February 1945
0600 Hours
Manus

As the Osage prepared to leave Manus, a squall raced across the island and harbor. For more than an hour, powerful gusts of wind blew horizontal sheets of rain across everything in its path. Smaller, lighter boats were capsized. Awnings and a few roofs were ripped from buildings on the shore. Sailors on the tanker and barge stayed below deck. Wind that strong could easily blow a man overboard.

When the storm settled down, crews aboard the Osage and its tow cleaned up. Afterward, Michaels doubled all of the duty watches on the tanker and barge before the ships resumed their journey.

19 February 1945
1200 Hours
Pacific Ocean, Micronesia, Near the Equator

Under partly cloudy skies, the ships lumbered north. At noon, one of the port lookouts called to the bridge and said he spotted two aircraft coming from the west. Without waiting to see if they were friend or foe, Michaels told the helmsman to sound general quarters.

Hearing the GQ alarm sound from the tanker, the team aboard the barge took cover. Only QM2 Silvonic and Chief Edwards remained on deck in the midship shack to steer the barge.

When the Japanese Zeros zipped over the slow-moving ships a few minutes later, every station had reported in. Both 20-mm guns starboard shot at the tails of the Zeros after they screamed over the Osage but neither gun hit their mark. The Japanese fighter planes circled for another pass.

At the 3-inch-50, Tipton told the pointer and trainer to lock onto coordinates that would intercept the planes as they banked into their turn. He fired. The shot fell far behind the second Zero. Tipton had to adjust his timing so he counted the seconds as the shell passed the place where he thought it would hit the Zero.

The Zeros came in again from the port side. One flew at the stern; the other flew toward the bridge. The 20-mm guns port fired at the enemy planes. Traces from the shells flew all around the incoming planes but none hit. Bullets strafed the bridge and fantail with loud, erratic pings. Everyone on the bridge dove for cover. Glass shattered. Morton looked up as the Zeros flew over the tanker. Wearing sound-powered phones, Hobbs lay on his back. His face and arms were cut from flying glass. The XO rushed to his side.

The starboard anti-aircraft guns fired again. The sky was filled with more 20-mm tracers. The noise on the bridge was deafening. Michaels stood and watched the planes bank and circle.

This time the Zeros came in from the starboard side. Like the previous pass, one came in at the stern, the other amidship. Turkin fired and Eggers fed the belt into the chamber. Bullets from the Zero flooded the aft gun tub. Turkin was knocked out of the gun's seat and Eggers dropped to the deck. At first, neither man moved. Then Eggers slowly looked up and saw Turkin on the deck. His eyes were closed and he wasn't moving. Blood flowed freely from Turkin's left shoulder and side. "Lord, God Awmighty," Eggers said aloud.

Eggers checked to see if Turkin was breathing. He was. Then he looked around for something to stop the bleeding. Finding nothing, he ripped off the sleeves of his shirt. With his pocket knife, Eggers cut the front of Turkin's shirt at the shoulder. He folded his own shirt sleeve, slipped it under Turkin's shirt and pressed it over the wound. Turkin's eyes opened. "Ow," he said.

"You been hit," said Eggers.

"That ain't no reason to make it worse," said Turkin. He winced in pain.

"Gotta stop the bleeding, Turk."

Eggers helped Turkin to pull his shirt tail out. Then, he lifted the shirt to reveal the other wound. The second bullet passed through Turkin's side. It was deeper than a flesh wound but not deep enough into his side to have hit an organ. Fortunately for Turkin, neither bullet hit a major vein or artery. Still, blood flowed freely. Eggers folded his remaining shirt sleeve and put it on Turkin's side. Turkin held it in place with his right hand.

"Stay here," said Eggers. "I'm goin' fer some help."

As the ship's steward jumped up, Turkin said, "Eggers!"

"Yeah?"

"Be careful."

199

The Zeros closed in from the port side. Bullets pelted the bridge and gun tub. Ritter squeezed the trigger of his 20-mm and Weston fed the ammunition belt into the chamber. The gun pealed off round after round. As the plane shot overhead, Ritter swung his weight with his feet and followed the Zero. Fire erupted under the plane just behind the cockpit. As the plane started to bank, it erupted in a ball of flames.

After strafing the bridge, the other Zero passed over the tanker and banked left for another pass. Estimating the time and distance the shell would have to travel, Tipton counted slowly, "Three, two, one." He fired. The 3-inch-50 erupted with a shattering bang and smoke billowed from its barrel. As the gun crew looked up, the tail of the Zero exploded. The crew yelled and waved their hands in the air as the plane spiraled down and fell into the ocean with a splash.

Eggers bounded into the engine room from the passageway. Becker looked at him. Eggers' clothes were stained with blood.

"Are you okay?" asked the engineering officer.

"Yeah, but Turkin ain't. He needs help," replied Eggers.

Billy Phillips and Hal Winthrop, a seaman electrician, jumped up and followed Eggers to the aft gun tub. Becker told the watch, wearing sound-powered phones, to call the bridge and tell them what was happening. The watch replied that he was unable to reach the bridge. Becker stared at him in disbelief.

Morton took the headset off Hobbs and helped him to his feet. "Are you all right?" asked the XO.

"I feel like I've been stung by a hive of bees," replied Hobbs.

"Can you make it to sickbay?"

"I think so."

Hobbs slowly walked through the glass on the deck and left the bridge.

"Great Hamlet's ghost!" exclaimed Michaels. "Ve are lucky to be alive."

Eggers, Phillips, and Winthrop ran across the deck into the gun tub. Turkin was lying there, holding his side. The blood soaked Eggers' sleeve and ran through Turkin's fingers onto the deck where it formed a small pool.

"Hey, buddy," said Phillips, "we're gonna help you to sickbay."

Seaman Ed Mayweather was sitting on the edge of the cot against the bulkhead in sickbay. Ganders had just finished applying mercurochrome to Mayweather's cuts from flying glass that hit his right arm, neck, and back. Hobbs stepped inside the small room.

"How soon before you can see me, doc?"

"I'm not a doctor. I'm a pharmacist mate and I can see you right away. Have a seat."

Gander turned to Mayweather. "Come back in a couple of days. I want to make sure those cuts don't get infected."

Mayweather stood. "Right, doc."

"I'm not a doctor, sailor. Didn't you hear what I just told this guy here?" Gander pointed to Hobbs.

"Maybe that's not your name, but that's what everyone calls you."

Hobbs sat on the cot and Mayweather stepped into the passageway.

"Gangway! Gangway!" cried Phillips. Mayweather backed down the passageway as Phillips, Winthrop, and Eggers arrived at sickbay carrying Turkin who winced in pain with every step his handlers took.

Gander pointed to Hobbs. "Jump up, sailor."

Hobbs quickly stood and stepped to the side.

The trio ducked inside. Phillips and Winthrop lay Turkin on the cot. His right arm dangled over the edge of the cot. His left arm was folded over his chest. Turkin took a deep breath and exhaled hard.

Gander looked at Hobbs. "What's your name, sailor?"

"Hobbs."

"Sorry, Hobbs, this man needs immediate attention. You're gonna have to wait."

Hobbs nodded.

"I can help, doc," said Mayweather from the passageway. "I saw how you cleaned the cuts on my arm and put the monkey blood on 'em. I can do the same for Hobbs."

Gander looked at Mayweather. "Okay, but you gotta do it in the head down the hall. First, clean the cuts with soap and water. Then, apply the mercurochrome with these cotton swabs." He pointed to a jar on a white cabinet near the hatch.

"Gotcha." Mayweather grabbed the vial of mercurochrome and the jar of swabs. He and Hobbs walked down the passageway.

Gander turned to the man lying on the cot and put his hand on Turkin's right shoulder. "What's your name?"

"Turkin."

"Well, Turkin, we gotta get that shirt off you. But first, I'm gonna give you a shot of morphine to ease the pain."

"You gonna use a needle?"

"Yes, I'm gonna use a needle."

"I hate needles, doc. Don't you have a pill?"

"Yes I do. He's lying on the cot in front of me."

Gander smiled. "Sorry, Turkin. You're just gonna have to suck it up."

"Damn!"

20 February 1945
1300 Hours
Pacific Ocean, Micronesia, North of the Equator

All hands mustered on the weather deck at 1300 hours. Michaels thanked the entire crew for its strength and commitment. Although half a dozen men were wounded in the brief battle, no one died. The captain extolled all of the gun teams for their steadfast dedication and heroism. The captain praised Lycovec, the gunnery officer. He then singled out Turkin and asked the crew to keep him in their prayers. When Michaels said Turkin would be eligible for a Purple Heart, the crew cheered. Michaels also commended Eggers who, with his quick response, probably saved Turkin's life. The crew cheered again.

Two destroyed Zeros, no deaths in battle, and tribute from their captain raised the morale of the crew.

22 February 1945
0700 Hours
Pacific Ocean, South and East of Palau Island

The Osage and its tow sailed north at four knots. The sky was overcast with low-lying grey clouds. A thick fog bank lingered a few hundred yards off the port bow, The air was heavy with a light mist.

In the past two days, the bridge was cleared of debris and electricians installed a temporary line for sound-powered communications. It was impossible, however, to replace the glass shattered by the Jap planes. A gentle wind and mist permeated the bridge through the glassless windows.

Michaels sat in the captain's chair. His right hand unconsciously fingered a bullet hole in the armrest. Morton stood forward with binoculars hanging around his neck. He tapped the barometer with his fingernail. Olsen wore the sound-powered headset and kept an eye on the radar monitor. Silvonic was at the helm, Miller in the radio shack.

"I haven't been a sailor very long, sir, but that fog bank this far out in the ocean is the strangest thing I've ever seen," said the executive officer.

"Ya, it is rare but it happens," replied Michaels. "I see it many times in North Sea."

"But that's the North Atlan…"

"Sir," interrupted Olsen, "I have a blip on the monitor."

Michaels looked at the enlisted man. Morton walked over and stood next to Olsen. He stared at the monitor. A grey line circled the face of the round screen. Each time it passed over the blip, a light green figure flashed and disappeared. Miller stepped out of his workplace and joined them.

"I think it's a sub periscope, sir," said Miller. "About 200 yards off the port bow just outside of the fog bank. It's running parallel to us, nearly dead even in the water."

Morton raised his binoculars and looked. Michaels stood and walked to the radar monitor. He, too, raised his binoculars.

"Periscope at 10 o'clock, about midway between us and the fog bank," said Morton.

"Ya, I see it. Sound general quarters."

Olsen punched the large red button on the console. The loud bong—bong—bong rang through the ship's 1MC.

204

"Hard port rudder," said Michaels.

"Aye, sir, hard port rudder," answered Silvonic. He spun the helm counterclockwise.

Olsen keyed the mike and repeated the orders. On the stern, a sailor with hand flags signaled the course change to the barge.

"Sir, we're heading right for the sub!" declared Morton.

"Sure, ve are."

"But sir, isn't that suicide?"

"The sub is parallel to us and too close to fire torpedoes. It vill come about for better angle and distance. The sub vill have to cover 800 yards at 8 knots. Ve have 400 yards at 4 knots to get into fog bank. It is our only hope." Michaels stroked the monitor with his hand. "Ellen, old girl, ve need more of your luck."

Slowly, the Osage turned toward the bank. The barge followed in kind. The officers on the bridge of the tanker watched the periscope submerge from sight.

"They have seen us," said Michaels. "All ve can do is vait and pray."

Michaels lowered the binoculars and let them hang from his neck. He walked to the captain's chair and sat. "Olsen, tell vatches to look for torpedoes—especially from starboard side."

"Aye, sir." Olsen keyed the mike and relayed the captain's orders.

"What do we do once we're inside the fog?" asked Morton.

"Ve turn starboard and head north again."

"Doesn't that take us closer to the sub again, sir?"

"Ya, it does. Maybe sub commander von't think ve vould head straight for them. And sub must surface to find us in fog. He must know by now that ve shot down the two

205

Zeros that reported our position. Perhaps, he does not vant to test his single gun against all of ours."

It took almost 5 minutes to reach the fog. The minutes passed like hours.

The tanker and barge slipped safely into the fog bank. Michaels waited almost ten minutes before he told Silvonic to turn hard to starboard. When the turn was complete, the captain cut the ship's speed to 2 knots and told the watch to pass the word that all hands had to be vigilantly quiet.

Morton did not ask why Michaels slowed. He presumed the CO wanted to use the fog as long as possible.

Miraculously, the fog bank endured until 2000 hours. Michaels never left the bridge. The ship's stewards brought him lunch and dinner which he ate in the captain's chair. As the Osage slipped out of the fog bank under a partly clear night sky, Michaels increased speed to 4 knots. Then he told the watch to pass the word that all hands make sure they used only red night lights—and only the lights that were absolutely necessary.

Michaels sat uneasily in the captain's chair until 0100 hours. Before he retired to his stateroom, the captain instructed the officer of the day, Ensign Russell, to wake him immediately if he saw or heard anything.

27 February 1945
0930 Hours
Ulithi, The Mackenzie Islands

Ulithi was captured from the Japanese in September 1944. It was a cluster of three coral atolls in the western Pacific. The main atoll had an excellent lagoon and served the United States Fifth Fleet as a base for operations during the invasion of the Philippine Islands and Iwo Jima, and attacks against Japan.

As the Osage approached the atoll, Miller picked up the microphone for the short-wave radio and called for anchorage berth assignments for the barge and tanker. He also told the harbormaster that they had a wounded man who needed medical attention, and asked for service from a tender to repair the glass on the bridge and in 6 portholes. When the harbormaster asked about the glass, Miller told him that they had been attacked by two Zeros.

The number of ships in the harbor was staggering. Battleships, cruisers, two carriers, destroyers, and a throng of support ships crowded Ulithi. Miller asked the harbormaster why there were so many ships. He replied that MacArthur had just taken Manila on the northern island of Luzon. US forces were now preparing to storm Mindanao, the major southern island of the Philippines.

Slowly, Emerson steered the vessels to drop off the barge. After it was disengaged, the tanker eased into anchorage 226. Two powerboats waited for the Osage to drop anchor. One, from a hospital ship, had a large red cross painted on the side. The other was from port command. Three officers were aboard to assess damage, talk to crew and officers about the battle, and file reports about repairs and the attack.

Hospital corpsmen came aboard the Osage first. After the corpsmen lowered Turkin—waiting in a gurney on deck—onto the powerboat, it sped off amid the shouts and waves of his shipmates.

One of the officers, who came aboard to assess battle damage, carried a camera. The ensign took pictures of the gun turrets, portholes blasted by strafing bullets, and the bridge. He used three rolls of film. While he took pictures, a lieutenant junior grade questioned the gun crews and a lieutenant interviewed officers. After two and a half hours, the officers left.

6 March 1945
0900 Hours
Ulithi

The Osage sat high in the water. For the past week, her crew refueled ships at Ulithi and emptied all of the storage tanks. Three days ago, a tender pulled alongside and workmen came aboard to replace the glass destroyed in combat. Yesterday, most of the ships left harbor and sailed east. Relatively few remained behind.

A powerboat pulled alongside the tanker. With thick white bandages around his waist and his arm in a sling, Turkin slowly climbed the ladder to stand on deck. He was greeted by a crowd of his fellow enlisted men and officers.

A Navy doctor stepped on deck behind Turkin but no one noticed. All eyes were focused on their comrade. The doctor, a captain, looked over the side at two sailors still in the powerboat and signaled them to come up. While the sailors climbed the ladder, Lieutenant Jackson stepped forward. He saluted.

"Lieutenant Rick Jackson, ship's first lieutenant. How can I help you, sir?"

The visiting officer returned the salute and replied, "Permission to come aboard."

"Permission granted."

"I'm Captain James Berg. I have a few boxes for sickbay. But I have this for your CO." He held out his left hand and revealed a small, clothbound box.

"Our CO is on the bridge. I'll take you to him." Jackson turned to the crowd. "Conway! Front and center!"

Jay Conway stepped out of the crowd and ran up to the officers. He stopped and saluted. "Sir!"

Morton returned his salute. "Help the sailors with these boxes and show them to sickbay. Then show them back."

"Yes, sir."

"And sailor," interjected Berg, "ask your pharmacist mate to come to the bridge."

"Yes, sir."

Conway turned to the two sailors and helped them bring aboard nine boxes.

The first lieutenant addressed the captain. "If you'll follow me." Jackson led the doctor to the commanding officer.

Michaels was reading the smooth log when Jackson and Berg stepped onto the bridge.

"Sir," began Jackson, "we have a visitor."

Michaels looked up, closed the log, and stood. He set the book on his chair and extended his hand. "Honas Michaels."

As the doctor shook Michaels' hand, he said, "James Berg. Pleased to meet you."

"And you as vell," replied Michaels.

"I brought the meds your pharmacist mate requested. Seems you saw some action a few days ago."

"Ya, ve did. Two Zeros strafed us. Ve downed both planes."

"That's the scuttlebutt that went around. Quite the gun crews. You were lucky no one was killed."

"Very true. Is there another reason you visit our ship?"

"Two, actually. I wanted to meet your pharmacist mate. He did a great job of patching your gunner. His was better than the work of some doctors I've seen." Berg handed the small clothbound box to Michaels. "And I have this. It's for Seaman Turkin."

209

Michaels took the box and opened it. A gold heart hung from a purple and white ribbon. In the center of the heart, a purple background held the gold profile of George Washington.

"The Purple Heart," said Berg.

"Ya, sure. Ve vill give it to him today after lunch. Vill you stay?"

"Sorry, I can't," answered Berg. "Hospitals—even floating in the middle of the ocean—are busy places in wartime. I took an early lunch to come out here."

The tanker's pharmacist mate stepped onto the bridge and saluted. "PH1 George Gander reporting as ordered. You asked to see me, sir?"

Berg returned his salute. "I did. At ease, sailor." Gander relaxed and stood at parade rest.

"You did quite an excellent job patching Seaman Turkin. When he told me a pharmacist mate did it, I was skeptical."

Berg paused but Gander remained silent.

"Do you have medical training?" continued the doctor.

Graduated from Johns Hopkins med school six months after the war started. Didn't get a chance to intern."

"You could have interned at a navy hospital, sailor. Or should I say, doctor."

"Didn't know I could, sir. I was called and I went."

"How'd you get to be a PH?"

"My first billet was aboard the Indiana. I was assigned to the black gang in engineering. Didn't like the heat so I talked to the engineering officer. Told him I went to med school. He spoke to the captain and they transferred me to sickbay. They signed off my paperwork and bumped me up to second class petty officer. I made first class a year and a half ago and was transferred here last month. I'm up for chief in a few months."

"Well, I'll certainly put in a good word for you. And with your captain's endorsement, chief petty officer won't be a problem."

"Thank you, sir."

"When this war is over, doctor, I hope you consider working at Bethesda. I was a surgeon there before the war. I'll put in a good word for you."

Gander eyes grew wide and he smiled.

"Thank you, sir!" Gander said emphatically.

"My name is James Berg. Remember that name when you show up at Bethesda."

"James Berg. Yes, sir. Thank you, sir."

Gander looked at Michaels. "With your permission, captain, I have to finish putting away the meds."

"Dismissed."

Gander saluted and left.

"I should be going as well," said Berg. "I have rounds this afternoon."

"I'll valk you down," offered Michaels.

"I'd be honored, commander," replied Berg.

1300

After lunch, Morton keyed the mike of the 1MC and told all hands to muster on deck. Fifteen minutes later, Michaels presented Turkin with the oldest military medal still in use. When Turkin took the Purple Heart from his captain, the crew cheered their friend and comrade.

8 March 1945
1000 Hours
Ulithi

"Whoo-hoo!"

When Michaels and Jackson heard Miller yell in the radio shack, they turned to see what was going on. Miller was taking off the headset for the short-wave radio. He picked up a piece of paper lying on the table and stepped onto the bridge. He handed the paper to his CO.

"Vhat is this?" asked Michaels.

"Those three officers who interviewed everyone and took pictures confirmed that we downed the Zeros, sir. It means we get credit for downing two more enemy planes."

Miller pointed to the paper.

"Their judgment was based on the visual evidence of strafing, reports of the gunners and officers, Turkin's wounds, and an intercepted Japanese radio message from Palau. The message said two Zeros did not return from a mission."

Michaels smiled briefly. "Thank you, petty officer. Now, back on the radio."

"Aye, sir," replied Miller.

The captain turned to Jackson. "Mr. Jackson, start repairing strafing damage. I think ve have all looked at it long enough."

"Yes, sir," answered Jackson.

Chapter 10
Spiked Beauty

22 March 1945
2000 Hours
Ulithi

A 23-ship convoy left Ulithi and headed to the Philippine Islands. The convoy formed 3 lines of 7 ships, 100 yards apart. The Osage sailed 100 yards behind and between the port and center rows. Another tanker sailed 100 yards behind and between the center and starboard rows. Six DEs—one in front, one behind, and two on each side—escorted the convoy out of Ulithi.

As a bright orange sun slowly dipped below an ever-darkening horizon, the contours of ships gradually faded into shadowed silhouettes rising and falling on the gentle swells of a sea that stretched without limit into the night.

Russell had the watch. Emerson was at the helm and Hobbs manned the sound-powered phones. Russell stood in the chart room and measured out the course heading: two-seven-zero. At four knots, it'll take a little more than two days to reach the Philippines, he thought. With binoculars hanging around his neck, he walked out onto the port flying wing between the anti-aircraft gun and the bridge.

Russell was lost in contemplations. Ever since Michaels talked to him about trusting his intuition, he thought about how the captain had changed course on, what seemed to be, a whim. Had Michaels already known about the reef and simply teased the ensign with some gibberish about listening to an inner voice? Or was the captain really connected to the spiritual heart and soul of the sea? The Osage had inexplicably escaped more than one encounter with the grim reaper. Was it coincidence? luck? fate? divine intervention?

Suddenly, Russell felt uneasy. He looked inside the bridge. Everything seemed normal. He raised his binoculars and scanned the sea off the port bow. He saw nothing. For no reason that he could explain, Russell quickly turned to his right and scanned the water in front of the Osage, between the rows of ships. Slowly, he raised the binoculars. As his eyes found a mine floating between the two ships ahead, a cold chill ran up his spine. If the ship were to hit it, the explosion would surely kill or maim crew members and possibly sink the ship. The tanker had precious little time to avoid the spiked beauty.

"Left full rudder!" he screamed into the bridge.

Emerson looked at Russell and saw the ensign's eyes wide.

"Left full rudder!" repeated the ensign. The helmsman quickly spun the wheel and the tanker slowly turned to port as the mine floated closer.

In his stateroom, Michaels had just stretched out in his bunk. Feeling the course change, he put on his trousers and shoes and ran up to the bridge.

"Vhat is it?" Michaels asked Emerson.

"I don't know, sir. Mr. Russell gave the order to change course."

Michaels looked at Russell on the port wing. Russell still had the binoculars to his eyes. The captain walked up to the glass and reached for a pair of binoculars hanging near the radar monitor. The captain lifted the glasses and scanned the sea in front of his ship. He quickly found the mine.

"Great Hamlet's ghost!"

The Osage was still heading hard to port and closing in on the floating explosive.

214

When the mine was 50 yards from the ship, Russell called to the helmsman, "Right full rudder. Come back to course two-seven-zero!"

"Two-seven-zero," repeated Emerson as he spun the helm again.

The Osage slowly turned back to its original course heading as it eased away from the mine.

The captain and the ensign did not look away from the mine until it floated harmlessly past the Osage—a mere ten yards off the starboard fantail. Russell let the glasses hang from his neck and walked into the bridge.

"Good vork, ensign," said Michaels.

"Thank you, sir."

"How did you know there vas a mine? It is almost dark and hard to see."

"Didn't know there was a mine, sir," replied Russell "Just had a feeling that something wasn't right."

"Ya, I know the feeling." Michaels smiled. "I do not have authority to promote you, Mr. Russell, but I can revard you. Choose the duty vatch you vant. You have it every day."

"I'd like the 8 to 12, sir." Russell smiled back at the captain.

"Then, it is yours beginning day after tomorrow."

"But that's Lieutenant Jackson's duty watch. He won't give that up."

"I vill deal vith Mr. Jackson. I am going back to my stateroom. Carry on."

"Aye, sir. Thank you, sir."

25 March 1945
0700 Hours
San Pedro Bay, Leyte Island, Philippine Islands

When the convoy arrived in the Philippines, each ship received orders and anchorage berths. The Osage sailed to an anchorage between Samar and Leyte Islands.

27 March 1945
0900 Hours
San Pedro Bay

A cruiser was scheduled to come alongside to be refueled. More than 600 feet long and 66 feet wide, she was armed with 8-inch guns, 5-inch guns, 40-mm and 20-mm anti-aircraft guns. Coming back from a run off the coasts of Mindanao and Palawan Islands, she had the scars of a ship who had been in more than one fight for her life.

Michaels stood on the bridge and his crew were at their stations ready to deliver fuel when the cruiser arrived. Olsen wore the sound-powered headset. The big ship eased next to the tanker's starboard side. Half a dozen Navy brass stood on the cruiser's observation deck high above the Osage and watched the approach. They were dressed in tropical whites. Michaels winced when he saw the admirals and captains. He believed many high-ranking officers lacked common sense, and he was not fond of them—not by any stretch of the imagination. The gold braid on the brim of their caps might as well be scrambled eggs for all the good judgment they had.

Michaels noticed the cruiser coming in too close so he stepped out onto the flying bridge and waved it away. No one on the cruiser seemed to understand him, and the big ship continued its propinquant approach.

Michaels ran back into the bridge and ordered Olsen to tell the ship to rig for impact. No sooner had Olsen finished speaking into the mike when the Osage received a jolt from its starboard side. The cruiser's port anchor, up and secured to its forecastle, scraped the front of the tanker's starboard hull and punched a hole in the bow. Michaels was livid. He screamed a litany of Danish curses as he waved his fist at the brass on the cruiser.

The big ship soon stopped. Almost immediately, deck hands on the cruiser dropped planks onto the rail of the Osage and a handful of welders walked briskly across with tools and portable acetylene tanks. They jumped onto the deck of the tanker and ran forward. Billy Phillips opened the hatch under the 3-inch-50 and waved to the welders. With his brow in a knot, Michaels watched them disappear below deck.

Moments later, a davit on the bow of the cruiser lifted a large piece of sheet metal and slowly swung it over the side until it rested against the hull of the Osage and covered the hole and scrape. The welders held it in place and fired up their torches. When they finished welding the sheet metal to the hull, another team came aboard from the cruiser and waterproofed the patch. By the time the Osage finished refueling the cruiser, repairs were complete. Although the repair was quick, exact, and efficient, Michaels ignored the brass on the observation deck of the cruiser while it was alongside.

1 April 1945
1700 Hours
San Pedro Bay

Michaels approved shore leave—day on, day off—for all hands. Two main attractions awaited the crew of the Osage: Tacloban, the principal town on Leyte; and the longest bar in the world near Balangiga on Samar.

Clark, Harkel, Lycovec, Jackson, and Russell settled into one of the tanker's powerboats and the coxswain shoved off for Balangiga. The longest bar in the world stretched west down the Samaran coast for more than a mile. Every 50 yards or so, a pier extended into the bay. Traffic was thicker than last-minute shoppers on New York's Fifth Avenue at Christmas Eve. A constant stream of powerboats dropped off and picked up sailors on shore leave, or tied up next to one of the docks and released a throng of thirsty and curious visitors.

Tents, set up contiguously, covered the bar and its patrons. Short, round-faced Filipino men and women stood behind the bar and served an almost unending flow of cocktails and beer. On the backbar, thousands of bottles of liquor were stored and arranged according to type and label. Filipino cocktail waitresses, carrying trays of glasses and beer bottles, walked among the tables, took orders, and flirted with American, British, and Australian GIs. Occasional tables of WACs, WAVEs, and nurses were surrounded by admiring officers and enlisted men begging to buy them drinks.

Above the backbar, loud speakers carried the swing tunes of big bands and the ballads of crooners. As the day slipped into evening, a string of lights lit up the bar, the tables, the sand, and the patrons sober, tipsy, or dead drunk. As employees clocked out and left work, more than one GI left the bar with a cocktail waitress or bartender. Sometimes it was attraction; sometimes it was for a few pesos.

Fights were not uncommon—especially after a few drinks—between men who had an eye for the same woman or between groups of soldiers, sailors, and pilots. Aussies fought Brits. Yanks exchanged blows with Aussies. Brits brawled with Yanks. Swabbies squared off against jar heads. Fly boys faced ground-pounders. MPs and SPs broke up the fights and escorted instigators from the area. The hours passed and many of the faces changed but the rhythm of the huge, international party never slowed.

After a few hours of drinking in the oppressive heat and observing the social mayhem in front of them, the officers from the Osage staggered back to the powerboat. The coxswain had just dropped off a group of enlisted men when he spied the officers walking down the pier. He laughed quietly when he saw them wobble up to the launch and half wished he was in the same inebriated condition.

Clark was the first to step off the pier. Talking to Lycovec, his head was turned and he failed to notice the powerboat sat much lower against the pier because the tide was out. He somersaulted in midair and landed square on his back. The coxswain and Clark's comrades on the dock howled with laughter. The lieutenant was not hurt. He quickly sat up and laughed with the rest—although the morning would probably bring a wide, tender bruise from the bench where he landed.

As inebriated as Clark was, Russell was more under the influence of alcohol. The ensign sat in front of the coxswain near the outboard motor. Lycovec saw him mumbling to himself but ignored it.

A few minutes after the coxswain pulled away from one of the piers, Russell stood and began to shout while he waved his arms in the air.

"Communications officer is not a fitting role for me in this man's navy," he exclaimed. "I should be a navigator." He pointed to Lycovec who sat two benches forward. "Don't you think I should be a navigator, Fritz?"

"Sit down, Pete," answered the gunnery officer. "You're rocking the boat. We don't need to fish you out of the harbor."

"So what if I keep a journal. Does that qualify me to be a communications officer? Nope. Am I a writer? Nope. I am a navigator by heart." He covered the left side of his chest with his right hand.

All eyes in the boat were on the tall, lanky, normally mild-mannered junior officer.

"My name should ring in halls of the great navigators: Vasco da Gama, Ferdinand Magellan, Francis Drake, John Paul Jones, Pete Russell. I was born to circumnavigate the world," Russell said loudly as he thrust his fist into the air.

"Russell, sit down before we capsize," demanded Jackson.

Russell sat and furrowed his brow. He turned to the coxswain. "Sailor, I want to navigate this boat back to the Osage. Step aside."

The sailor looked at Jackson. The first lieutenant nodded. The coxswain throttled down and traded seats with the ensign. Russell gassed the throttle and the boat sped forward.

"Easy does it, ensign," said Jackson. We're going back to the Osage—not San Francisco."

"Sir?"

"We have plenty of time. Throttle down."

Russell eased the throttle and, for a few minutes, was content—albeit somewhat dejected—to steer the powerboat around the myriad of ships between the Osage and the longest bar in the world.

As the powerboat approached an aircraft carrier, the communications officer perked up. Slowly, he increased speed. Russell angled the tiller slightly and the powerboat eased to the right.

At first, the only one to notice the speed and course change was the coxswain. He was the only one sober. He looked where the boat was heading and then glared back at the ensign holding the tiller.

"Sir, do you see where we're heading?"

220

"I'm in complete control, sailor. Just enjoy the ride."

Lycovec overheard the brief conversation and looked where the powerboat was heading. He turned around to Russell. "What the hell are you doing, Pete?"

"I'm a navigator, Fritz," said Russell. "Damn the torpedoes. Full speed ahead." He laughed out loud and gassed the throttle again. The powerboat lurched forward and the motor hummed at full volume. The others in the boat quickly took note of what was happening.

Lycovec stood to walk to the rear of the small craft but Russell shifted the tiller side to side quickly. The boat danced back and forth. Lycovec was forced to sit or be thrown into the water at high speed.

Jackson turned and glared at the ensign as the small boat ran alongside the carrier. "Russell, ease the throttle!"

Russell pointed to his ear and shook his head.

On all fours, the first lieutenant climbed over the benches toward the rear of the boat. The gunnery officer followed his lead.

As the boat zipped between the 60,000 ton carrier and its huge anchor chain, Jackson and Lycovec reached Russell. Lycovec restrained the tiller so Russell could not shift the rudder. Jackson pulled Russell away from the outboard and the coxswain scrambled to reclaim his seat. He took the tiller and throttle in hand. Lycovec released the tiller and turned to help Jackson subdue the communications officer. Harkel came back to help. The three of them forced Russell to lie face down on a bench. Then, Lycovec sat on his back, Jackson sat on his rump, and Harkel straddled his legs.

"Let me up!" demanded Russell.

"Sure thing, Magellan," said Lycovec. "Just as soon as we circumnavigate the bay and arrive safe and sound in Portugal. The queen awaits thee."

13 April 1945
1000 Hours
San Pedro Bay

Miller walked somberly onto the bridge from the radio shack and handed Michaels a message he received over the short-wave radio. President Roosevelt died the day before. Harry S. Truman, FDR's vice president, was sworn in as commander in chief. Michaels ordered the flag on the stern to be flown at half mast for the rest of the day.

29 May 1945
1400 Hours
San Pedro Bay

For the past few weeks, the Osage refueled warships and troop transports in San Pedro Bay, Leyte Gulf, and the Mindanao Sea. The crew enjoyed shore leave at the mile-long bar when not on duty.

Early in the afternoon, Michaels received orders to sail to Ulithi for a load of oil. From there, the Osage would be part of a convoy to Okinawa.

1 June 1945
0800 Hours
San Pedro Bay

Since March, the weather steadily warmed as the rain subsided. The Osage, with empty storage tanks, sailed east for Ulithi under a cloudless blue sky.

4 June 1945
1600 Hours
Ulithi

High, wispy cirrus clouds blew leisurely in from the southwest as the Osage pulled into Ulithi. After the tanker settled into anchorage, Michaels authorized Clark and two enlisted men to lower one of the powerboats and shuttle to the administration center to pick up mail.

8 June 1945
1500 Hours
Ulithi

Miller stepped out of the radio shack and handed Michaels another message that came over the short-wave. Michaels looked out at the sea for a moment and then picked up the microphone to the 1MC.

"Attention all hands, this is the captain. Yesterday, Germany surrendered unconditionally. Hitler committed suicide. The var in Europe is over. President Truman proclaimed today V-E Day." He paused as the shouts of more than 100 men rang through the ship.

Michaels keyed the mike as the noise subsided. "Let us all pray the var here ends soon." He set the microphone in its cradle and turned to Lycovec who had the watch. "I vill be in my stateroom."

"Yes, sir," replied the gunnery officer.

14 June 1945
0600 Hours
Ulithi

With a full load of oil, the Osage left Ulithi in a six-ship convoy headed northwest for Okinawa, the principal island of the Ryukyus. Two DEs provided escort.

The scuttlebutt among the convoy was that nearly half a million Allied personnel were engaged in the attack against 100,000 Japanese. Although the crew knew rumors were prone to exaggerate, they were awed by the significance of the campaign. Okinawa was strategic because it lay only 350 miles south of Kyushu, the southernmost of the main Japanese Islands.

16 June 1945
1900 Hours
Crew's Quarters Forward

Lewis dealt the next hand. He enjoyed playing hearts—cutthroat, not teams. Card games were playful exercises for his mind. Lewis counted cards. He counted tricks. He measured every card passed and played by those who sat at the table. Lewis understood individual strategy in card games. Good strategy, he believed, could often balance a bad hand. Lewis seldom lost—when he played without a partner.

Partners, to Lewis, were like anchors: they kept him from sailing quickly to victory. Only two or three others aboard ship counted cards like he did. But they did not understand how to use the information to their advantage. Knowledge, with reflection and application, became wisdom. Wisdom, with reflection and application, was better than luck. If opponents were lucky to draw good cards but didn't know how to play well, it wouldn't save them the time or the humiliation—not to mention the money—from his shrewd and precise technique.

Lewis, Phillips, Elson, Pelk arranged the cards in their hands.

"Okay, gentlemen," said the dealer, "pass three to the right." Each drew three cards, set them face down on the table, slid them to the right, then picked up the cards on their left.

"Who has the deuce?" asked Phillips. He always seemed to be in hurry to play—whether or not he had good cards. Phillips liked to run the tricks: take all the hearts and the queen of spades during a hand. The player who took all of the points had the option of removing 26 points from his score or adding 26 to his opponents' scores. Phillips tried to run them even with marginal hands.

Elson drew the two of clubs and set it in the middle of the table. Pelk followed with the eight. Lewis put the ace on the stack and Phillips slipped the king beneath it.

Lewis gathered the trick and said, "Let's go hunting for the bitch." He set the ten of spades on the table.

"The war in Europe is over," said Pelk. "Can you believe it?"

"Seems like we've been at war ever since I can remember," replied Elson. Trying to finesse the trick past the first two players, he dropped the king on Phillips' six and looked at Pelk.

"It won't be long before we're goin' home, boys. We're knockin' on Japan's back door," said Phillips triumphantly.

Pelk lay the ace on the stack and raked the cards in. Elson smiled. Everyone figured Pelk probably did not have the queen of spades because he did not unload it on Elson.

"Hey, Lew," said Elson, "how long do you think it will take to capture Okinawa?"

"I don't know, Frank," replied Lewis. "It took more than a month to take Iwo Jima and that was only 8 square miles. Okinawa is almost 545 square miles with 6 times as many Japs. They'll defend it to the last man because it protects Japan's southern islands. They know that once we take it, Japan will be subject to more than just occasional raids. Okinawa is big enough to accommodate a lot of the big planes that carry the big bombs."

"When is the killing going to stop?" asked Pelk. "I don't understand why humans feel the need to kill each other. It seems we have a callous disregard for life."

"The human race still has a gladiator mentality, Pelk," said Lewis. "As much as we'd like to believe we have a more sophisticated society than the Romans, we just have more sophisticated ways to kill each other."

"I guess that's true, Lew," said Phillips. "Only 20 years after WWI, Hitler invaded the countries around him. Seems like no one learned any lessons from the first world war."

"Well, there were problems with the way the Allies forced the Germans to accept responsibility for that war. They didn't start World War I. Austria and Russia did. Germany just honored the treaty it had with Austria. And because they lost, they were forced to bear the responsibility for the war and much of their industry and territory was handed over to non-Germans. For a long time, Germans were very poor. That created a lot of bad feelings in the fatherland. I think Hitler wanted to regain respect for Germany. He wanted to recapture its land, commerce, and capital, and he wanted revenge against those who forced Germany to accept terms it didn't deserve.

"Sounds like you're defending Hitler," said Elson.

"No. I am not defending him or what he's done. But I understand why he did it. I just hope we don't make the same mistakes that Woodrow Wilson, Georges Clemenceau, and David Lloyd George made after World War I. Otherwise, we'll be doing this again and again until we learn and accept a better way."

"God forbid," said Pelk. "I don't want my kids to fight a war. Too many people die horribly. It's crazy."

"Thank God that Turkin and the others who were wounded are alive," said Phillips. "And thank God no one else aboard the Osage has been wounded."

"No one escapes war unwounded, Billy," said Lewis. "No one."

23 June 1945
1030 Hours
Okinawa

As the Osage approached Okinawa, Miller received word through the short-wave radio that the island was completely in US hands as of 22 June. Casualties were high. During nearly three months of fighting, the US lost 11,000 men and more than 30,000 were wounded. More than 100,000 Japanese men died and almost 5,000 taken prisoner. US general Simon Bolivar Buckner was killed four days before the island was taken. The huge bay on the southeast end of the island was named after him.

Buckner Bay was a large c-shaped anchorage formed by a natural curved land mass and several miles of manually extended landfill. The narrow entrance to the bay was protected from enemy subs by a steel, underwater net. Tugs opened and closed the net for ships entering and leaving the bay.

2 July 1945
1400 Hours
Okinawa

The Osage had half a load of oil when Michaels received orders to join a convoy leaving Okinawa. A Pacific typhoon approached the island so the Navy sent its fleet away from the storm. Typhoons often traveled south to east in a wide arc along the eastern coast of Okinawa. To avoid these occasional and dangerous storms, ships formed convoys that sailed east, then south, to circle around and behind them. The evasive excursions lasted three or four days.

7 July 1945
1000 Hours
Okinawa

When the Osage returned to Okinawa, she emptied her oil tanks into other ships and took a fresh load of oil from a commercial tanker. For the next several days, however, few refueling ops were scheduled.

Every night, electricians set up a projector to show movies on a makeshift screen in front of the forward superstructure. Each movie was shown for two nights. That way, crew members who had duty the first night a movie was shown could see it the second night. Jackson traded movies on hand or swapped supplies with other ships in Buckner Bay for flicks the crew had not yet seen. He kept a list of movies and the dates they were shown. With hundreds of ships at Okinawa, the supply of available movies seemed endless.

The first lieutenant made arrangements with a cruiser to swap a Marx Brothers comedy and a John Wayne western for a Charlie Chaplin film and a musical with Fred Astaire and Ginger Rogers. As deck hands lowered the longboat into the water, Lycovec and Russell walked up to Jackson and asked him to drop them ashore so they could look around the island for a couple of hours and take some pictures.

Okinawa was decimated from the three-month battle and the typhoon. Nothing lay untouched from the ravages of humanity and nature. When the officers stepped onto the island, hollow roofless buildings stood amid piles of ash and rubble. Craters from bombs and large-caliber shells dotted the ground and surrounding hillside. More than one palm tree was stripped of fronds by the rain of bullets and mortar shells.

Sea Bees and the Army Corps of Engineers were clearing debris and trees that had fallen across roads. Tractors and bulldozers pushed and pulled wreckage into bulky piles that were scooped up and dumped into hefty grey-green trucks. Thick, knobbed treads of over-sized rubber tires kicked up clouds of dust as the trucks drove away, out of sight.

Lycovec and Russell walked on the shoulder of the road. Covering mouths and noses when a truck passed, they unhurriedly marched toward the remains of a village they saw from the longboat when they were close to shore.

The village was deserted. A single row of demolished huts and mud buildings lay on a kop of grass between the dirt road and a low dirt cliff that descended to the sea. On the other side of the road another row of ruins stood at the foot of a steep, barren rise littered with caves.

The two ensigns took turns taking pictures of each other in front of skeletal huts. As Russell stepped through the debris to pose in front of one building, he accidentally kicked a bottle, intact but empty. He picked it up and examined it.

The bottle was almost a foot high, about three inches wide at the base, and tapered to a slender neck not much larger than Russell's thumb. It was clear brown glass with no label. However, symbols of the Japanese alphabet encircled the base. Another row of symbols encircled the bottle just below the neck. They were not etched into the bottle. The characters were raised on the glass, probably part of the original mold.

Russell held the bottle high for Lycovec to see. "Hey,

229

Fritz. Look what I found."

The gunnery officer snapped a picture. "The spoils of war, Pete."

"What do you think it is?"

"From here, it looks like a bottle," Lycovec said dryly.

"Very funny. I mean, what kind of bottle?"

"A brown one."

"God, you are in rare form, today. Seriously, what do you think the Japs used it for?"

"They put little messages inside bottles like that and throw them into the sea." Lycovec pointed to the water beyond the low cliff. "They float back to Japan in the tide and people read them. I'm surprised you don't know about that. It's how all the famous navigators sent notes home." Lycovec started laughing aloud.

Russell couldn't help but smile. "You guys aren't going to let me forget that are you?"

"Not bloody likely, Pete."

The junior officers stepped behind the collapsed walls of a hut and stood near the base of the barren rise. They looked up and saw a myriad of caves in the face of the cliff.

"Can you imagine what it must have been like to live in these caves, Pete?"

"Actually, I can't imagine what the fighting must have been like in the three months it took to capture the caves on this island."

Lycovec turned to his left. "Did you see that?"

"See what?" answered Russell.

"Something moved near the entrance to that cave." Lycovec pointed to a cave near the ground.

"I don't see …"

"Holy shit. What is that?" asked the gunnery officer.

230

A white, round shape, almost two feet in diameter, slithered out of one hole and into another just below it in side of the rise. The officers stared at it in disbelief.

"It's got to be a tree root," said the communications officer.

"Tree roots don't move through the ground like snakes and worms!"

"Whatever it is, it's coming down the side of this cliff."

Both men backed slowly away.

"It's huge!" said Lycovec.

"Let's get the hell outta here!" said Russell.

Slipping and stumbling over the rubble, the men turned and ran back to the road. They did not stop until they were nearly a mile a way.

10 July 1945
0900 Hours
Okinawa

"I'm telling you, Lewis, it was nearly two feet in diameter." The gunnery officer held his hands apart, palms facing each other, in front of him. "It was crawling through the face of a cliff. What the hell was it?"

"Why are you asking me?"

"Because you're the resident Einstein. If anyone here knows, you do."

"It was probably just a giant worm."

"A giant worm? Two feet wide?"

"Giant worms in South America—rhinodrilus—grow to be seven feet long."

"You're kidding. Seven-foot-long worms?"

"They aren't the largest. Megascolides in Australia grow up to twelve feet long. The one you saw was probably spenceriella, native to Malaysia. They also grow up to twelve feet long."

"Are you shittin' me?"

"No, sir. Twelve feet."

Lycovec pushed up the brim of his ballcap. "Good God, that'd catch one helluva fish."

"Providing you could find a big enough hook—and a rod to hold it."

"I can dream, Lewis."

21 July 1945
0600 Hours
Okinawa

While the Allies regrouped and prepared to advance north to invade Japan, the Osage saw very little duty. More than 200 ships were anchored in or around Buckner Bay. Occasionally, kamikaze pilots tried to fly into troop transports. Some were shot down before they reached their mark; others slipped through and crashed in violent fireballs.

Via short-wave radio, Ron Miller received word that another typhoon was heading toward Okinawa. He relayed orders to Captain Michaels that the Osage would sail around the storm in another convoy, three rows of ten ships each.

After leaving Buckner Bay, Michaels found the convoy leader, a light cruiser, and maneuvered his tanker behind a cargo ship at the end of an outside row sailing southeast at 6 knots.

22 July 1945
07300 Hours
Pacific Ocean

Rain fell steadily under low-lying, dark grey clouds. The Osage rolled and pitched in a choppy, almost angry, sea. Gusts of wind whipped the tips of white caps across the tanker's deck. Jackson stood watch on the bridge.

With a cup of steaming coffee in hand, Pete Russell stepped onto the bridge to relieve Jackson of the watch. The ensign arrived a few minutes early to get course, speed, weather conditions, and to chat a bit with the lieutenant. Since Michaels gave his 8-12 watch to Russell, Jackson seemed a bit distant and terse with the ensign. Although the first lieutenant never said anything directly, Russell thought Jackson was a little peeved that Michaels gave Jackson's 8-12—the most favorable time to stand watch—to him.

The first lieutenant course, speed, and weather to the ensign but did not stay to chat. He left the bridge immediately after giving Russell all of the information. Russell just shrugged his shoulders and picked up the binoculars hanging near the radar monitor.

After a few minutes on the bridge, Russell noticed that it seemed the Osage was gaining on the ship in front. At first, he dismissed it as an illusion of how the tanker was rolling and pitching in the heavy sea. A few minutes later, he was certain it was no illusion. They were much closer to the ship than when he took over the watch. Russell asked the helmsman for course and speed.

"Bearing one-four-three at 9 knots, sir," answered Silvonic.

"Nine knots? Are you sure?"

"Yes, sir."

"Who told you to increase speed to nine knots?"

"Mr. Jackson."

"When did he tell you to increase speed to nine knots?"

"About two hours after he told me to decrease speed

to three knots, sir."

"Three knots?"

"Yes, sir."

"Did the rest of the convoy decrease speed to three knots?"

"Not that I'm aware of, sir."

"Why would Jackson decrease speed, then increase speed, and then tell me our speed was six knots instead of nine?"

"I don't know, sir."

Russell did not have time to think about it because the Osage was rapidly gaining on the ship ahead. He ordered the helmsman to decrease speed. But momentum still carried the Osage so close to the cargo ship that Russell was forced to order the helmsman to use the rudder to avoid a collision. The tanker's bow missed the starboard side of the cargo ship's stern by a scant 15 yards.

During radio silence, ships of the line flashed Morse code on large round lights with blinkers to communicate long distances or during inclement weather. The watch who manned the sound-powered phones was usually responsible for sending and receiving the code via blinkers. When the Osage pulled close to the cargo ship, their watch flashed a message asking whether or not the tanker had someplace special to go. Russell could not relay a lengthy explanation so he offered a sheepish "sorry."

No sooner had Russell finished his reply than the cruiser blinked a course change and Michaels stepped onto the bridge. The captain quickly noticed his ship was not where it should be.

"What is going on, Mr. Russell?"

"We are changing course, sir."

"Why are we so far out of position?"

"I'm trying to figure that out, sir."

234

"Figure it out and get it under control. Vhen you are relieved from vatch, come to my stateroom and tell me vhat happened."

"Yes, sir," replied the ensign.

Michaels turned to the helmsman. "I vill speak with you as vell, Mr. Silvonic—after your vatch."

"Aye, sir."

Michaels left the bridge.

"Damn!" said Russell.

The ensign spent almost the entire watch adjusting course changes and speed to get back in line.

1400 Hours

Michaels sat at the table under the porthole in his stateroom. He had just finished the rough log of the morning's events when he heard a knock.

"Enter."

Lieutenant Jackson opened the hatch and stepped inside.

"You sent for me, sir?"

"Have a seat, Mr. Jackson." Michaels pointed to the chair on the other side of the captain's small table.

Jackson closed the hatch, walked to the table, and sat.

"Can you tell me vhat happened on Mr. Russell's vatch this morning?"

"Well, sir, I turned the watch over to Mr. Russell and left the bridge. I don't know what happened on his watch. I was below deck."

Lightning quick, Michaels reached across the table and grabbed the first lieutenant by the collar of his shirt. Jackson tried to pull away but Michaels held fast. The captain leaned over the table, his face expressionless.

235

"Mr. Jackson, you go too far. If you do not like my decision to revard officers and crew then come to me. If ever again you put my ship or crew in harm's vay, I vill rip off your head and shit down your neck before I turn you over to fleet command for court martial. Am I clear?"

Jackson swallowed hard. "Yes, sir."

Michaels released his grip and Jackson straightened his shirt.

"Next time ve are in port, you vill not leave this ship. Send someone else to trade movies. For next month, you have mid vatch, 12-4, every day and night. Do you have anything to say?"

"I am very sorry, sir. I did not mean to put the ship or crew in danger."

"Great Hamlet's ghost! Vhat did you think vould happen?"

"I thought it would just be a prank on Mr. Russell."

"Next time, do not think vith your shriveled little dick. Dismissed."

"Aye, sir."

7 August 1945
1000 Hours
Okinawa

Holding a cup of coffee, Miller sat at his small metal desk in the radio shack. He blew on the hot steaming liquid before taking a sip. The short-wave radio beeped and he slipped on the earphones. He wrote the message down and reached for the code book. In a few minutes he deciphered the message. The day before, the United States dropped an atomic bomb on Hiroshima, the Chugoku Regional Army headquarters, on the southeastern coast of the island of Honshu. According to follow-up reconnaissance, devastation was widespread. The bomb blast covered 4 square miles. The blast and shock wave that followed destroyed an estimated 60,000 buildings and killed tens of thousands of people. He passed the information to Michaels.

"Mr. Miller, vhat is atomic bomb?"

"I don't know, sir. Perhaps it's some kind of super bomb. According to recon, one bomb destroyed quite a lot."

"Better super bombs to bring Japan to its knees than invade its home islands vone by vone."

10 August 1945
1000 Hours
Okinawa

Miller received another message via short wave. He deciphered it and handed it to the captain.

Michaels read the note. The US Air Force dropped another atomic bomb—this time on the major ship building and industrial city of Nagasaki on Kyushu Island. Again, details of the destruction were staggering.

"Vhat have ve done?"

"Sir?" asked Miller.

"Just thinking out loud." He tucked the note in his pocket. "Thank you, Mr. Miller."

"Aye, sir." The radioman returned to his desk.

18 August 1945
1900 Hours
Officers' Wardroom

After dinner, the officers on the Osage gathered in the wardroom. Only Lycovec was absent because he had the watch on the bridge. Seated, they waited for the captain to arrive.

"Why does Michaels want us here?" asked Harkel.

"Maybe we have another bonehead towing mission," replied Becker.

"Doubtful," answered Morton.

Michaels walked through the hatch and the officers stood to greet him.

"As you vere," said the captain. He pulled out a small box from his pants pocket and turned to the communications officer. "Ensign Russell, front and center." His voice was flat.

Russell's eyes grew wide. He stood and walked up to the captain.

Michaels looked him up and down. Everyone in the room thought Russell was going to get chewed out.

"Mr. Russell," began Michaels, "a few months ago I forwarded your paperwork for lieutenant junior grade. You vere approved. Michaels handed him the small box.

Russell took the box and opened it. Inside were the bars of a lieutenant jg.

"Congratulations, lieutenant," said the captain. "You are vone step closer to be navigator." He laughed and held out his hand. Russell shook it.

"How do you know about that, sir?" asked Russell.

"I have my vays."

Jackson was the first to walk up to the new lieutenant. "Congratulations, Pete." He held out his hand and Russell shook it.

"Thanks, Rick."

"No hard feelings?"

"No hard feelings."

All of the officers stepped forward and congratulated the communications officer. Most stayed to chat and play cards. Harkel left to relieve Lycovec on the bridge.

3 September 1945
0800 Hours
Okinawa

Michaels received a short but poignant message from fleet command: The war in the Pacific is over! Yesterday, 2 September 1945, the Japanese signed an unconditional surrender aboard the USS Missouri. Terms will follow. He looked up from the note and took a deep breath. His entire body seemed to relax all at once in the captain's chair. A wry smile came across his face. Michaels stood, walked to the console and picked up the microphone for the 1MC. He pressed the key and spoke. His voice was calm and steady.

"Now here this. This is the captain speaking. I have just received message from fleet command. The var is over. I repeat, the var is over. Yesterday, the Japanese signed unconditional surrender."

Michaels returned the microphone to its cradle.

For a moment, an unearthly silence blanketed the tanker. Some stood or sat in disbelief; some waited for the punch line; a few thought they had not heard correctly. Then, suddenly, a tumultuous roar grew from the belly of the ship. Men shouted, danced, cried, banged tools on pipes in unruly syncopated rhythms, and hugged good friends. The war was finally over.

For the next few days, one question loomed in the minds and conversations of everyone aboard ship: When were they going home?

9 September 1945
1900 Hours
Okinawa

Although the war was officially over, pockets of Japanese army, navy, and air force resisted the end of hostilities. Almost 1 million Japanese soldiers still fought in China. More than half a million Japanese were in Southeast Asia.

Kamikaze pilots continued to harass navy ships in Buckner Bay. Almost every day at sunset, a Japanese pilot flew his plane low and tried to crash into a troop transport, aircraft carrier, or battleship. When the plane was spotted, all ships—including the Osage—were forced to go to general quarters because it was never certain that the pilot would not lose control or change his mind and attack a different vessel.

16 September
0900 Hours
Okinawa

Another typhoon headed for Okinawa. Instead of joining a convoy to circumvent this hurricane of the Pacific, Michaels chose a different strategy. Typhoons usually moved northeast along Okinawa's east coast. Out of Buckner Bay, the captain of the Osage wanted to sail southwest, directly toward the storm; scuttle around the south end of Okinawa; and sail north up the west coast to use the island as a shield.

As the rest of the fleet sailed away from the approaching storm, the tanker broke away from the convoy. A little more than an hour after leaving Buckner Bay, the Osage was in trouble. Swells rose to more than 50 feet. The tanker rolled side to side and pitched forward to the point that the giant propeller came out of the water and spun freely in the air. With every roll and pitch, Ellen groaned and squealed as though she were in pain.

Torrents of rain poured on the tanker while it was tossed around like a large, helpless cork. Waves close to 90 feet high crashed over the deck. Life boats were splintered. Metal ducts and pipes were torn loose. Hatches shook violently in the raging winds that pummeled the Osage. Salt water drenched the sound-powered outlets on the weather deck and cut off communication between watch stations. Almost every man aboard felt like an island about to be swallowed by the sea in one long gulp.

A few hours into the storm, the skipper had to know if the engine room was taking water so he sent Russell aft. From the bridge, the newly promoted lieutenant could not go below to transverse the length of the ship because the forward superstructure had no access to the 'tween deck. Russell had to walk the weather deck and cling to the lifelines to keep from being hurled overboard by wind or water.

After he left the safety of the bridge, Russell tightly gripped the rail of the metal stairwell as he slowly stepped down to the main deck. His best chance to survive was to take it one stage at a time—with self-assurance and respect for the power of the ocean. If he made one mistake, he would not get a second chance to do it right.

Clinging to the rail and standing on deck, he studied the rhythm of the ship as it rose and fell with the swells. When the fantail came up out of the water on top of a swell, the ship seemed to hover for a moment before it fell. Then, he thought, was the best time to run.

First, he had to get to the aft superstructure—200 feet of open deck away. Russell looped his left arm around the lifeline and grabbed his right wrist. He grabbed his left wrist with his right hand. With arms interlocked around the lifeline, he waited for the ship to rise.

Slowly, the ship rose on the front of a swell. At the apex, the ship hovered. Russell yelled, "Shit!" and ran as fast as he could. The ship fell on the back of the swell. Midway to the superstructure, he took a deep breath and held it as a wave washed over him. His feet were swept from underneath him. Russell clung to the lifeline and prayed it would hold.

The ship rose again. Slipping, Russell struggled to stand. At the apex of the pitch, he ran until he reached the mast. He wrapped his arms and legs around it. The ship fell and another wave crashed over the deck.

The tanker rose. When the ship hovered, he ran until a wave knocked him off his feet. Russell found his footing and, when the ship rose, he ran to the aft superstructure. He lunged for the hatch, opened it quickly, jumped inside, and closed it. Russell was soaked and breathing heavily. He slogged to the other side of the superstructure. The ship rose and fell one more time before he opened the hatch and wrapped his arms around the lifeline that stretched to the fantail. One stage at a time, he thought. Be confident. Get there.

Russell clung to the lifeline. As the ship lingered at another apex, he dashed 50 feet to the hatch on the fantail that led below. He waited for the ship to rise again before he opened the hatch and ducked inside. Russell breathed a sigh of relief.

As he stepped down the ladder, Russell noticed a vile, putrid odor. "Aagghh!" he said, wrinkling his nose and pursing his lips. "What the hell is that?"

At the bottom of the ladder, Russell slipped and fell in a puddle of vomit. Some seasick sailor failed to make it to the head. "God damn the luck!" he said aloud.

Inside the engine room, the officers and enlisted men stared in disbelief at the communications officer dripping from head to toe.

"Mr. Russell," said Becker, "looks as though you've

had a bath. Smells like you took it in a vat of horse vomit." Becker waved his hands to ward off the smell.

"Looks like the entire Sixth Fleet threw up just outside the crews quarters. I found it the hard way."

The black gang laughed.

"The captain wants to know if you're taking water," continued Russell.

"Tell the captain that everything is fine. Except that all of us are seasick to high heaven."

Russell looked at the crew in the engine room. Everyone was listless and pale.

"Would you please leave," continued the engineering officer. "You stink to high heaven. Jesus, the smell is making me more nauseous."

"Sure thing, Becker." Russell walked to the hatch. Before he stepped out, the communications officer turned and said, "I know something that'll help your queasy stomach. Think of soft-boiled eggs and wet toast."

Becker looked at Russell for a moment, doubled over and dry heaved.

The journey back to the bridge was as dangerous and wet as the trip aft. However, it had one redeeming feature: it washed off all of the vomit. When Russell arrived at the bridge, he reported everything in the engine room was shipshape.

1800 Hours

With the strongest and most dangerous part of the storm behind them, officers and crew began to clean up and repair damaged fixtures, fittings, and equipment. Twenty-four hours after leaving Buckner Bay, the Osage was back in the harbor. The rest of the fleet returned three days later.

243

Chapter 11
Home

28 September 1945
0800 Hours
Okinawa

Late Thursday afternoon, Miller received orders for the Osage to return stateside and gave them to the skipper. The following morning, Michaels, Morton, Jackson, and Becker met in the captain's stateroom to discuss the voyage home. They crowded around the small table. Notebooks, pencils, ballpoint pens, and cups of coffee rested on the tabletop.

"Mr. Jackson," asked Michaels, "do ve have all typhoon damage repaired?"

"Yes, sir. Deck hands have restored everything."

"Good." The captain turned to the engineering officer. "Mr. Becker, how is engine room?"

"With the exception of the water pump for the diesel, everything is shipshape."

"Vhat is problem?"

"The water pump is frozen, sir. It happened this morning. The pump cools the diesel. Without it, the internal temperature would gets hot that the oil breaks down and the pistons freeze in the cylinders. We couldn't sail across Buckner Bay—much less all the way back to the States."

"Ve have orders to leave in less than three veeks. Can you fix it by then?"

"If we're lucky enough to find a water pump for that old diesel. It's big and it isn't standard Navy issue."

"Ya, it was refit in Sydney," said Michaels.

"If it's Australian, the depot here might have it for

244

the Aussie navy. If not here, Ulithi would surely have it."

"With all of the paperwork, it would take more than a month for a replacement pump to get here from Ulithi," offered Jackson.

"You have better idea, lieutenant?" asked the captain.

"I don't know yet, sir," replied Jackson. "Let me go ashore and see what they have. Then, we can talk about our options."

"Do it," said Michaels.

Jackson rubbed his hands together and smiled. His eyes narrowed. "Excellent." The first lieutenant turned to Becker. "Henry, I'd like to take a look at the pump. When can I visit you and the black gang?"

"Any time, Rick."

"How about 1100 hours?"

"Fine." Becker looked at the CO. "Sir, we have to shut down the diesel to replace the pump. We'll be cold for two or three hours."

"Understood," replied Michaels.

"The pump weighs 500 pounds. We'll need a few strong backs to lift the old one out of the engine room and lower the new one in."

"I am certain Mr. Jackson has qualified team."

1100 Hours

Holding a notebook, the first lieutenant ducked into the engine room and walked to the console where Becker sat. "Ready to go, Henry?"

"Go where?"

"We're going to take a look at water pumps in the depot."

"Why am I going?"

"Because you know the pump. I can write down the serial number and ID number on the name plate and check them against the stock on hand. But you know what pumps we can substitute if we don't find a match."

"Can't you take Frederickson?"

"How's it going to look when an officer from Deck and a first-class from Engineering go sifting through salvage? We're going to attract attention. Two officers won't attract attention—especially if we play it cool and nonchalant, see."

"Okay. Gimme ten minutes. I'll meet you on deck."

Jackson lifted his paper and pencil. "I'll copy the numbers."

Twenty minutes later, the two officers headed toward the depot on Okinawa. Turkin was the coxswain. By the time they reached the dock, Jackson gave Becker a couple of pointers about how not to be obvious. The secret to investigation, he explained, was to remain nonchalant about everything you encountered—including the item or information you sought.

Turkin tied the longboat to a short cement pier, ideal for loading and off-loading heavy equipment. Becker and Jackson stepped onto the pier. The first lieutenant turned and looked at the coxswain who nodded.

The three men walked up to the chain-link gate of the depot. It was open. Turkin lit a cigarette and casually leaned against the high chain-link fence that surrounded the storage facility. He exhaled the smoke through his nose. The officers continued inside.

The depot resembled a one-story warehouse Jackson remembered from his days in San Francisco. The building was wide and long. The walls were cinderblock, ten feet high, with a row of windows around the entire building—except the entrance—just below the sheet-metal roof. They let a flood of natural light into the spacious building and, when opened, helped a breeze stir the stale smell of wood, metal, oil, and rust.

Becker wondered why the building had no doors. The entrance was broad, approximately 20 feet wide and all the way up to the roof. Wide aisles separated rows of machinery, drums, boxes, and crates plainly visible from the entrance. The Engineering officer thought it resembled a graveyard for things industrial.

Just inside to the left, a young army corporal sat behind a wooden counter waist high. He stood when he saw the officers step inside.

"Mind if we look around?" asked Jackson.

"Help yourself, sir. Looking for something specific?"

"Maybe a cargo net—if it's thick enough. Cash and carry okay?"

"For some of the smaller stuff. For the larger equipment I need paperwork."

"How long to process it?"

"About three weeks."

"Thanks."

"Where's the head?" asked Becker.

"All the way back to the right. It's a grey metal door. Japanese letters are still on it."

Becker nodded. He and Jackson walked down the center aisle, deeper into the storehouse.

Approximately half way back, Becker spotted a group of water pumps. "Over there," he said pointing.

"Put your hand down! Don't point!" Jackson demanded.

The engineering officer lowered his arm. "Why not?"

"We don't want to give ourselves away. Now, let's walk over there. But if you see the pump we need, don't point and don't stop at it right away. Stop at two other pumps before you look at the one we need. After we look at water pumps, we'll look at a few other things. And for God's sake, act disinterested."

"Why are you making this so difficult?"

"Because we're going to steal the pump."

"Now?"

"No, Henry. We're casing the joint so we can plan a perfect crime."

"Does the captain know?"

"He practically ordered me to do it."

The officers zigzagged between rows of crates and equipment until they were in the general area of the water pumps. Jackson stooped to look at what he thought was a generator. Becker stood next to him and casually looked around without focusing on anything in particular. They moved and stopped a few times before the engineering officer knelt next to a large water pump.

"This is it," he said softly. "a perfect match."

Jackson leaned over and patted the machine with his palm. When he pulled his hand away, a small disc was stuck to the side of the pump. It was black with yellowish numbers from 1 to 12 evenly spaced around the inside circumference.

Becker saw it and asked, "What is that?"

"I took my watch apart. It's the face. It glows in the dark."

"Why'd you stick it to the pump?"

Jackson looked at his partner. "When we come here at night, it'll be easy to see. We'll know which pump to take without turning on all of the lights and letting the entire fucking base know we're here." His voice half growled. "Let's go."

Jackson walked toward the center aisle but Becker

248

walked deeper into the giant storeroom.

"Where are you going, Henry?"

Becker answered without turning around. "To the head."

Jackson walked up to the counter to wait. Becker arrived a few minutes later carrying a large, folded cargo net over his shoulder. "How much for this?"

"Five bucks," replied the corporal.

"I'll give you four."

The corporal hesitated. "Okay, four."

The engineering officer pulled a few dollar bills out of his pants pocket and handed them to the corporal. "Thanks," he said.

They walked outside and met Turkin who immediately reached for the cargo net. "Let me carry that, sir."

"Thanks, Turkin." Becker handed it to him as the men walked down the concrete pier.

"What did you find out, Lem?" asked Jackson.

"Gate's locked from 1700 to 0700. Simple padlock. No alarm and no outside lights. A cake walk, sir."

Jackson rubbed his hands together and smiled. "Excellent!"

2200 Hours

The night was clear and cool. Surrounded by stars, a white half moon rose high in the sky. Jackson, Turkin, Williams, Phillips, and Reasoner met on the fantail near the aft davit. Becker, Edwards, and Conway just finished unscrewing the deck plates that covered the engine room. Reasoner hopped into the davit's seat, grabbed the handles, and lowered the hook.

Down below, four seamen each had a corner of the cargo net Becker bought at the depot. Hours earlier, Becker

249

and the black gang drained the pump of water and oil. Then they lifted the pump onto the middle of the cargo net. When the hook was close enough, each sailor placed his corner of the net onto the hook and Reasoner lifted it onto the deck of the Osage. The officers and enlisted men looked at the big, heavy machine.

The pump was more than 2 feet high, and approximately 3 feet wide by 4 feet long. It wasn't massive but it was heavy—nearly 500 pounds. Edwards double-checked the net before Reasoner eased it into one of 2 longboats waiting.

"Okay, Here's the plan," said Jackson. "The depot has a concrete pier. Chief Edwards made a four-wheeler from 4x4s and casters. When we get there, he'll put it on the pier. We lift the pump onto the four-wheeler and roll it into the storehouse. Turkin, the padlock on the gate is yours. Inside we swap pumps, roll the new one back to the longboat, and head back to the Osage. Becker, Edwards … you're in the boat with the pump. Turkin, you're the coxswain. Everyone else with me. Phillips, take the helm. Any questions?"

No one spoke up.

"Let's go. And be quiet. If we get caught, it's the brig."

Everyone scrambled into the boats and the coxswains shoved off. By the time they reached the pier, it was nearly midnight.

Turkin was first to leave the boats. He walked to the gate and knelt in front of the padlock. Edwards set the four-wheeler on the concrete. He and the rest of the team, using the cargo net, hoisted the pump onto the skid. Turkin swung the gate wide open and they pushed the water pump into the warehouse all the way to the row where the replacement waited.

Leaving the cargo net on the skid, they lifted the old pump onto the floor. Then they carried the new one and placed it on the four-wheeler. Finally, the sailors carefully substituted the old pump where the replacement sat on the floor. As quickly as they entered, the group left the depot, loaded the new pump into a longboat, and returned to the tanker. By 0330 hours, the new equipment rested on the deck of the engine room and the team retired for the night.

29 September 1945
0800 Hours
Buckner Bay

Michaels and his officers met in the wardroom after muster to follow up on the pump. Becker told the captain that the pump was in the engine room and ready to be installed.

"Typhoon vill be here this afternoon. Ve do not have enough time to install pump and leave vith fleet, so ve must ride out storm in Buckner Bay." Michaels looked at the refueling officer. "Mr. Harkel, oil tanks are empty, ya?"

"Yes, sir. Port and starboard."

"How long to fill tanks with seavater?"

"Seawater?"

"Ya."

"Sir, why do you want to fill all of the oil tanks with seawater?"

"Ballast. Ve need to be low in vater."

"It'll take about an hour."

"Good." The captain turned to the engineering officer. "Mr. Becker. can you give me any power?"

"Without the pump, the diesel will overheat in five to seven minutes, and the oil in the cylinders will start to break down. I don't recommend moving quickly. The hard-

251

er the diesel has to work, the faster it will heat up."

"Fine."

"Mr. Morton, I vant all hands at GQ stations during storm—except gunners and lookouts. Find place for them below main deck. Everyone in place at 1000 hours."

"Yes, sir."

Michaels explained the plan he had to ride out the typhoon in Buckner Bay and dismissed the officers to prepare.

1000 Hours

Almost all of the ships had already left the bay. The few that remained with the Osage were not seaworthy. Because the tanker would be without power while the diesel was cold, Jackson borrowed a gas-powered generator from the depot. It provided electricity for limited areas of the ship. The crews' galley offered only sandwiches and coffee for officers and enlisted.

All hands aboard the Osage were at their stations. With the wind quickly increasing in intensity, Michaels wasted no time to right his ship for the typhoon. He told Becker to engage the diesel and go all ahead slow. The captain headed for the center of the bay.

Becker monitored the diesel carefully. The temperature rose faster than he anticipated, so he called the bridge and informed the captain. Michaels told him to do whatever was necessary to keep the engine cool because he needed power a few more minutes. The engineering officer ordered a couple of seamen to stretch a hose and siphon water from the harbor onto the diesel. When the cool seawater hit the overheating engine, it hissed and evaporated in a cloud of steam that rose to the ceiling.

Once in the center of Buckner Bay, Becker fired up

the generator and shut down the diesel. Michaels called for bearings, port and starboard, so he could chart the ship's position in Buckner Bay. Then he told the starboard anchor detail to drop anchor. As the heavy metal links fell into the choppy water, the wind pushed against the hull and super-structures, and the ship turned around the chain.

As soon as the ship's bow faced the wind, the captain told the port detail to drop anchor. Then he called down to the 'tween decks to tell Harkel to open the valves and fill the oil tanks.

The wind continued to pick up. The anemometer registered 105 miles per hour and the barometer sank to 28.33. As the tanks slowly filled with seawater, the ship eased lower in the water. With less metal for the wind to push against, the tanker lessened its roll and pitch. Although the harbor protected the Osage from huge swells, the wind still increased and buffeted the tanker. Soon, the rain fell in thick, grey horizontal sheets.

After a few hours, the wind suddenly stopped and the sky directly overhead was clear. Many of the crew crawled out of their stations to look. Michaels gave a stern look at his executive officer and Morton picked up the microphone of the ship's 1MC and told the men to get back to their stations. The crew quickly scrambled back into place. A few minutes later, the wind slammed into the helpless tanker from the opposite direction.

30 September 1944
0800 Hours
Buckner Bay

The Osage was one of a few ships in the harbor that survived the typhoon. Of the 70 ships that tried to ride out the storm, only 15 remained afloat. Some were washed ashore. Some ran aground on a sandbar. A few sank. The tanker did not emerge unscathed. The wind tore pipes and fittings loose and blew the tanker, dragging both anchors, 1500 yards from its original anchorage.

After muster, Becker and the black gang installed the water pump. After a few checks to ensure everything was running properly, he shifted power from the emergency generator back to the ship's diesel. The captain ordered the crew to prepare for a short cruise outside of the harbor to test the pump and discharge the water from the storage tanks.

18 October 1945
0700 Hours
Buckner Bay

With no refueling ops scheduled and the date to depart Okinawa well in mind, time passed slowly for the officers and enlisted men of the USS Osage. But the crisp, clear dawn of this Thursday morning carried the excitement of a final voyage.

Before the ship could leave port, however, Michaels filed his route and estimated time of arrival in Panama with the port authority in Okinawa. They relayed the information so the canal zone authority knew when to expect the home-bound tanker.

Coffee in hand and legs apart, Michaels stood on the bridge and looked beyond the harbor to the open sea. With the crew at duty stations for leaving port, the captain picked up the microphone of the 1MC.

"Now hear this. This is the captain speaking. Mr. Jackson, hoist anchors. Mr. Becker, all ahead one third. Mr. Emerson, set course for Mobile, Alabama."

The hurrahs of more than a hundred voices

drowned out the clang-clang-clang of the metal chain slowly winding up into the forecastle.

24 October 1945
1300 Hours
North Pacific Ocean

The Osage set a northerly route that took the crew south of the Aleutians, then down the west coast of the United States. The course was actually shorter to Balboa and the Panama Canal than south along the equator.

Just after lunch, a school of dolphins swam alongside the tanker. The slender mammals averaged 7 feet in length. With a small black ring around their eyes, they sported longitudinal green, grey, and brown stripes on the sides of their bodies. Officers and enlisted men on deck stood along the rail and watched the graceful animals jump out of the ocean and dive back in while they easily kept up with the plodding tanker. After a couple of hours, the school swam ahead and left the ship in its wake.

30 October 1945
1430 Hours
North Pacific Ocean

A sudden squall blew across the stern of the ship. The crew marveled that the bow was dry and the fantail was wet. Amidship, a few sailors danced in and out of the rain and laughed at the odd event and each other.

11 November 1945
1230 Hours
North Pacific Ocean

The crew had not seen land for weeks. Every morning, Russell plotted the position of the ship in the chart room. He noticed this morning that the ship would be at the apex of the long arc home. The lieutenant reasoned that the Osage was too far south to see the Aleutians from the deck, but the archipelago might be visible from the top of the mast.

After his morning watch, the communications officer went to boson's locker and signed out a vest that deck hands used to climb the mast. More than once he watched Fiore climb the tall, slender pole. Step and clip; step and clip. What one man could do, thought Russell, he could do.

The first third of the trek up was easy. The rungs were wide and the distance from the deck was tolerable. He stepped and clipped with the ease of an apple picker harvesting ripe fruit on a crisp October morning. The second third required more concentration. As he climbed higher, the mast narrowed and the rungs became smaller. Russell slowed his ascent to make certain his footing was sure. He also began to feel the roll and pitch of the ship as it rose and fell on the open sea.

A third of the way from the top, Russell stopped and looked down. The top of the mast appeared to lean over the side of the ship with every roll. A cold tingle ran up the back of his legs and through his spine to the back of his head. His stomach was queasy. He ignored the small crowd of sailors who gathered beneath to watch him. Russell swallowed hard and looked at the rungs that led higher. They seemed much too small for his size-12 deck shoes.

The newly promoted lieutenant decided to descend. The crew would certainly tease him about not reaching the top. Better, he thought, to face down the men on deck than to fall and wind up face down on the deck.

5 December 1945
0900 Hours
The Bay of Panama

As the Osage advanced toward Panama, Russell noticed the Osage would arrive two hours behind schedule—not unreasonable for the distance and time traveled. Looking at the chart, Russell figured a way to cut the two hours out of the approach. A slight shift in course took the tanker out of the normal shipping lanes and more directly toward the canal. He sent word to Michaels that they were close.

Michaels arrived on the bridge and Russell proposed the course change. The captain readily agreed and the tanker arrived almost to the minute of Michaels' original ETA. With Panama in sight, Michaels petitioned canal authorities to enter the inland waterway and received instructions to get in line. Directly in front of the US tanker was a French cargo ship.

From deep water to deep water, the Panama Canal was 51 miles long—including the distance sailed in Gatun Lake and Miraflores Lake. Although the Danish captain had never been to the Panama Canal, he knew it would take roughly 8 hours to cross the isthmus via the lakes and half dozen large locks—providing no large ships, like aircraft carriers, were crossing in the other direction.

1715 Hours

With night quickly descending, the Osage eased out of the canal zone and steered a course across the Caribbean Sea, the final leg of the long voyage home, for the gulf port of Mobile in southwestern Alabama.

9 December 1945
1930 Hours
Gulf of Mexico

A day out of Mobile, the enlisted men had an informal party in the mess hall after work. The mess hall often served as a common recreation room. The cooks prepared quarter-cut sandwiches and bowls of pretzels and placed them on four large tables. Each table also held two tubs of chilled sodas and an urn of hot coffee. Although still wearing work dungarees, the men were relaxed but eager to see home.

Barry Olsen stood at a table and reached for a pretzel. "Hey, Melvin, got any mustard?"

"Why you want mustard?" replied Wilson standing on the other side of the table.

"I wanna dip these pretzels in it."

"Man, that's just wrong."

"Does that mean no?"

In a corner of the room, Tex Akins sat on a stool with a guitar across his knees. With one hand, he picked a string and, with the other hand, turned a small key at the top of the neck. Herb Pelk stood next to him and pulled a harmonica out of his back pocket. He licked his lips and put the harmonica to his mouth. He blew softly and played scales to warm up while Akins tuned his guitar.

Harold Booth, Billy Phillips, and Buck Williams stood a few feet away from Pelk and Akins. Each held a can of soda.

"I don't know," answered Phillips. "What are you going to do, Harold?"

"I'm going back home to Kentucky and work on my grandfather's horse farm."

"Mucking horse stalls won't be much fun," said

Williams.

"He's a breeder and my father's the trainer. I'm gonna learn how to do both and win the Kentucky Derby someday."

"I thought they only let horses run in the Derby," quipped Phillips.

Emmet Weston backed slowly down the metal staircase. With every deliberate step, a deep thud resonated throughout the mess hall. Almost everyone in the room turned to see who and what were making the noise. When Weston reached the bottom, viewers saw him easing a barrel, step by step, into the room. Once the barrel was on the floor, he rolled it over to the musicians and stood it on end. Then he found a chair and set it behind the barrel. Sitting, Weston asked, "You guys ready to go?"

"Shoot fire, boy, I was born ready," replied Akins.

"Let's give'm a little bit o' Texas. How 'bout Cotton-Eyed Joe?" said Pelk.

It's a good one fer a starter and we've played it fer 'em before. They know it." said Akins.

Weston pulled a pair drumsticks out of his back pocket and counted down. "5-6-7-8."

On the next beat, Akins strummed a chord and Pelk blew a single note. With everyone's attention, the three-man combo kicked off the country-western two-step. Their audience clapped to the beat and, at the end of each refrain, Weston yelled, "What's that spell?" The crowd responded with a resonant, "Bullshit!" At the end of the song, the small band received a thunderous ovation. They bowed and began the next song softer. The men turned to friends and comrades and struck up conversations.

Chief Stacek stood at the bottom of the staircase leading into the mess hall. He looked up to see Captain Michaels descending. "Attention on deck!" he called.

Everyone in the room immediately stood at attention.

"As you vere," said Michaels as he took the final step. The musicians picked up where they left off and the enlisted men settled back into their stories, rumors, and jokes. The Dane turned to his chief boatswain's mate. "This is social call, not vork detail."

"Glad to have you, sir,"

Michaels walked up to a group of men standing nearby. They seemed to be arguing. "Vhat is the fuss, gentlemen?"

Tipton responded. "Nothing serious, captain. Turkin says we—him especially—were awful lucky on this tour of duty. Lewis says there is no such thing as luck."

"Everything that happens is a result of actions and decisions that put a series of events in motion," said Lewis. "Luck is merely a subjective perception of a beneficial outcome of those events."

"But the outcome is never certain," answered Gander who came to Turkin's defense, "because we cannot control all of the variables. We can only respond to events as they present themselves. And, at any given moment, our responses might change depending on the influences around us."

"That's not luck," responded Lewis. "That's free will."

"But luck helps us choose the best course of action," countered the pharmacist mate emphatically.

"That's just good decision-making based on experience and all of the information at hand," said the yeoman smiling.

The captain's head moved back and forth with each proposition offered by the debaters. Finally, he interrupted.

"Vhat do you think, Mr. Tipton?"

"I really don't know, captain," he answered.

Michaels nodded. "Perhaps ve can reach compromise."

All four men looked at their captain.

"Vhen ve found this old whore, she vas floating shithouse, ya?"

His four-man audience smiled and nodded.

"Ve vorked hard and made her elegant lady of the sea. Ve changed this ship and took good care of her, and she took good care of us vhen there vas trouble. So, you could say that ve created our own destiny or luck or vhatever you call it."

"I can accept that," said Lewis.

"Sounds good to me," said Gander.

Michaels smiled and walked to a table near the hatch that led aft to steerage. He pulled a can of soda out of the tub of ice, shook off the water, and opened it. Taking a drink, he looked around the room and saw Earl Frederickson and Chief Edwards playing darts on the other side of the mess hall. The chief boatswain's mate held a dart shoulder high. With a snap of his wrist, the dart flew toward the target and landed inside a small, slightly curved rectangle.

"Double 16, Earl. I'm gonna wipe the floor with yuh behind."

"It wasn't that good of a shot," replied Frederickson.

Edwards let another dart fly. It stuck in a larger inner circle not far from the first dart.

"Two more points, chief," chided the first class petty officer. He whistled.

Edwards loosed his third dart. It hit his first dart and both fell to the floor. "Damn!"

"That's a mighty powerful round. I pray to God I

can beat two points," laughed Frederickson. He lifted the blue-feathered dart to his shoulder and tossed it at the board. It landed in the outer circle of the bull's-eye.

"Damned Yankee," cursed Edwards.

"Damned Yankee, indeed."

"I'll be glad tuh see the lot of yuh go."

"Why not come with me to the Great Lakes? We'll find an easy-going freighter or tanker and sit pretty until we retire."

"I got a year and a half left in this man's navy an' I ain't goin' north when I retire. I'm goin' back tuh Georgia an' hook me some catfish."

Michaels saw Sam Chance and Lev Holland kneeling side by side facing a corner of the room. Jay Conway and Hal Emerson stood behind them. Chance was shaking his closed fist over a pile of dollar bills on the floor. Holland, Conway, and Emerson held handfuls of cash. The captain walked up and stood behind them

"Gimme an eight!" Chance said as he opened his fist. A pair of dice rolled into the corner. "Four and one," he said. Chance picked up the dice and rolled again. Each die had a single dot on the side up.

"Snake eyes," cried Holland. "My turn, fish." He picked up the dice and shook them in his fist.

Chance picked up the pile of money on the floor and distributed the bills among the other three men. "Damn the luck. Eight's an easy point."

Chance, Conway, and Emerson dropped a bill or two into a pile on the floor. Holland matched them and let the dice fly into the corner. One die had five dots on the side up. The other had two dots. "Yes!" he said. Holland scooped the pile of money in front of him and reached for the dice. Each man dropped another bill or two into another pile and Holland matched the bills again.

This time, Holland blew on the dice before he tossed them into the corner. The dice rolled and stopped. Both had a six showing.

"Boxcars, Dutch," said Conway. "My roll."

"Crap!" said Holland. He picked up the bills on the floor and handed them out. Michaels watched.

"Must have been an ill wind that blew across those dice," said Emerson as he dropped more money into a newly formed pile.

Conway matched everyone's bet, rubbed the dice between his palms, and pitched them into the corner. A six and a three lay face up.

"Nine's a hard point, Jay," said Emerson. "Why don't you just hand the ivory to me and save yourself the embarrassment?"

"That's not going to happen, Hal."

Conway picked up the dice, rubbed them like before, and let them go. A two and a three lay face up in the corner. He picked up the dice and rubbed them again. "Come on, nine." He dropped the dice on the deck. A four and a one faced up. Again he tossed the dice and a five and a four lay face up. "Point!" he cried and picked up the bills.

The three men formed another pile of money as Conway reached for the dice. Michaels turned and walked up to another group of men on the other side of the room.

10 December 1945
1500 Hours
Mobile Bay

From the Gulf of Mexico, the Osage eased between Mobile Point and Dauphin Island into Mobile Bay. In the center of the bay, a one-story white house sat on thick wooden pillars that stretched about 10 feet out of the water.

The roof housed a large revolving light. Locals called it The Mobile Lighthouse.

Officers and crew who did not have duty, lined the rails of the tanker. Wearing dark-blue Navy peacoats to ward off a cold wind blowing in from the northwest, the men tossed bits of food in the air to gulls, waved to passing boats, laughed, and pointed to ordinary frame houses and buildings on Dauphin Island.

The final mail call, before the Osage left Okinawa, carried to each man's home the news of the tanker's departure and estimated time of arrival in the tiny gulf port. The entire crew wondered who, if anyone, might have come to Mobile to welcome them back to the States.

As the ship edged next to the dock, the sailors searched the crowd of coat-wearing civilians for familiar faces. On the pier, men, women, boys, and girls looked for sons, husbands, fathers, and lovers. When eyes recognized a loved one, a name was called out and a hand raised to catch someone's attention. Soon, a sea of hands—aboard ship and on land—waved eagerly in the sunny but brisk winter afternoon.

As soon as the ship was tied to the pier in the navy shipyard, deck hands and electricians hauled large electrical cables aboard so the Osage could be rigged with shore power. When electricity was finally hooked up and turned on from shore, Becker shut down the old diesel for the last time.

Michaels allowed those who did not have duty to go ashore—with the knowledge that everyone had to muster aboard ship at 0800 the following morning. Almost before the plank was laid down and secured to the pier, sailors rushed off the ship into the outstretched arms of family and friends. Michaels sat in the captain's chair and watched from the bridge. Morton stood next to him. After all of the enlisted men on the bridge secured their equipment and left, the lieutenant turned to face his commanding officer.

"Permission to go ashore, sir."

"Permission granted," replied the captain.

"Thank you, sir." The executive officer saluted and, before waiting for the salute to be returned, ran off the bridge.

Michaels smiled. Alone on the bridge, he softly patted the arm of his chair and said aloud, "Thank you for bringing all of us back alive, Ellen."

11 December 1945
0800 Hours
Mobile, Alabama

The northwest wind brought layers of grey clouds and a threat of rain. Ship's company stood at parade rest between the superstructures and waited for their captain to speak. After two years of warm tropical weather, the cold damp morning was unusual and unwelcome.

Michaels was a man of few words and emotional farewells were difficult for him. This morning he wanted to be as brief as possible because this was, essentially, a good-bye address to his crew. Morton called the crew to attention and stepped back. Michaels walked forward.

"Today is last day ve are a crew. Tomorrow, many of you receive orders to report to temporary barracks and personnel office for discharge. Some vill be transferred to other ships." Michaels paused briefly. "On Thursday, the shipyard vill start to gut this old sea whore. It is strange to take her apart on the thirteenth because she has been very lucky lady for all of us." He paused again. "If you vant to take a little something from this ship vith you, I vill turn a blind eye to it. But it must be small enough to fit in duffle

265

bag. Mr. Fiore, that means the masts are off limits."

Knowing Fiore's willingness—even, enthusiasm—to climb the masts in any kind of weather, the crew smiled.

Michaels continued. "It has been honor and pleasure to be your captain. You are fine men. Officers in vardroom in twenty minutes. Dismissed." The Dane brought his heels together and saluted his crew. They returned it.

For a moment, unsure of what to do or say, no one moved. Then, from the ranks, someone cried out, "Three cheers for Captain Michaels. Hip, hip …"

The men answered, "Hooray!"

"Hip, hip …"

"Hooray!"

"Hip, hip …"

"Hooray!"

Unlike days previous, the crew did not rush to duty stations. They dawdled on deck and turned to friends and compatriots with whom they shared the past two years. Firm shakes of hands, quick hugs, questions about plans for the future, and vows to keep in touch peppered the next few minutes between the two superstructures.

Officers headed to the wardroom to meet for the final time as a group. One by one they stepped inside and took their seats. Michaels was the last to arrive. As he entered the room, the officers stood.

"As you vere," said the captain. He walked to his chair and sat. The other officers sat as well. Michaels shuffled uneasily in his chair.

"It has been good to vork with each of you. Thank you for making my last command a pleasure."

"Your last command?" asked Morton.

"Ya. The var is over and the navy has no use for this old sea dog. I vall go back to Lokken to see vhat is left of my uncle's farm."

"We're sorry to hear that, sir," said Jackson.

"Ya, me too. It has been too long since I have valked on dry land. I am afraid I vill fall over." The captain and officers laughed.

"I invite all of you and your vives for little party on Thursday night at club just outside shipyard gates. Nothing formal. Eight p.m. Name of club is The Blockade Runner."

The officers all nodded.

"Mr. Russell, vhat is blockade runner?"

"If I remember correctly, during our civil war in the 1860s, the North tried to bottle up the South's shipping. They sent warships to block Confederate ships and ships from other countries from entering or leaving Southern ports. Mobile was the heart of the Confederate navy's counterattack. They built fast ships here to run the blockade and bring in badly needed supplies."

"Ya. I understand."

Cook spoke up. "It's also the name of a drink made with gin and fruit juice, sir. I think they created it in Mobile. Perhaps, even at the club we're going to."

Michaels looked at the warrant officer. "Thank you, Mr. Cook. Maybe I vill try vone on Thursday night." The captain looked around the table. "If there is no more business, you are dismissed." The officers rose and, before leaving the room, each walked to the captain to shake his hand.

13 December 1945
2000 Hours
The Blockade Runner

Pete Russell stood in the corner of the tavern with his wife, Marianne. The tall, lanky lieutenant towered over the petite blonde with crystal green eyes wide with incredulity. She was talking to Beverly Becker, pudgy wife of the Engineering officer, Henry. Beverly had brown hair, brown eyes, and a shrill laugh which pierced the low murmur of steady conversation surrounding the officers and wives of the USS Osage. Much to the surprise and chagrin of the couples with the Harkels, Beverly laughed at just about everything.

Sitting at a table nearby, Susan Lycovec watched Fritz tell Rose and Phil Harkel a story about how he and Pete Russell discovered a giant earthworm on Okinawa. Susan did not tire of watching her rugged, usually laconic, husband tell stories because he became very animated. His voice rose and fell and he waved his hands and arms to exaggerate parts of the story. Rose and Phil leaned over the table to hear above the background voices. They seemed to drink in every word like tavern patrons more thirsty for gossip than whiskey.

A long, dark wooden bar was only a few feet away. Men and women dressed in weekend threads sat on barstools, leaned on the bar, or stood with a foot on the rail that ran around the foundation. Holding glasses of beer or highballs, they smoked cigarettes and laughed at the slightest amusement offered by partners in idle conversation.

Four Coast Guard officers stood near the center of the bar, not far from the table where the Lycovecs and Harkels sat. One, a tall lieutenant with one blue and one green eye, was talking to a long-legged brunette wearing a light-blue dress. She suddenly threw her head back and laughed. As her head came forward, she lifted a cigarette to her red-painted lips and took a shallow drag.

"Rick Jackson, you are the funniest man I have ever met. To think anyone could make up a story about talking a Japanese soldier into surrendering. Where did you come up with that?"

Behind Jackson, another officer, wearing horn-rimmed glasses, leaned around and interjected. "It's a gift, really."

Jackson turned to Clark and both men laughed.

On the other side of Clark, the third officer stood at the bar and nursed a glass of beer. With his back to the bar, Morton sipped occasionally from the frosty mug in his hand. He didn't seem to have much to say. He was content to watch the commotion around him.

Chief Warrant Officer Cook sat on a barstool behind the brunette. With his elbows on the bar, he silently stared into his highball, distilled spirits in fruit juice with a wedge of orange on the rim of the glass and a small confederate flag for a swizzle stick. His shirttail was tucked unevenly into his trousers and the dingy elastic brim of his skivvies was plainly visible above his left back pants pocket.

"Did you tell that story to anyone aboard ship?" asked Rose.

"This is the first I've mentioned it. Didn't want to spend the rest of the tour explaining why I ran like a schoolgirl from an earthworm."

Lycovec and his three companions laughed.

"On a more serious note, ladies," said Phil, "our captain has a colorful and rather unpredictable vocabulary. He speaks three languages: Danish, English, and profanity."

"And he mixes his languages freely," added Fritz.

"Why are you telling us that?" asked Susan.

"Forewarned is forearmed, honey," replied Fritz. He slipped his arm around her shoulder and she leaned into him.

"What's that about the captain's vocabulary?" asked Marianne standing behind the Harkels.

"The boys were telling us that Captain Michaels has a dirty mouth," replied Rose.

"Oh, for heaven's sake. It's not like we've never

heard foul language," said Marianne.

"Isn't that the truth!" said Beverly. Her shrill laugh sliced through the noise, the smoke, and the smell of beer, whiskey, and cigarettes.

"Speak of the devil," said Henry. The group looked up to see Honas shouldering his way through the crowd. He carried his cap waist high in front of him and held it like a shield. He walked up to the table and smiled broadly.

"You must be Marianne Russell," he said and held out his hand, palm up.

Marianne placed her hand in his and the Danish captain lifted it high enough to kiss.

"Your husband said you vere attractive but failed to mention you vere so striking." He allowed her hand to fall away.

"Well, thank you captain," Marianne replied almost blushing.

"Please, call me Honas. It is a name cursed to me by my father. It vas his father's name."

"It sounds noble," said Beverly.

Honas turned to face the plump wife of the Engineering officer. "How kind of you, Beverly." He held his hand out again. She wasted no time to put her hand in his. After he kissed it, the woman squealed with delight.

"Your laugh is enchanting," he said. Everyone's eyes in the group grew wide—one with delight, the others with astonishment.

The captain turned to the table. Mrs. Lycovec sat closest to him so he bent over and held his hand to her. "So this is the angel you spoke of so affectionately, Fritz. It is clear why she is so dear to you." He kissed her hand and Susan turned immediately to her husband.

"You called me an angel?"

Before Fritz could answer, Honas looked at Phil

Harkel's wife and said, "A rose by any other name would smell as sweet. It is pleasure to meet you." he held his hand to her.

Rose offered her hand and replied, "Shakespeare. How refreshing, captain."

"I insist you call me Honas."

"What about me?" came from a voice behind him. The Dane stood up and turned. A brunette in a pale-blue dress had her hand, palm down, in front of her. Michaels kissed it.

"I beg your pardon, madam, I don't believe ve have met."

"Edie LaPonte. My father owns the shipyard."

"How do you know these fine people?"

"I just met Ricky, here." Edie pointed to the first lieutenant who smiled and nodded. "He's funny."

"Ya, I've heard."

Everyone in the group smiled.

"Ladies, you must allow me to buy you drinks."

Before anyone could finish an objection, the captain held his hand up and said, "I insist. It is a small mark of respect to the enchanting vomen of such fine officers."

The women half smiled, half giggled—except Beverly, whose shrill titter again rose above the din. The men rolled their eyes.

"Excuse me, Honas," asked Edie, "You talk funny. Where are you from?"

"I am from Denmark. Do you know vhere it is?"

"Sure. Northern Europe. I guess that makes you a great Dane. Do you bark?" She smiled, obviously pleased with herself.

The women looked at her in disbelief. Expecting their captain to go off the deep end, the officers cringed.

"Ya, but my bite is much vorse."

271

Everyone laughed.

Jackson turned to Morton. "Well, waddaya know. The captain's a real charmer."

"Yeah. He's got the women eating out of the palm of his hand. That's a side of him we never saw."

"Personally, I think that's a good thing because his palm is probably pretty salty."

The two men laughed.

Carrying a small round tray, a cocktail waitress walked up to the table. She was about thirty years old and wore her dishwater blonde hair up in a bun kept in place with a pencil. Her makeup was so thick it looked like pancake batter on a cold skillet. She asked if they were ready to order a round of drinks.

Honas leaned into her ear and said something no one else could hear above the noise. The woman turned and shouldered her way through the crowd to the waitress station at the end of the bar.

The women crowded around Honas and asked questions about his homeland, his family, and what their husbands did on shore leave. The Dane answered the questions with humor and an occasional whisper that the men were unable to hear. Exiled to the bar, the men were comfortable to chat about how good it felt to be home and see their wives again. And they asked each other about plans for work, now that the war was over.

The cocktail waitress returned and set a round glass with a short stem in front of everyone in the captain's group. Each glass held a light brown liquid two fingers deep. Honas lifted his glass and said, "To Ellen Hagerman." He took a drink. Others in his group drank from their glasses.

"Ooh, that is very warm," giggled Beverly. She licked her lips and sipped again.

272

"Who is Ellen Hagerman?" asked Susan.

"She is the voman who kept your husband alive in the South Pacific," answered Honas.

She looked at Fritz.

"I'll explain later," said the gunnery officer.

The group stayed until midnight. The couples were the first to leave. The women gave the captain a polite hug and the men shook his hand. Then, Rick and Edie left arm in arm. Under his coat, the first lieutenant carried a paper bag twisted at the top. Outside, he lifted the top of the bag to his lips and handed it to Edie. She followed suit. Laughing, they half walked, half stumbled down the street.

Michaels was next to leave. Hinting that he had a big day on the morrow, the Dane bid good-bye, shook each man's hand, and slowly walked away. At the door, he turned and waved. The three remaining officers saluted.

15 December 1945
0900 Hours
The Mobile, Alabama, Shipyard

Wearing his Navy-issued black dress shoes, a pair of dungarees and sweatshirt under his peacoat, Michaels stood at the head of Pier 7. A navy-blue stocking cap covered his head and his khaki-green duffle bag stood on end beside him. His ruddy face was covered by the thick, rough stubble of a beard started the day before.

For a moment he stood and watched unfamiliar men dismantle what had been his home for the past two years. A large crane sat in the middle of the pier. As it hoisted a massive sheet of metal off the hull, Michaels thought back to when he had first seen the rusted hunk of a ship in Noumea harbor. Two men carried a small motor from the deck onto the gangplank and the Dane remembered the problem they had with the winch during first shakedown cruise. Someone threw a small object off the bridge. It landed in the water with a splash he could see but not hear. He wondered what that might have been.

With each object that left the ship, Michaels felt a small piece of himself being carried away. He opened his duffle bag and pulled out the bottle of brandy he found in his stateroom only a year and a half ago. He uncorked the top and raised the bottle toward the tanker. Without saying a word, Michaels nodded and took a long swig.

The Dane corked the bottle and stuffed it back into the bag. He stooped and slid the strap over his shoulder. "Good-bye, old girl." As the ship's former captain picked up his duffle bag, a cold wind blew in from the west. Michaels pulled the collar of his peacoat up around his neck, turned, and walked slowly toward the shipyard gates.